BURIED HEART

Visit us at www.boldstrokesbooks.com

By the Author

Forsaken

Bitter Root

Buried Heart

BURIED HEART

by
Laydin Michaels

2017

BURIED HEART

ISBN 13: 978-1-62639-801-6

This Trade Paperback Original Is Published By
Bold Strokes Books, Inc.
P.O. Box 249
Valley Falls, NY 12185

First Edition: January 2017

CREDITS
EDITORS: VICTORIA VILLASENOR AND CINDY CRESAP
PRODUCTION DESIGN: SUSAN RAMUNDO
COVER DESIGN BY MELODY POND

Acknowledgments

I want to thank the great people at Bold Strokes Books who help with every step of this process. From our senior editor to our many proofreaders, you make great things happen. Thank you to Vic and Cindy for their care in editing, even when it hurts.

I hope you enjoy the read.

Dedication

For MJ, always.

PROLOGUE

The light hit her eyes and her world went white. She dropped to the asphalt, squeezing her eyes shut against the glare. She became aware of footsteps drawing near. Someone was coming. She threw her hands up, blocking any attack from above.

"No, no! Let me go! No!" she screamed.

Her voice cracked. Hands grabbed at her, and she fought against them. She head-butted the hard surface of someone's face.

"Ow, damn. Cut it out, hear me? You're okay. I'm trying to help you," the voice said.

It wasn't the voice she'd become accustomed to in the dark. This voice was loud, but somehow not as frightening as the other one.

"My name is Bill. I'm going to give you some water. Quit fighting me. I called the cops when I saw you running down the highway. They should be here anytime now. Just relax, kid," he said.

She felt something round push against her lips, and she sipped cautiously. Water. Cool and fresh. She drank heartily, pulling until container made a loud pop. Startled, she jumped.

"It's okay. That's just the plastic bottle. What's your name?"

She stared at him. *What is my name?* She didn't have any answer to give him, so she stayed quiet.

"Okay, here's an easier one. Why are you out here running on the highway in the middle of the night? I almost ran you over."

"I don't know. I had to get away from the voice," she said.

"The voice? Where's your house? Can I call your parents?"

Call? What did he mean? She watched him, not comprehending. Piercing sounds ruptured the silence between them. She tried to get up, to run again, but the man held her fast.

"That's just the cops. They're going to help you. It's okay."

They're going to help me. It's okay. Where am I? Who am I?

Soon there were others moving around her. People in dark clothes with shiny shoes.

People carrying guns. There were noises she had no understanding of, crackles and disembodied voices. Then a woman helping her to sit on a cot of some kind. She was shining a light in her eyes and wrapping something around her arm. The strap tightened and she wanted it off, but when she tore at it, a man held her hands still. Panic started to rise inside her, and she began to scream. Then, a sharp stick in her leg and everything dimmed.

She could still see people moving around her, could feel the cot being lifted into a bright metal box. She heard them talking, felt the movement and knew they were taking her somewhere. And then she must have fallen asleep. She came to awareness in a bright room. The sounds of people talking nearby made her freeze. But they weren't the voice, the bad voice. She stayed quiet and still, hoping to discern where she was and what was happening.

"She was running down FM 1431 in the middle of nowhere. Closest place to there is Lago Vista, but she wasn't walking distance from there. She's not carrying any ID. Have we got any missing kids that we know of?"

"None in the county. I'll search neighboring counties, but there aren't any active Amber Alerts. Hey, she's moving."

They were standing above her now, and she felt panicked again. She tried to sit up, but her arms were strapped to the bed.

"Hold on, calm down. You're safe. This is Seton Northwest Hospital. I'm Officer Morrell. This is Officer Bates. Can you tell me your name? What happened to you?"

She stared at him.

"I don't know. I can't remember," she said.

"Okay, how about your name, honey? Can you tell me that?"

"I can't remember." Her voice cracked as the panic rose.

"Shhh, it's okay. You've had a trauma. I'm sure it will come back to you. Just rest now. One of us will be here, so you're safe. We're going to find out who you are, and get you back to your mom and dad."

Mom and Dad. *Dad.*

CHAPTER ONE

Drew Chambliss paced her living room as she argued with her best friend.

"Come on, Drew. You can't miss this. I'm telling ya, the SXSW is the best festival ever. You won't even believe who's going to be there."

"Preston, you know I hate being out in the heat."

"This isn't hot. Come on. I've got my CamelBak. There will be so many people there. We might even hook up with Tom and Jenn. I spent a ton of money on these tickets. You can't let 'em go to waste."

"I didn't ask you to buy me one."

"I know you didn't, but I owed you. City Limits, remember?"

"I didn't buy you that ticket so you'd owe me. I knew you really wanted to go, and I had the money, so…"

"And now I want to return the favor. Mersey's Cow is going to play. You'll be lying if you say you don't want to see them. So get over yourself and get dressed. I'll be there in fifteen to pick your ass up. If you aren't dressed, plan on going naked."

"I'll be ready. Do you have ponchos in case it rains?"

"Ha, you're funny. If, by some miracle, the heavens decide to finally grant some mercy to our drought-baked city, I will be happy to give you the shirt off my back to keep dry."

"That's okay. I'll bring 'em."

Drew disconnected and rummaged around in her front closet for two nylon ponchos. They weren't any bigger than her wallet when they were all folded up like this, and Pres would be happy to have one if it did rain. She slipped them into the side pockets on her shorts and pulled out her wallet. *Pretty thin.* Maybe he'd stop at the ATM so she could grab some extra cash. She was happy Preston had pushed the issue of the festival on her. It would be awesome. She liked being home on the weekends to rest, but mixing it up once in a while was healthy.

When she'd first awoken on the highway fourteen years ago, she had no memories of anything but a voice in the dark. She had gradually remembered bits and pieces of her early life, but they didn't make sense. It was like she was watching a movie about some little girl. She didn't recognize herself in those images, but she had remembered her name. Her adoptive parents were happy to use her name, in hopes that it might help her unlock more of her past.

That had never happened. The only thing that seemed to change was the intensity and terror of her nightmares. She'd wake up screaming more nights than not, but couldn't hold on to what caused the fear. She didn't have a lot of friends, and she cherished what she had with Preston, who seemed to know when to push and when to let it go.

She slipped out the door to wait on her porch. It wasn't long before Pres's blaring moombahton music announced his arrival. She jumped off the porch rail and ambled over to the car. She gave in to the rhythm of the music and let herself move. He jumped out of his door and gyrated in an equal display of musical appreciation.

"Man, that's awesome. I wish Major was doing a set this year," she said.

"Ha. That'd be freakin' amazing! We are totally going to save up for EDC next year. Vegas, here we come, baby," he said.

"Yeah, right. We'll see. I'm happy to catch whoever comes to town. We're so lucky to live in new music central. I read there's going to be this awesome band from South Africa throwing down some tunes on the Radio Day Stage. I'd like to check them out."

"That's cool with me. I like just about any music. Well, anything but twangy country."

"Let's boogie. You know the crowd is going to be thick. Would you run by the bank? I need some cash."

They piled into the car and headed to the festival by way of an ATM. The traffic started jamming up well before their exit.

"This was a sucky idea. Why did I think driving was the way to go?" he said.

"Don't sweat it. Jump off at Riverside. We can grab some mountain bikes at the park and bike over," Drew said.

"Damn, no wonder they say girls are the smart ones. Think Truman will mind us bugging out of the park with two service bikes?"

"He won't as long as we don't let him know about it."

"Excellent point."

They struggled through another ten minutes of stop-and-go traffic before they caught the Riverside exit. Once on the surface streets, it only took a few minutes to get to Zilker Park and a few more to check and see if the bike garage was attended. Working for the city had some advantages, and being rangers at Zilker had even more benefits.

Drew left her customary bandana hanging on the rack in case anybody came by while they were out. Truman might get pissed, but at least that way he'd know the bikes were basically safe and in good hands. Hopefully, they'd get them back in with no one the wiser.

They cut through the park and got on the bike trail. It took them less than twenty minutes to get to Buffalo Billiards for the first showcase. There were a ton of choices of music style, but they both loved TrancenDance, who was the featured DJ at Buff's. He'd open the venue, and then they could hit some of the other stages as the night wore on.

Drew jumped in the queue while Pres locked up the bikes. It wouldn't do to lose them or have them wander off with strangers.

There were people everywhere, and the atmosphere was all peace and party. No ill will to be seen. They watched Wallslidr at Maggie Mae's and grooved on her amazing sound. It was kind of a reggae/bluegrass fusion, and Drew let herself go with the sound, feeling the bass pulsating from her feet through every nerve ending. She rolled and shifted with the beat, eyes closed and hands high above her head.

She sensed more than felt the presence of someone in her personal space. Normally, she'd have stopped moving and walked away in disgust. Boundaries were sacred to her. But something about the energy of her invader held her in check and she stayed in the moment.

Damn, I hope when I open my eyes it's not some drunk frat dude slinging his sweat on me.

She didn't think that would be the case, though, and as the music fell off and a new groove kicked in, she braved a peek at her dance partner. What she saw made her clench deep inside. Her mouth went dry, and she could hear the beating of her heart warring with the bass. The woman was drop-dead gorgeous, so uniquely beautiful Drew lost the rhythm of the music for a few seconds.

"Hey, you're making me look bad, hottie. Keep moving or I'll have to slip away."

Her voice was like a silk ribbon running across Drew's bare skin. Smooth and soft, but rich in tone and resonance. Drew liked what she heard and made her body fall into the rhythm again.

This time she kept her eyes wide open. The light played on her partner's ebony skin, refracting and sliding down her long frame. She was tall, a good five inches taller than Drew. Her hair was close shaven, so tightly curled Drew twitched with the desire to touch it.

She felt a jolt as the thought struck her. *This isn't me.* She didn't randomly want to touch strangers or have them anywhere near her. It took her own folks a good two years and lots of expensive therapy to reach her.

Drew moved closer to her partner, their bodies so in sync that the rhythm seemed to flow through one and into the other. She lost herself in the beauty of it. WallSlidr transitioned into a techno track that increased the tempo, but not the intensity of her connection to the woman. Drew felt as if they were in their own space, she and her mystery dance partner. She had a moment of panic and glanced around, looking for Preston. He was there, too, dancing with a beautiful brunette. It was all good.

As the next set started, the woman leaned into her. "So, I'm Cicely and you are?"

"Drew, Drew Chambliss."

"Well, Drew Chambliss, you know how to move, baby. Don't stop now."

Drew felt her face heat as she nodded in return. She wasn't used to this kind of attention, but it felt good. The music wrapped around them again, and they moved together through set after set.

She was about to suggest stopping for a break when Cicely turned toward her, smiling.

"I'm thirsty. Let's go get something to drink, huh?" Cicely said.

"Yeah, that sounds good. Let me grab my friend."

Drew tapped Preston and signaled him to follow, and let the woman lead her away from the crowded dance space. When there was finally room to turn and face her, Cicely smiled. It was like the sun coming from behind a cloud, and it warmed Drew to her core. It turned out that Pres had been dancing with Cicely's best friend, Kallie.

"This place is packed. How about we grab something to eat and then head back to Beerland?" Pres said

"I could use a bite to eat," Cicely said.

"There's a little place a few blocks from here. Puco's Mex Mex. Sound good?" Drew said.

"Lead the way."

She took them to the quirky, fun little hideaway. Drew loved this place, with its good food and awesome staff. It was a total locals place, so it wasn't too crowded. They only had to wait ten minutes for a table and were soon seated in the eclectic eatery. Drew was both tense and excited to have Cicely sitting so close to her. The occasional brush of her skin against her was making her nipples tighten. She hoped no one noticed, but it was beyond her control. Something about her set off all kinds of reactions. It was so new she didn't know how to react or how to cover it. She moved a little away from her and ordered a grapefruit infused beer. Something cold would help.

Everyone ordered margaritas and Drew did her best to push the heated sensations from her consciousness. She felt thickheaded, unable to think of something to start a conversation. Why did this happen to her so often? She wasn't shy by nature, but being around beautiful women always had this effect on her. She smiled sheepishly at Cicely, hoping she'd say something.

"So, tell us about yourselves. What brought you out to the SXSW? The music, the tech conference? What's your angle?"

"Oh, totally the music. I could care a flip for the latest in social media," Pres said.

"What he said. I'm all about the music," Drew said. "What about you two?"

"Honestly? We were at the tech con today. Social media is relevant to what we do for a living. We have to stay up-to-date."

"Really? What do you do?"

"I—" Cicely started.

"We work for the Travis County court system. We advocate for the mentally ill, particularly the indigent," Kallie said.

"Cool. That sounds like interesting work."

"It is. What do you two do?"

"We work for the city," Preston said. Drew was about to add that they were park rangers, but Pres kicked her under the table.

What was he up to? There was no reason not to be upfront about their jobs. She looked at him and he frowned, slightly. *So less is more, as far as information goes. Okay.*

She avoided the topic altogether and started talking about who they most enjoyed listening to that night. Cicely and Kallie had been front and center at TrancenDance. They had been blown away by the energy he sent out as he worked his set. Drew and Pres groaned when they heard how awesome it had been. They had only been able to get in the door and never made it anywhere close to the stage.

When their food arrived, they ate and talked about their favorite songs and DJs. When they had paid the bill, they walked back to Beerland. Drew surprised herself by wanting nothing more than to be with Cicely. She generally stayed clear of strangers, but there was something about Cicely. When she moved it was like light through a prism, refracting and expanding, holding Drew captive to the movement. She was beauty and elegance, and Drew couldn't resist the pull of her charisma. Even more surprising, she found herself comfortable with that. She wasn't anxious, didn't shut down. *I like being with her.*

They stopped in front of the venue. Crowds of people were flowing out.

"Looks like we missed the last set. What time is it?" Cicely said.

Drew was shocked when she saw that it was well after midnight. She had assembly at eight the next morning and dinner with her family after work.

"Man, how'd it get so late? We've got to get going."

She was about to grab Preston when she felt Cicely's arms encircle her. She turned toward her.

"So, kiss me first."

Drew flushed, her throat tightened and her stomach did flip-flops. This was going to happen. She leaned in and touched her lips to Cicely's. The flashes of excitement from dinner were nothing compared to the earthshaking intensity of that kiss. The velvet softness of Cicely's lips was intoxicating. She wanted to live in that kiss. And then, it ended. She felt like the ground had dropped away from her and she was falling. She held tight to Cicely to regain her balance.

"You okay?" Cicely asked.

"Yeah, that was amazing. Thank you," she said.

"I think my coach is going to turn into a pumpkin if I don't get home soon. I enjoyed spending time with you."

"I know what you mean. I have to be at work bright and early. It's been really special. I'd like to see you again, if that's okay?"

Cicely smiled again. That smile that could light the sky with its brilliance.

"I'd like that. Why don't you come over for dinner next Friday? Here, give me your phone."

Cicely quickly entered her number.

"There. If you want to have dinner, call me. Okay?"

"I will."

She grabbed Preston and they headed back to the bikes. They rode back to the park and stowed the bikes in the garage. Drew saw that her bandana was still in place and hoped that meant their pilfering had gone unnoticed.

"Come on, I'm beat. Let's go," Preston said.

"Right behind you," she said.

They slid into the car seats, worn out from the day. Drew punched Pres in the arm.

"Ow. What was that for?"

"Why did you stop me from saying we were park rangers? What's the deal with that?"

"I don't know. I mean, they were hot. I felt some real chemistry with Kallie, and I didn't want her to think we were glorified Boy Scouts."

"Seriously? Come on, dude. You know our jobs aren't only important, they're hard. Not everyone can handle the crap we do. Besides, it's better to be up front."

"You think? Maybe for a chick like you, but trust me, a woman like Kallie isn't going to give a park ranger the time of day."

"You're wrong there. She was totally into you. You going to see her again?"

"Maybe. I hope so."

"Did you exchange numbers?"

"I gave her mine. Left it in her hands, you know?"

"Yeah, that's cool."

"What about you and Cicely? You guys seemed to connect."

"Yeah, we did. She's so…" Drew found herself drifting in the sensation of what Cicely was. She felt those lips on hers again, the laugh that was deep and sexy and ran down her spine like silk. Her beautiful face, piercing brown eyes, and the deep cut of her cheekbones. She was lost in the memory when she was pulled back to the moment by Pres's nudge.

"Drew, snap out of it. I get it, you like the woman. Did you get her number?"

"I sure did, my man. That, and an invitation to dinner."

"You dog. Man, you slayed me. I hope Kallie calls."

"Aw, buddy, she'll call. Who could resist your charm?"

"Whatever." He shook his head doubtfully.

In no time, he was dropping her off at her house.

"See ya in the morning."

"Night."

Drew kicked the door closed behind her and went straight to the kitchen. *Damn, I'm sore. I'm not as young as I used to be.* She filled a glass with water and drank it down with a couple of ibuprofen. That should help with the muscle aches, and she'd be grateful for that in the morning. She dropped onto her couch and thought about her evening. It was unlike her to react to someone the way she had with Cicely. She didn't do instant attraction; in fact, she avoided attraction. Why had this been different? What was it about her that made it so easy?

It had to be something unexplainable. Nothing else made sense. The more she thought about it the more discomfited she became. She dissected the night, taking the bits and pieces that didn't fit with her normal self and tried to pinpoint what had been different. *Let it go. Don't overanalyze it. Just enjoy it. Don't make it into something bigger than it was...*

But when she climbed into bed, Cicely's kiss was all she could think of. The sense of wholeness she felt in that moment. The sweeping loss of balance as it ended. That was real. That was solid. Whatever it was, she wanted more of it. She lost herself as the memory of sensation flooded through her. With that in her mind, there would be no room for nightmares tonight. She closed her eyes and lost herself in the memory of velvet.

CHAPTER TWO

Cicely was exhausted. She loved dancing, and Drew had been a treat, but she couldn't wait to curl up in her bed. Kallie was going to crash on her couch. They had cabbed it back to her apartment, since neither of them was okay to drive. They pulled out the couch and loaded it up with pillows and such for a comfy night's sleep.

"So, that was different," Kallie said.

"How so?" Cicely said.

"Well, for one thing, you don't usually stick with one person all night."

"Okay, that's somewhat true. Not completely true, since I always stick with you all night, so there's that."

"That doesn't count and you know it. I'm talking about you and Drew."

"I like her. What can I say?" Cicely said.

"And I'm pointing it out. You were relaxed and comfortable, even though you'd just met. You usually have to do a background check on someone before giving them that much of your time." Kallie poured another glass of pinot.

She had no idea how right she was. Cicely did run background checks on prospective dates. Ever since Jacki, she hadn't been able to stop herself. She needed to know that the people she let into her life weren't going to lie and steal from her.

Damn you, Mom and Dad. You made me this way. You took away my trust, and Jacki made it even worse. I can't let people matter to me if they're going to hurt me. I can't take that kind of pain again.

"You want?" Kallie asked, lifting the bottle.

"No, I'm good. It was different, I guess. It felt...I don't know, right?" She didn't do fantasy or magic. Cicely Jones was rooted in reality and truth. Kallie told her she needed to work on her trust issues, but it wasn't easy. She had her reasons for not taking people at face value. She'd trusted Jacki. That had felt right, too. Look what happened. She'd let Jacki in, started building toward a future together, and then what? One day she'd come home to an empty apartment and a cleaned out bank account. Trust was overrated. She wouldn't be a victim of that again.

When she and Kallie had bumped into Drew and Preston, something had clicked. It was that simple. Besides, it was a night of dancing, not a marriage proposal. She knew how to build walls and keep things superficial. She could date Drew and not have it mean anything. Just because they felt right didn't mean she had to open everything up to her.

"What are you going to do if she ends up being less than you hope? When, and I'm sure it will happen, she proves to be more human than ethereal being? How are you going to handle the disappointment?"

"Damn, Kallie. Can't you give me a night to enjoy the fantasy?"

"No. If you were prone to fantasy, and could handle reality when it bites, sure. But no. I know you, Cicely. I'm not going to stand by and watch you implode. As your friend, it's my job to ask the tough questions."

Cicely looked at her. Kallie wasn't just a friend; she was a practicing psychiatrist who moonlighted as Cicely's best friend. She couldn't help pointing out when things didn't jibe, and Cicely loved her more for it.

"Of course you're right. I'm sure when I wake up in the morning I'm going to be panicking about tonight. But what's done is done. She has my number. If she calls, I'll have to reevaluate, but for now, I'm going to go to bed. It doesn't have to mean anything, or go anywhere."

"Okay, honey. I'll see you in the morning."

Cicely headed to her room. *She's absolutely right. I acted completely out of character. What was I thinking? She could be the world's most superficial woman, and I've given her my number. Ugh.*

She dropped her clothes into the hamper and washed her face. She caught her reflection in the mirror. *Why? Do you want to be shredded again? Is it worth it, just because there's something about her?*

So much for sleep. Cicely knew herself well enough to know she wouldn't manage any tonight. She pulled on her oversized T-shirt and sat on her bed. She grabbed her tablet off the table beside her. Might as well find out what she could since she wouldn't sleep.

She ignored the twinge of conscience as she pulled up the Zobot search engine and entered Drew's name. There wasn't much there. Two addresses, three relatives. She moved on to Pepl. Here there was more. She found links to Drew's Facebook and Twitter accounts. Her place of employment was there.

Cicely's gut twisted as she held her finger above the touch pad. *Should I really do this? Why can't I trust my instincts? Everyone else does. How did I come to the place where I want to run a background check on anyone I let in?* It had become second nature, and she hadn't felt qualms about it in years, but tonight, it felt wrong. It was like she was the one betraying Drew by finding out all she could about her. But she had a compulsive need to know the people around her weren't scammers or liars, even if they were only on the periphery of her life.

People who had something to hide didn't usually seem as open as Drew had, though. Unless they were very skilled at lying. What if that was Drew's game? What if she was a scammer?

Stop it. She didn't come on to me. I was the aggressor here. I broke into her space and announced my presence. I didn't give her any opportunity to charm me or con me.

The hell with it. She needed to know. She tapped the submit key and the search began in earnest. She watched the flow of files on her screen. Would she be someone Cicely could get to know? Time would tell. She felt bad, dirty even. That hadn't happened before. Typically, she'd run a check without even thinking about it. It was safe. She was protecting herself, right? She thought about why this time was different.

Going to a festival or out to a club and flirting wasn't anything new. She was all over that. But like Kallie said, she usually didn't narrow her focus down to one person. She usually lit a spark with three or more girls, dancing with them alternately, and making sure they all knew they were interesting to her.

It wasn't like she was playing games with them, either. She was totally upfront about her divided attention. Often, they knew each other, and she and Kallie would join their group for the night. She might give one more attention than another, but she didn't leave with any of them, ever, and she didn't give her number up. If she felt an attraction deeper than casual, she might get their number. It was off-putting to a lot of women, but she never gave a piece of herself away. On the rare occasion she wanted one-on-one time, she didn't go there without thorough research. If, and only if, they checked out to be who they claimed to be, Cicely was cautious, and inevitably found some kind of fatal flaw in the person. Hence the fact that she was perpetually single.

She was lucky she had Kallie. Not many straight girls would stick it out with such a messed up lesbian friend. They'd met when a former patient of Kallie's had been incarcerated and ended up a client of Cicely's. *It's been four years. How has time escaped me that way?*

They had become really good friends as they'd helped him through the system and made sure his mental health needs weren't neglected. Her instincts had been on the mark. She'd trusted Kallie from the beginning, and she hadn't been disappointed. She'd thought maybe she could trust her instincts after all.

But then there was Jacki. That had been brutal. And Kallie had been there with her the whole time. She'd even sensed that Jacki wasn't being honest before Cicely had. She'd felt so right, but she was a con artist.

Kallie had alerted her to her misgivings, but Cicely had been blind to it. She wanted to believe Jacki was who she said she was. She'd ignored Kallie and gone with her own feelings. It had ripped the rug out from under her, completely. Kallie was there to pick up the pieces, thank God. She was the backup system that kept Cicely from giving away too much of herself too soon. But Kallie also worried about Cicely's inability to trust. How often had they talked it out? At times it seemed to be the only conversation they had.

And she *had* worked on it. She tried every day to be open to love. But she simply couldn't let go of the distrust yet.

She wanted her instincts to be right this time, but this was about her need to feel secure and in control. If Drew ever found out about it, it would have to be okay. That was how she had to be. If she couldn't accept that about Cicely, then they weren't meant to be.

The program signaled completion and she tapped the file icon to find out who Drew Chambliss was. She was a park ranger with the city. *That's kinda cool.* She'd probably enjoy outdoor sports. *I love to camp and hike, so that's good.* Her parents were teachers, and she had two siblings. Cool. Family was good. She'd ask her about them when they got together next time. *Huh? Where'd that come from?* She had no idea if Drew would even call her. She was renting a two-bedroom house in Rosewood. *Nice.* Cicely had always liked the idea of living in a house. One day, maybe. If she could find the right place to buy. If she was going to rent, she wanted a maintenance department to handle issues.

The more she read about Drew, the more convinced she was that her instincts had been right. Drew seemed to be a pretty normal person. Cicely was cautiously optimistic that something could develop between them. She put the tablet back on the table and settled into her comforter. Now she could release herself to sleep.

As she drifted off, the last thought in her head was of the kiss she had shared with Drew. How right and good it had felt to trust her in that moment. *Don't let me down. Please.*

Chapter Three

*T*he sound of her breathing was all she knew. Rough wood ground into her arms and legs. The weight of the darkness surrounding her pressed in. "I can't breathe. I need out."

She wrenched her arm upward, tearing the skin of her knuckles on an unyielding barrier. Pain shot through her hand like fire. "Help, someone let me out."

No one came. She fought for shallow breaths, knowing there wouldn't be many more. Cold like a killing frost seeped in around her. She screamed for someone, anyone, and then there was a pinprick of light. It cut through the darkness with blinding strength, increasing and ripping the black away.

She couldn't see him, but she knew he was there, standing above her. The sour smell of his sweat fell like a cloud around her.

"Did you learn your lesson? I'll close you right back in if you can't behave, hear?"

"Please, let me out. I'll be good. Please."

"Come on out then. But remember, this hole is for you."

Drew woke covered in sweat, throat dry from screaming. She kicked off the tangle of covers and sat up. With no idea who her attacker was, there was no way to really deal with the nightmares. *Coffee.* She needed coffee and a shower to clear the cotton from her head. She stumbled into her kitchen, avoiding the desperate attempts of her cat, Kashka, to trip her.

She thumbed on her coffee maker and splashed some water from the sink over her face. The dreams were more intense these days. She wished she could remember details, but they were all lost when she awoke. Her adoptive parents had taken her to a long line of psychiatrists and psychologists to try to help her. They had done everything from behavior modification to diet regimens with little effect. Nothing worked. Believing the trauma that caused her dissociative amnesia also caused the night terrors, her psychologist suggested regression therapy via hypnosis. Her parents refused. They thought the risk to her overall mental health would be too great. When she was ready, her mind would unlock and she'd remember on her own. They figured her amnesia was her protection, and if the memories were so awful, it might be best that she didn't retrieve them.

As an alternative, and to give them all some well needed rest, the doctor prescribed sleeping pills. Her parents agreed even though they weren't recommended for someone as young as her. The medication and her night terrors kept her from connecting with the world. By the time she entered high school, Drew had her bubble well established. She walked through her days in a fog. She had friends, a motley group of other rejects and dopers who didn't fit in. They all just went along to get along.

Drew wiped her face on a clean kitchen towel and pulled her favorite mug out of the cabinet. Wy had chosen it for her the last time they were together. It had been a cold February day, and she had taken her to Genuine Joe's for a hot chocolate. Wy had seen the mug and insisted Drew buy it. It was the shape of Captain America's head and held a good 20 ounces of coffee. He was her sister's favorite comic hero, and the size was right, so she'd bought it.

She smiled thinking about Wy. When her parents adopted Wynika, Drew had been starting her senior year. Wy was five. She had stolen Drew's heart the minute they'd met. Her parents had also adopted her brother Javon at the same time. He was ten and had oppositional disorder. They had their hands full with him and left Wy to Drew more often than not. Being responsible for her sister had saved her. She devoted all her free time to Wy. When Drew moved into the dorms at the University of Texas, she made a point to spend weekends home.

Having responsibility for her sister woke Drew up to the clouded reality of her life. She wanted to stop the sleeping pills right away, but the authorities in charge of her dorm didn't feel the same. They looked somewhat unfavorably on students waking other students with blood-curdling screams on a nightly basis. So Drew worked as many hours as she could at Pepe's Wonder Pizza and saved every cent. After six months, she was able to put a deposit on a garage apartment and stop the pills. Her parents also supplemented her earnings by paying her for babysitting Wynika.

After she earned her degree in environmental science, she got a job with the park service and was able to move to a bigger place. She lucked into it; one of her professors was moving and wanted to rent to someone he trusted. He thought twenty-four-year-old Drew was a good risk. Two years later, she still loved her little bungalow with its low-slung porch. And she had an extra bedroom for Wy when she stayed over.

Drew poured her coffee, adding a little cream and sugar. As soon as she sat at the table, Kashka jumped into her lap begging for attention. She scratched him under the chin and ran her hand across his silky fur. She sighed. *Time to hit the shower.* She downed her coffee and headed that way.

She was all about business when it came to showering, as she was in most areas of her life. Get in, get clean, get out. Her new hairstyle helped. It was close-cropped except for six inches on the right side, which hung to just below her ear. Everyone had complimented the cut but Wy. She said Drew looked like an anime character.

She toweled off and dressed in her park service uniform. She grabbed her helmet and headed to the garage. She slid into the saddle of her Harley Softail Classic. It had been a graduation present from her parents. Her dad had bought it when he turned forty and kept it in prime condition. He hadn't ridden it much since Javon and Wy had joined the family. Drew knew it was a big deal for him to let it go, though. The only thing they made her promise was to never ride without a helmet. She could live with that.

Drew didn't like riding in wheeled metal boxes like most folks. They were too confining. It was okay when the windows were open and she had the wind in her face, but if it was raining or something and the windows were up, claustrophobia set in and the need to claw her way out surged through her. When she drove the park service trucks alone, she kept a towel under the seat for rain and left the windows down. She didn't mind being hot or getting a little wet. Much better than the anxiety that gripped her otherwise.

She pulled into the park a good fifteen minutes before weekly assembly. The work assignments had been posted, and she was happy to see she had no overnights that week. She wanted to see Cicely again. She was also happy she had drawn Barton Wilderness Patrol today. That meant she'd be on an ATV all day.

Poor Pres hadn't been so lucky. He had overnight tonight as well as next Friday. *Bummer for him.* She grabbed a bagel and a juice from the counter and slid into a front row seat for assembly. The other rangers sauntered in in twos and threes until Truman finally walked in, pulling the door closed behind him. Before he'd reached the podium in front, Pres had quietly toed open the door and entered. He had a hard time with punctuality, and unfortunately, Truman used overnight patrol as punishment. He'd probably just guaranteed himself yet another night tour.

"Okay, people, listen up. Not much to cover today, but it's important. There was a little spill over from the SXSW last night. Apparently, some folks didn't think partying till two was enough. A fair-sized group gathered in the Town Lake Greenspace. Schiller and Ramirez handled it appropriately. They called in APD and broke the group up without too much commotion. Good job."

"Tonight we are going to double our overnight patrol, since this is the last Saturday of the event. Everyone look sharp and be respectful. These guys are in our town. That makes it their town, too. They aren't here for trouble, so let's help make sure it doesn't find them.

"A housekeeping note. Park service bicycles are for authorized use only. It seems someone borrowed a pair yesterday. Don't let it happen again. Chambliss and Vasquez, the ATVs are all at the mechanic being inspected. Pick yours up there. Now, head out, be safe and careful out there."

He dismissed them to their duty assignments. Drew detoured to the bathroom while the crowd thinned out. It was nice to have the number advantage when it came to the facilities. She liked giving the room a chance to clear. The guys jostled her a little too much in a crowd. While she waited she slid her phone out of her pocket. She stared at the number Cicely had left the night before. She clamped down on her self-defeating inner voice and hurriedly shot off a text.

I really enjoyed last night, and I don't have to work Friday night, so if the invitation to dinner is still open, I'd love to see you again.

As she was putting it back in her pants it buzzed in reply.

Awesome. How about I cook for you?

Sounds good. What time and where?

My place, 8:30. She included her address and a note to bring her swimsuit. She had no idea where her swimsuit was, but she'd have to find it later. Now, it was time to head to work.

She smiled as she pushed the door open.

"What are you so happy about?" Preston said.

"Hey, I can't help it if I'm happy. Sorry you drew the night shift."

"Not once, but twice? Come on. Who's he trying to fool? He's got it out for me for some reason."

"You know the reason. You need to be at work on time, buddy. He won't let up until you show him you can do it."

"It's not like it's my fault the roads are full of cars. I can't change that."

"No, but you could leave ten minutes earlier. It's not so bad. At least you have today and tomorrow off."

"Right, but I'm here, so now I get to turn around and fight my way back through traffic."

"Bummer. I have to run. Vasquez is probably waiting in the truck for me. I'll catch you later."

He grunted and looked like a sour-faced two-year-old. He had no one to blame but himself. She climbed into the truck, and Vasquez headed to Chuy's to get the bikes. In no time, they were out at the Wilderness area. Vasquez directed her as she backed the bikes off the trailer. She had more experience with them than he did.

"You run the perimeter, east to center, making sweeps," Drew said. "Note any hikers or illegal campers. It's the time of year for that. Be polite. They don't usually know they're breaking the law. I'll take west to center. Radio in any contact, or if you run into any trouble. If all goes well, I'll see you back here in about four hours. Take plenty of water."

Drew headed out to the far western edge of the park. She loved this land. The prickly pear cactus and scrub oak that defined the hill country. This was where she felt her best. Most at home. She had discovered her love of the outdoors during her first year at UT. Some of her dorm mates had gathered up a crew to go on a school sponsored camping trip near Canyon Lake. Drew had been surprised to be invited, but was happy to go.

As soon as the bus had driven into the hill country, she'd felt this deep sense of belonging. When they'd unloaded and started setting up camp, the tents confounded her, but picking the best spot to set them up was a no-brainer. She'd impressed the advisors by digging a fire pit and getting a fire going without being directed, and without the Sterno they had brought.

After that experience, they'd encouraged her to be more active in their group and steered her toward environmental science. It was a natural fit. She'd traveled to many places as an advisor with the Outdoor Recreation Program. Places she never would have discovered on her own. She'd had job offers in Arizona and Montana, but her heart belonged to the hill country, and she made it her goal to work with the park service.

She eased back on the throttle and let the bike slow to a stop. She looked down into what she playfully called Preston's Canyon. It was a small ravine, no more than twenty-five feet deep, full of cactus and boulders. When she had gone out with Pres on his first wilderness patrol, he had reached this ravine and radioed. What should he do? Technically the end of the ravine, some thirty feet west, wasn't on park land. Should he take the bike onto private property? Or follow the thing to its easterly end?

She had agreed with him that it was against regulations to take the bike off land, but it was his call. She didn't tell him it would add an hour or more to his trip if he went back. Seasoned rangers knew it was no big deal to take the fifteen feet, but they always waited to see what newbies would do. As she suspected, he had dutifully run the length of the ravine to its end at a wash and picnic area, before crossing and running back out to the western perimeter. Drew had waited a full two hours at the truck before he made it back. She didn't say anything to him, but at the next assembly, she gave him an award for thoroughness in patrol to the guffaws of the rest of the crew. Pres had turned bright red, but handled it with his customary poise. It was an initiation of sorts, and they'd all had their turn.

She gunned the engine and scooted west around the ravine. Back to work. Her headset went off as she turned for her first full sweep.

"Chambliss, I have a situation here. Need your assistance. Copy."

"What's your twenty?"

"I'm at Sculpture Falls. I have what appears to be an abandoned car in the water. Repeat, vehicle in water."

"On my way."

Shit. This happened periodically. It usually turned out to be one of two things. A drunk who got a wild idea about driving the creek at night, or kids who'd ripped off a car and dumped it where they expected it would never be found. Both wrong. You don't drive Barton Creek. It's rocky, it's steep in places, and it's protected, for fuck's sake. And if you want a hot car found within the first twelve hours, dump it on park land. Anywhere on park land. Drew knew a hundred places you could leave a car and it wouldn't be questioned for months. But park land wasn't one of them. The city of Austin treasured its natural resources, and sweeps of city parks happened every day, without fail.

She took the quickest route to Sculpture Falls and soon joined Vasquez, who stood ogling the predicament they were going to have to deal with. *What the heck?* How in the world had they gotten that car out to the center of the falls? It didn't look like a 4x4. Those limestone knobs would tear out the undercarriage of nearly any car. But there it was. A relatively new looking VW Beetle, jammed out in the center above the waterfall.

"I already called base for the wrecker. Truman said it should be about half an hour," Vasquez said.

"Did you walk out there?" she said.

"You kidding? That water's damn cold and I don't have my waders."

"Wimp. Here, hold my radio."

She handed him her phone as well, and stuck her helmet on her ATV. She shimmied out of her boots and socks and rolled her pants as high as she could. She stepped into the cold, fast-moving water, mindful of her footing. Most accidents around the creek happened when folks underestimated the strength of the current or the slipperiness of the limestone. The grooves that gave Sculpture Falls its name only increased the danger.

It took her about five minutes to reach the car. The windows were cracked and she immediately noticed the figured slumped over in the driver's seat.

"We've got a victim out here, Vasquez. Radio for paramedics, and let Truman know."

She started walking around to the driver's side of the car, the current pushing her into its bumper. It rocked and bobbled. She worried it would slip farther down the falls. It wasn't that the falls were steep. They weren't. It was the deep pool that gathered at their base. No way would she be able to get to the driver before the car filled with water if it reached the pool. For a minute, she froze, praying the thing would settle. And then, with grating vibrations she felt through her feet, it hung up on the limestone again.

Relief washed through her and she started moving again. When she reached the driver's door, she was able to snake her hand through the window and lower it farther. She slipped the top half of her body into the car and assessed the woman behind the wheel. She was unconscious, but had no visible injury. Drew figured the best thing to do was to tie off the car to prevent slippage and wait for trained medical personnel.

She waded halfway back to Vasquez and had him toss her a line. He secured the other end to a nearby oak. She soon had the car anchored on one side and had him meet her to hand off a second line. She tied that one to a tree on the opposite bank. The car wasn't going anywhere now. She sent Vasquez to the nearest parking area to wait for the ambulance. She headed back to the car in case the woman went into distress or woke.

She was still out cold. Drew wondered why, but kept monitoring her breathing. It was hard to do nothing, but she knew from experience it was for the best. The EMTs would have to hump into the park from the nearest entrance. It would take them a while to get here. The park wrecker was really just a Yamaha Rhino Side-by-Side with a powerful wench.

She heard the returning ATV and knew help had arrived. Vasquez dropped the first paramedic and headed back for another. Soon she heard the Rhino engine, and knew the wrecker had arrived. Joe Stovall was driving, and he had an APD officer as a passenger.

Drew was relieved when the paramedic took over. She didn't like how still the woman was. Other rangers and police arrived via ATVs and mountain bikes. She sure hoped someone was handling access at the highway. This amount of activity was going to bring looky-loos from all directions. She moved to the bank of the creek and waited. When they had the woman secured to a backboard, the paramedics signaled, and she and everyone else took positions in the creek and along the bank. They handed the woman down the line in a human chain. Unreasoning panic filled her as the board touched her hands and she passed it on to the guy next to her.

Why does it feel like I'm in danger? Nothing here is going to hurt me. Shake it off.

She tried to push the panic down, but it stayed with her. When the woman reached the bank, they carefully carried her to a flat surface where a waiting paramedic assessed her more completely. They decided she was stable enough to move further and loaded her on the Rhino. Drew and three other rangers were asked to walk beside the vehicle to help steady her journey.

Drew couldn't make herself walk over to the woman and help.

"Chambliss? What gives? You get a chill from that water?" Truman said.

Drew knew it wasn't the water, but she didn't have an explanation, so she nodded, allowing him to believe she needed a break.

"Okay, get back to headquarters and get warmed up. Vasquez, you take Chambliss's position."

Thankful for the reprieve, Drew climbed onto her ATV and headed back to the locker room. *What the heck was that about? What's wrong with me?* Humiliated by her weird reaction to the accident, she changed uniforms and headed back to where she'd left Vasquez's ATV to wait for him. They still had to sweep the rest of the park.

By the time her shift was over, she was sore and tired. Going anywhere but home and to bed was less than appealing. She gave some consideration to canceling, but her mom was counting on her, and it'd be nice to see her dad and the kids.

On the drive to her parents' house, Cicely's smile filled her imagination. The sway of her hips as she danced, the feeling that being beside her gave Drew, were what she focused on. She did her best to push aside the memory of panic she'd felt at the crash site. Her nights were hard enough; she didn't need to add panic during the day to the mix.

By the time she was headed home late that evening, she felt miles better. Dinner with her family had been just what she'd needed. Good food, lots of laughter, and hugs from her parents made all the stress of the day melt away. She fell asleep thinking about Cicely's lips, and wondering if this was how it felt to be reasonably normal.

CHAPTER FOUR

The workweek had been grueling, and Drew was more than ready when her day ended. She fought traffic to get home and went straight to the shower. When she was drying off, she heard her text alert going off. Probably Wy. She had texted her earlier about going to see a movie tomorrow. Drew grabbed her phone off the bedside table and looked at the message. It was an unrecognized number. Must be an ad. Those guys never gave up texting random numbers.

She opened the message to be certain and frowned.

I've been looking for you, and now I've found you. You'll be back with me very soon.

No name, just that bizarre statement. She deleted it and blocked the number. *Must be some kid playing a prank.* She shook it off and dressed for her date with Cicely. She debated wearing jeans or slacks, but knowing she was going on her bike, the denim made much more sense. She chose a chestnut brown western shirt. It had flourishes embroidered on the front and cuffs as well as a six-inch sugar skull on the back. She pulled on her engineer boots to finish the look. *Nice.*

Now she just had to find something to swim in. She found her tank crammed in the back of her drawer, but her trunks were AWOL. She looked in her closet and in the dryer, but they weren't there. She pulled open the drawer under her bed and started flinging out her work shorts. Maybe they'd gotten mixed in with those. She finally gave up and grabbed a random pair of workout shorts. *They'll do.*

Her room looked like it had been ransacked, but she didn't have time to fix things right now. She'd deal with it in the morning. She rushed out the door and hit the road. It was after eight twenty by the time she made it to the address Cicely had given her. The place looked pretty unimposing from the outside. A low stack, three-story apartment building without a lot of grandeur. She knew that looks could be deceiving, but she was truly surprised by the interior courtyard.

The pool and recreation area took up the majority of the space, and it was clear the residents were given lots of opportunity for community bonding. There were wall mounted grills and outdoor day beds all around the pool. *Nice for them.* Drew couldn't stand the idea of apartment living for herself. She couldn't get out of the dorms quick enough. She needed land around her. Land she didn't have to share with a community of fellow dwellers. It was her dream to move out west of town, out to Lake Travis, where she could have some acreage and a home.

She was feeling claustrophobic and antisocial when she found Cicely's apartment and rang the bell. *C'mon. Let it go. Don't be stupid.* When the door opened, her misgivings were blown completely away. Cicely stood in the doorway, dressed in a flowing cream tunic top and matching Capri pants. She wore a leather cord with a large amber pendant that fell just between her breasts. The subdued sconce lighting highlighted the warm rich color of her skin. Drew felt herself clinch with desire. She was absolutely the most beautiful woman she had ever seen.

"Hi there, come on in," Cicely said. Even the sound of her voice was beautiful. So rich and seductive. Drew walked in, feeling nervous, but excited.

The apartment was lovelier than Drew had imagined. The floors were some kind of engineered wood. *Probably ecological and sustainable.* The wraparound kitchen had dark wood cabinets and black granite flecked with blue mica. The room opened to a great room that functioned as part dining, part living space. There were sliding doors opening onto a balcony above the courtyard.

Everything was clean, minimalist. Cicely had excellent taste from what Drew could see. The colors in the great room were as dynamic as her beauty. Oranges and reds, by way of throw pillows on the ash colored sectional. What looked like an old barn door had been repurposed into a coffee table. On one wall hung what looked like old wrought iron fencing of some sort. It now held little votive candles every foot or so, which were giving the room a nice ambient glow.

"What is the candle holder made from? An old fence?" Drew asked.

"Actually, it's from an old screened door. I drove by a junk shop in Marble Falls and there was this door, sitting there saying, 'Hey, Cicely, you know you want me. Come on and buy me.' I'm such a sucker for talking doors. I bought it but couldn't figure out how to use it. At first, it leaned against the wall in the bedroom. Then I had this brilliant idea to scrap the wooden frame and make the candleholder out of the iron. I'm pretty proud of that piece."

"So you should be. It's lovely."

"Come on, let me show you everything."

Cicely led her on a tour of the apartment, which really only had the great room and her bedroom, aside from the laundry and powder rooms. The balcony was an added bonus, and she clearly put a lot of thought into its setup. There was bench seating on one side, covered in overstuffed pillows, and an apartment safe fire pit in the center. The far side had a large vase with bamboo and a mini sand garden. Drew could see the appeal. Not her cup of tea, but nice. Really nice.

"Would you like to sit out here and have a drink? Or would you prefer being inside?"

"Oh, I'll always take outside if it's a choice. Thanks."

"Great, me too. How about a mojito? Or a beer? Wine?"

"I'll have a mojito. Can I help?"

"That's okay. I know you had to work today. I was off so I've been a lazy bum. You rest and I'll get the drinks," Cicely said.

As Drew settled back on the cushions, she heard music begin to play. She recognized the soft ballad and found herself quietly singing along with the lyrics. She leaned deeper into the bed of softness surrounding her, kicked her boots off, and pulled her feet up onto the bench.

The first song transitioned into the next, a little grittier, but still fun. She felt her shoulders and hips moving with the beat. Major chair dancing.

She stopped and looked around sheepishly. There was Cicely, holding their glasses and moving across the living space with the same shimmy in her hips that Drew had just stopped. She started moving again, and saw Cicely smiling. She had to. There simply was no option. She rose from her cushy spot and danced across the floor to her. She took the glasses and set them on the coffee table and moved into her.

They danced as one, so in sync Drew felt heat flow through her. Her flesh rippled with pleasant surges, like the sun hitting her skin on a cool morning, waking up every nerve and washing her in electric energy. The feeling intensified as Cicely's hands ran up her back, and her nails ignited a fire in Drew. Leaning her head back, she effectively pushed her body into full contact with Cicely's gorgeous form. And then her hand was on Cicely's neck, urging her forward, and they fell into a kiss that matched the rhythm of their bodies.

Then the music transitioned again, and the song, an anthem for their generation, made them fall away from each other, laughing. Then they were bouncing to the beat, arms hitting the air and singing at the top of their lungs.

When it ended and another ballad began, they collapsed on the couch.

"That was fun. I can't get over how everything is easy with you," Cicely said.

"I know exactly what you're saying. It's effortless. At least for now, it is."

"I hope it lasts. It's amazing to have this. I don't want it to go away."

"No, me either. But the truth is, we really don't know very much about each other."

"True, we have a lot to discover. So let's start now. Tell me about you."

Drew was unprepared for her delivery. She coughed and cleared her throat. "Me? Uh. Okay. So, I'm twenty-six."

"Thirty-two," Cicely interjected.

Drew was surprised. She looked much younger, but then again, she had that indefinable something that people called timeless beauty.

"I'm a park ranger. Master's in environmental science. I love my job. I love being outside."

"I like that. That's a good thing. I'm mostly stuck in an office. I'm a social worker with the Travis County Mental Health Public Defenders Office. So yeah, lots of fun and games."

"But that's such important work. I mean, the number of people who need that kind of advocacy is staggering."

"That's exactly why I do the work I do. Heaven knows it can be brutal, but it's also rewarding. I always thought I'd work with families, you know, with kids. But I wasn't built for that level of pain. That work is for the hearty."

Drew was quiet. She knew exactly how brutal that could be. She'd lived some of it. Cicely didn't need to know that, though. She pushed down the urge to talk about her experiences with social services.

Cicely must have picked up on her reticence, though. "What? What are you trying so hard not to tell me?"

"It's nothing." She took a long sip of her drink.

"No. We aren't going to do that."

"Excuse me?"

"Lie. Prevaricate. Avoid difficult discussions. I don't do that."

She didn't seem upset, just absolutely serious. Drew evaluated the situation. Tell her about her youth in the welfare system, or make an excuse. *Should I tell her?* Would it be a mistake to let it go? Or would laying it out there be the mistake? There was really only one choice she could make, if she wanted to truly connect with someone.

"Okay. I'm not real comfortable talking about this, but I don't want it to come between us."

"Yes? I'm listening." She slid closer to Drew on the couch and put her hand gently over hers. Their shoulders touched, and somehow, that simple human touch made it easier.

"I was in foster care for a year when I was a kid." There, she'd said it.

"Drew, I'm sorry. Why were you removed from your home?"

And there it is. The inevitable follow-up question that threw everything into chaos. No one ever believed her when she said she didn't remember. It had earned her many unfair punishments from her foster siblings. They thought she was saying that for attention. She felt herself tensing, pulling in, closing off to any external emotions.

"I don't know."

"What? How can you not know? How old were you?"

"Best guess? Twelve. I guess I lied to you about my age. I'm not sure if it's twenty-six or twenty-seven at this point."

Cicely looked puzzled, but not angry. No anger. No rejection. It was a different reaction than she was used to, and it unsettled her. She started to pull away, to stand up and leave, but Cicely's hand closed on hers and held her fast.

"No, don't go. Help me understand, okay?"

"Okay."

"So, you went into foster care around the age of twelve," Cicely said.

"Yeah, that's the doctor's best guess at the time."

"What do you remember?"

"I remember running. Running down a road, I guess. Then someone found me and the police took me to the Center for Child Protection. They made sure I was okay, you know, physically. Then they started trying to help me remember," Drew said.

"Did you? Remember?"

"No. I mean, I didn't remember anything. Cars scared me. Electric lights. Everything. It was like I was born that day. Born, running down the road."

"What did the doctors say? About why you didn't remember?" Cicely said.

"They figured out I had some type of traumatic experience that made me forget."

"Dissociative amnesia."

"Yeah, exactly that," Drew said.

"But that's usually temporary. Most patients recover their memories in the first few weeks or months."

"Yeah, so they tell me."

"That didn't happen for you?" Cicely said.

"Not yet. I'm still waiting for the grand epiphany," Drew said.

"Wow. That's got to be so hard for you."

"Nah, not so much anymore. I mean, it's been fourteen years. I wasn't in the system too long. My folks adopted me a year after I'd turned up. They gave me history, you know? And love, and family."

"Well, that's good. I'm glad you have them."

"It's pretty awesome. My family is pretty much built from foster care. Me, my brother, and, sister are all fosters who fell into a family that loved us. We're the lucky ones."

"Yes, you are. Tell me about them? Your family?" Cicely said.

"My parents are reformed hippies. Or maybe hippies born a generation too late? They're both professors at UT. They adopted me when my mom made tenure, and when my dad made it, they adopted Javon and Wynika," Drew said.

"Javon and Wynika? Nice names. How old are they?"

"Javon is eighteen this month, and Wy is thirteen."

"Are you close to them?"

"Oh yeah. I spent a lot of time with Wy when she was little. Javon had some struggles, and he kept my folks pretty busy the first two years. So I kind of stepped in with Wynika. She was pure sunshine, you know? A total love. She still is, really. She gives me a run for my money sometimes, but still that same pure soul."

"I think it's pretty amazing that you're so connected to them. That's great."

"What about you? What's your family like?"

Cicely looked sad suddenly, and then angry. *What did I say to upset her?*

"No, no family."

"No? Should I not ask?"

"They…they kicked me out when I came out to them. Same old story I'm sure you've heard a million times."

"Seriously? I didn't think that happened so much anymore." Drew could see that Cicely was in pain. It was like a wall fell between them, and she didn't want to let that stand. She ran her hand down Cicely's tight shoulders.

Cicely turned away from her touch. "Yeah, sucks to be me. Their religion says I'm an abomination, and if they were to maintain any relationship with me, they would imperil their immortal souls. Big scary lesbian. That's me."

"Wow. I'm so sorry. They're wrong, of course. You know that, right?"

"Yeah, I know, but say it anyway. It makes me feel better."

"I'll share my family with you. They're all about sharing the love. You'll fit right in." She smiled at that, and Drew felt it in her soul. A warm punch of sunshine. "I love it when you do that."

"What? Do what?"

"Smile. You have the world's most amazing smile. I find myself only wanting to do and say things that end with you smiling at me. Are you a wizard?"

Cicely laughed at that, and the tension surrounding her family situation dissolved. "Come on, get up and dance with me, you freaking hippie child."

She pulled Drew up from the couch and they danced their way out to the balcony. *It wasn't a one-off.* This was real, this feeling of belonging, of rightness. It might not always feel like this. Something could happen to change the way one or both of them felt, but for now, Drew was going to trust it. She was going to believe it.

They danced until the timer started buzzing in the kitchen. "Time for dinner. Come help me," Cicely said.

"Sure."

She directed Drew to the drawers for silverware, and she set the table while Cicely served.

"Whatever that is sure smells delicious," Drew said.

"I'm glad you think so. I hope you don't mind a vegetarian dinner. I try to limit my intake of meat."

"No, I don't mind a bit. What are we having?"

"It's cauliflower gratin with Manchego and almond sauce."

"Mmm, sounds great. If it tastes anything like it smells, it is going to be fabulous."

"I have a tabouli salad, as well. Here, take these plates to the table and I'll grab the salad."

Drew's taste buds were completely happy with the delicious meal Cicely had prepared. She had eaten vegetarian a few times, but nothing came close to this.

"This is so good. How often do you cook without meat?"

"At least three times a week. I'd love to give meat up entirely, but I can't resist a good steak."

"My favorite, but this is so delicious it makes me believe I could go without."

"That makes me happy. I'm glad you're enjoying it. Did you remember your swimsuit?"

"I did indeed," Drew said.

"Good, after this we can go down to the hot tub. Would you like that?" Cicely said.

"Sure. How crowded does it get this time of year?"

"Some days it's pretty full, but with the festival and it being a Friday, there shouldn't be many others tonight."

"That sounds even better. I get kind of antsy around a lot of strangers. I don't know why, but small groups are better for me."

"No problem. We can check it out, and if it's not comfortable, we can come back up here," she said.

"Thank you." Drew appreciated Cicely being sensitive to her feelings. She was really enjoying this time with her. The magic that took hold of her hadn't faded one bit. In fact, it was even more pronounced now that she knew a bit more about Cicely.

They cleaned up after dinner and changed into their suits. Drew looked down at her faded blue workout shorts and hoped Cicely wouldn't be embarrassed to be seen with her. Oh well, it couldn't be helped. She pushed through the door of the powder room and almost bumped into Cicely. She was a knockout in her gold colored string bikini. Drew closed her mouth when she realized it was open, clicking her teeth together.

"I take it you like my suit," Cicely said.

"Um, yes?" Drew said.

"Good. I don't wear it very often, and it's nice to know it's appreciated. You look all kinds of handsome in that outfit, as well."

"You're so full of it. I look like a Goodwill reject."

"No. You're wrong. You look like a rugged individual, unfettered by convention and comfortable with yourself. That, my dear, is sexy."

Heat flashed across Drew's face at the compliment. "That's nice to hear. I'm glad you don't mind. I couldn't find my regular trunks, so these shorts had to do."

"They do, nicely. Come on, let's go get wet."

She led them down to the pool. It was empty except for a couple sitting on one of the day beds. The hot tub was set into one edge of the large pool with a constant flow of water. Drew stepped into the warm water and settled on the bench seat. She held a hand up to Cicely and steadied her as she joined her.

"This is really nice," Drew said.

"This pool was the selling point for me when I was deciding on a place to live."

"Yeah?"

"I'd really prefer to be in a house, but it's hard to find anything affordable so close in. One day I'll have my house and a garden, maybe near one of the lakes. That's my dream."

"Mine, too. I'd love to live up near Pace Bend Park, or Marble Falls. Something away from the city where there's land."

"Nice. I could go for that, as long as it wasn't too far to commute."

Drew smiled. It was nice to imagine that they had that in common. She felt ridiculously childish, checking off boxes of how they fit. She chuckled.

"What? Why are you laughing?"

"I'm just amusing myself. I don't understand why, but I feel so right with you. That's something I've never had happen before. That's all."

"I get that feeling, too, but honestly? I've learned not to trust it. This is our first date, and yeah, it feels right, but we don't know much about each other yet. Let's see where we are in a few weeks, huh?"

"I'm good with that. I like how this feels, though."

"I like it, too. I want to be clear about my expectations. That's all."

"Okay, tell me about them."

"I want this to be fun, you know? I'm not looking for anything more than that."

Drew was confused. She didn't have a lot of experience dating, but never had things felt so easy. *Does this mean she wants a one-nighter? Do I want that?* She felt sick to her stomach. This was a lot more complicated than she'd expected. She liked Cicely and wanted to be with her, but she wasn't sure she wanted to be in a casual relationship. *I want this to lead to somewhere solid, even if short-term. Can I say that to her?* She had to try. "Your idea of dating and mine are different, but that's okay. I want to be able to trust that what we have together is something I can count on, even if it's short-term. So should I leave? Am I asking too much?"

"I want you to stay, but understand this is just a casual night, okay? I'm not planning to run off into the sunset with you because it feels good to be together, but I won't disappear either. Let's take things slow."

"So does that you mean you're not interested in a relationship?"

"Well, no, that's not exactly what I mean. I just want to keep this light and easy. I have trouble getting emotionally involved."

"I get that. I have a hard time connecting to people, too. When you say you want light and easy, does that mean not to get my hopes up?"

"It means giving you my trust isn't going to happen for a long time."

Ouch. I get not wanting to get serious too fast, but not to trust? "Am I wrong to trust you?" Drew traced circles in the water, trying to figure out the subtext of what was going on, something she wasn't good at generally.

"Not at all. I've been burned, more than once. I'm not in a hurry to get burned again, that's all. My ex, Jacki...she messed me up pretty bad. Cheated on me, left me financially ruined, the whole bag of clichéd crap. I don't take risks on people lightly anymore."

"Damn. I'm sorry to hear that. But you know, not everyone is like that, and I'm not her. I mean, I don't have any guarantee that you'll turn out to be the way you seem tonight, but I trust my instincts. I'd like to see how things develop between us." It sounded naïve once she said it out loud, but Drew felt the need to be open.

"That's exactly what I'm saying. I just don't want to give you false hope. If you don't turn out to be what you appear to be, I want you to understand why you're suddenly not a part of my life. It's about being real. Upfront and clear."

It sounded a little strange and a little extreme, but Drew figured she could deal with it unless it got weird. "I think I get what you're saying. I'm fine with going slow and all, and trust is something you build, right?"

"Having you come over tonight is huge for me. I feel vulnerable. Don't make me regret it. That's all I'm asking."

Relief loosened the knots in her stomach. "Slow is good. And we can always just be friends, right?" She grinned and splashed Cicely slightly, trying to lighten the mood, which felt way too heavy for a first date.

Cicely stood and held out her hand.

"Let's go dry off."

"Sounds good to me."

They went to the apartment and changed out of their wet things. Drew changed as quickly as possible, pulling her jeans up over wet thighs. *What am I getting myself into? Is this what I really want? Yeah, I like her and she's beautiful, but is there something real here or not? Do I want to spend time getting to know her better if she's only interested in temporary? Stop it. She said she wouldn't disappear, and she's worth the risk. I've never felt this kind of connection before, and I want to see where it goes.*

She snapped her shirt closed and shoved her wet things into her backpack.

Entering the great room, she saw Cicely leaning against the balcony rail. She was so beautiful and seemed so perfect. Drew cleared her throat, and Cicely turned toward her.

And then they were kissing, as perfectly as they had embraced before, they kissed. No frantic realization that this was happening, only the sense of intoxicating rightness. Drew was vaguely aware that they had moved through the apartment and were now in Cicely's bedroom. The hard point of her nipples through the thin fabric of her gown had Drew's complete attention.

She worked open the buttons of the gown, and Cicely's skin was under her hand. Her pale alabaster hand was a stark contrast to the mahogany of Cicely's chest. She ran her fingers down her sides and back up to those taut nipples. She caressed them and squeezed gently, causing them to harden further.

She felt the tug as Cicely gripped and pulled both sides of her shirt, unsnapping it in one clean motion. And her mouth was on Drew's breast, an extension of the kiss that started on the balcony.

"God, don't stop," Drew said. She slipped her hands into the tight curls of Cicely's hair and held her in place. The exquisite tension that gripped her from her nipple to her clitoris was electric and she wanted it to build and build before she released it. She kicked furiously at her boots to knock them to the floor and squirmed out of her jeans, naked but for her cotton underwear, and those were quickly becoming an unbearable annoyance.

And then Cicely sat up, astride her. Her gown was open down the front, her nipples peeking out from the silky fabric. She rolled her hips and ground her pelvis into her. She wasn't wearing anything but the gown, and she painted Drew's belly with her essence. Her hands slid under the edges of the gown and slipped it from her shoulders. The silk tickled Drew's thighs as it landed. Then she leaned over her, her eyes alive with the heat of their desire.

"Take me," Cicely said.

Drew slowly ran her hand between Cicely's legs and parted her tender flesh. She was hot and wet, and the tension Drew was holding threatened to break free. When she entered her, Cicely embraced her and held her, little spasms of excitement pressing into her. She moved her hand, gently at first, and then with abandon as Cicely rode the crest of her orgasm. Drew had to let go when she saw the look of elation flash on Cicely's face and her hand was flooded with the evidence of their passion. She felt herself slide over the edge into the pool of raw energy that engulfed her.

Cicely collapsed onto her, then slipped to her side and Drew pulled her hand free to hold her. She was completely at peace and happy as she closed her eyes and fell asleep.

Someone was screaming.

Cicely pulled herself from sleep as Drew started flailing beside her. She was breathing so strangely, Cicely wondered if she was having some kind of allergic reaction. She sat up.

"Drew, wake up," she said. She shook her gently, her own heart pounding. "Come on, wake up."

She thrashed even harder under the sheet, acting as if something was holding her down. Her scream became frightening, her terror evident.

"Drew," she shouted. Someone was going to call the police if she didn't get her to stop. She stood, thinking maybe a bit of water on her face would rouse her. Before she could step away from the bed, the scream abruptly stopped. Frightened, she moved to Drew's side. Her eyes were wide open, staring at nothing. No sound, not even ragged breathing. Cicely felt her own panic rising.

"Drew, are you awake?"

No response. *She's not breathing.* Cicely pushed her hand against Drew's chest, hoping to hear a deep inhalation.

"Come on. Breathe, damn you."

She leaned forward to give her a rescue breath when Drew gasped, took a huge breath, and closed her eyes. Cicely watched as she fell back asleep without waking at all. *How did that happen? How did she go from screaming to not breathing to sleep? Was it a night terror? Like children have?* She needed to understand, but would wait until the morning. For now, she'd watch over her. She climbed back into bed and wrapped her arms around her knees. She watched the subtle rise and fall of Drew's chest as she slept. She couldn't imagine what Drew had been through to cause the kind of terror she'd seen so clearly in her face, something so awful it would take away the memories of her entire childhood. She felt twisted inside, like her nerves were exposed and something was rubbing against them. *I'm not sure I can handle this.* But the vulnerability she saw in Drew's sleeping face was so compelling.

She slid down under the sheet and pressed herself against Drew. *I'm here. I'm not going anywhere. You're safe with me.* She willed Drew to hear and believe her thoughts. Before long, her own eyes started closing and she gave in to sleep.

❖

Drew woke and felt the warm presence of Cicely beside her. The changing light in the room lauded the arrival of morning, and she knew she needed to get moving. She rolled toward her and kissed Cicely's bare shoulder. She was rewarded with the sweetest sound as Cicely balked at the idea of waking.

"Good morning, beautiful. I have to get going," she said.

"Why? Can't you stay with me for a while?"

There was something in Cicely's expression, like she was trying to figure out how to say something. But Drew didn't have time for a long chat. "I could, but then my sister would be disinclined to make friends with you. I'd really like for you to be friends."

She sighed and opened her eyes. "You drive a hard bargain. Okay. I'll get the coffee going."

The sheet slid down, exposing her pert nipple. Drew found it impossible to resist and wrapped it in the warm comfort of her mouth. She loved the way Cicely's nipple reacted when she sucked it. It tightened and felt like a ripe berry against the roof of her mouth. Cicely mewled and pushed her hips into her.

Drew shifted until she was above her and kissed her way down Cicely's body. She felt jolts rock through her as Cicely's skin reacted to the kisses. She was dusted with gooseflesh and Drew wanted nothing more than to create the same reaction all over her. She reached the place where she most wanted to be. She leaned back to drink in her beauty, but Cicely was impatient.

"Come on, baby, please," she said.

And she couldn't hold back any longer. She indulged herself in the glory of this amazing woman, sucking and kissing and giving it her all. It was over too soon as the spasms rocked Cicely and she cried out Drew's name. Sliding up beside her, Drew was content. *This is good.*

The need to leave was still there, on the edge of her awareness. She knew, rationally, that Wynika would be texting her in the next half hour or so to confirm when she'd be picking her up. She should go, really, but this was so nice. She closed her eyes. *Just a catnap.*

She woke an hour later to the sound of her phone going off. *Damn.* She fumbled to her feet and found her jeans. She silenced the phone and checked to be sure Cicely was still sleeping. She pushed out of the room and into the great room.

"Good morning, Wy," she said.

"I thought you'd never answer your phone. Where are you?"

"I'm just waking up. Sorry. What time are we going to the show?"

"You said we could go to lunch first, remember?"

"Yes, I remember. You wanted to go to Freebirds, right?"

"Can we eat after the movie instead?"

"Why?" Drew said.

"Oh, um, there's an eleven o'clock showing. You know I've been dying to see the new Avengers movie. I don't want to wait until one."

Drew wondered what the real reason might be, and suspected it might have something to do with that boy, Charles. Wy had mentioned that he was working at the cinema now.

"Okay, no problem. I'll be there at ten thirty," she said.

"Yay. I'll be ready to go. Thanks, Drewsy."

"You got it, squirt. Let me get going."

"Bye," Wy said.

Drew quietly made her way back into the bedroom and picked up her scattered clothes. It was nine forty-five now. She dressed quickly and walked to Cicely. She looked so beautiful, curled into her pillow, sleeping soundly. Drew bent down and kissed her softly.

She left a note on the kitchen counter asking Cicely to call her when she woke and headed to her bike. Her phone buzzed in her pocket. Hoping it wasn't Wy, she pulled it out. Not a number she knew. She opened the message.

Where were you last night? You didn't come home, naughty girl. I'll have to punish you.

The hair on the back of her neck stood up. *What the hell?* She started to delete it, but hesitated. This was too weird. It sounded like someone was watching her. If she deleted the message she wouldn't have any proof. She blocked the number but saved the message. She wished she had time to run by the house, but as it was, she'd be pushing it to make it to pick up Wy on time. Kashka was going to give her shit and she knew it. She couldn't keep leaving him alone. She'd invite Cicely to her house tonight, then he'd be appeased.

She filled her ride with memories of Cicely the night before and this morning, the touch and taste of her so powerful that she was afraid she was going to have to pull over. She'd never had such a deep sense of connection with anyone. *Not a girlfriend, not my parents, no one.* It was almost surreal. It was a relief to pull into the driveway and park. She needed to feel the solid ground under her.

She was later than she wanted to be but had made up some time on the highway. Wy was standing at the door waiting.

"You're late," she said.

"Where's your helmet?"

"I'll get it," she said and ran to the garage.

Wy had ridden with her often enough that she didn't need to be reminded how to be safe, but Drew told her anyway. She'd never forgive herself if anything happened to Wy. They took surface streets to the Greenway Cinema. She never went over thirty-five with Wy. When they had parked and locked the helmets, Wy gave her her customary hug.

"Umm, thanks. I thought you were getting too big to give hugs. I thought I was going to have to beg."

"Nah, I'll never be too big to hug you, Drews. Come on. I want to get some popcorn before the show," she said.

"Seriously? Aren't we eating lunch after the movie?"

"Yes, but I want popcorn for brunch."

Drew shook her head. She knew Wy could eat popcorn and still enjoy a good lunch, so she agreed. At the counter, Drew watched as Wy made eyes at the young man helping them. *This must be Charles.* Nice looking kid, but he seemed too old for Wy. She waited, but as soon as they sat down, she was going to have to ask some serious questions. This was her baby sister they were talking about.

Drew handed Wy a twenty to pay for the treats and she actually giggled when she handed it to the boy. *Ugh.* She was growing up too fast. She led the way to their theater and chose seats in the middle tier. Wy liked to sit close, but it gave Drew a headache.

"So, tell me, who's the boy?"

"What boy?" Wy said.

"The boy you were drooling over at the counter? Remember him?"

Wy blushed and Drew felt bad for teasing her. "It's okay, Wy. I just want to know more about him. He seems really nice," Drew said.

"Isn't he gorgeous?"

"Well, I don't know about—"

"Of course you don't. I forget you like girls. He's gorgeous, trust me."

"Okay, but how old is he? He seems a bit older than you."

"He's only sixteen. That's not too old."

"Wynika. You're still in middle school. If he's sixteen that means he's in high school. How do you even know this guy?" Drew said.

"I know him from around."

"Around where?"

"Gosh, Drew. Who are you? The FBI?"

"No, I'm even scarier. I'm your adult sister who knows your parents and has their phone number."

"You're not going to tell on me, are you?"

"What's to tell? That you have a crush on a boy? I'm sure Mom's already aware of that."

"Not that. Are you going to tell that he's older than me?" Wy said.

"You haven't told Mom already?"

"No."

"How come?" Drew said.

"She wouldn't let me see him if she knew he was sixteen. But, Drew, he's so nice and so sweet. He just turned sixteen and I'm almost in ninth grade. I'll be fourteen way before he's seventeen. Please don't tell, please?"

"Where do you see him?"

"At the library. And sometimes at Ginger's house. She's his cousin."

"Ginger? Javon's girlfriend?"

"Yes."

"Is that where you met him?"

"Yes. At their Christmas party."

"So his parents were there? And our parents?"

"Yes."

"Does Javon know you like this boy? What's his name, Charles?"

"It's Charlie. And yes, he knows."

"What does he say about it?"

"He says Charlie better never try anything with me or he'll break his nose."

"Have you ever been alone with Charlie?" Drew said.

"No. Javon won't let me. If I go to meet him at the library, Ginger or Javon have to go with me. And when I see him at their house, Ginger's parents have to be home." Wy looked put out by the amount of chaperones involved in her little crush.

"Okay, I'll make you a deal," Drew said.

"What deal?"

"I won't tell Mom and Dad that you're seeing a boy who's older than you if—"

"If what?"

"If you tell them yourself. I don't think they'll have a problem if you keep things the way they are. I actually think they'll be proud of Javon for watching out for you. But you have to tell them. Lying is only going to lead to trouble," Drew said.

"Hmph. I don't like your deal."

"Suit yourself. You come clean or I do. That's how it works, kiddo."

She could tell Wy was going to pout about it for a while. Luckily, the movie started. Hopefully, she'd accept it by the time the show was done. Drew really didn't relish being the snitch, but she wouldn't let Wy play games with their parents, either. Javon would be heading to college in the fall and wouldn't be there to keep an eye on her. She needed to be upfront with their folks. Drew would see to it that it happened. Her family had saved her, and she'd do everything she could to keep the people she loved safe, always.

Chapter Five

He sat behind them in the darkened theater. Some action movie was blaring across the screen. She was still so perfect, even more perfect now that she had reached the fullness of womanhood. He felt the familiar stiffening in his pants as he thought of their reunion. Not long now. She'd be his again very soon.

He lost himself in the memory of her room last night. It had been such a mess when he entered. Clothes strewn in every direction. He carefully collected each item and neatly folded and replaced it in her drawer. He took his time, smelling each piece in hopes of catching her scent. When he remembered discovering the soft cotton of her underclothes in their little drawer, he slid his hand down to caress himself. *Soon.*

The sudden quiet of the film brought him back to the present. He had replaced the phone he had last texted her with, knowing she'd block access to that line. He had learned so many things during their time apart. The harsh education he had been afforded courtesy of the department of corrections had opened his eyes to a whole new level of entertainment. His cellmate had made him his special friend. Along with pain there had been pleasure and mentoring. He'd taught him all about modern communication devices and social networking. That was how he had found her. The contraband cell phone market in Luther Unit had been profitable in many ways.

His cellmate helped him make an online profile and presence that hid who he really was. He'd first flirted with a variety of women and men, teasing and exciting them. When he gained confidence with the medium, he'd begun to actively search for her. It'd been difficult.

Her name was wrong. But he'd done it. He found her. Her face was so vivid in his memory that even the passage of time couldn't keep him from recognizing her. That smile. Those eyes. Did she miss him? Did she cry out for him in her sleep as she had when they had been together? He had to know.

The first thing he'd done after parole was to stake out the ranger station at Zilker Park. He had watched her coming and going, day after day. He imagined sliding behind her on that big noisy motorcycle and pulling her against him. They belonged together. He bored quickly of the activities she engaged in at the park service, though. How could she stand such repetitive, dull work?

Deciding it was worth the risk, he'd grown bolder. He'd followed her to her home. That had been pure ecstasy. Watching her in her little house, with her bossy cat. Her routines became second nature to him. He knew when she woke, when she went to sleep, how long her showers lasted. He knew her, oh, how he knew her. And then he finally accessed her cell phone number. She was his. He'd tease her a while, and when the time was ripe, he'd reclaim her.

When she failed to come home the night before he had been angry with himself for not tailing her. Where had she been? With the tall man? The ranger?

He didn't like the hulking man who worked with her. He was always showing up at her house. He was a rude thing, never calling, just suddenly appearing. It had taken some maneuvering to avoid discovery every time the man stopped by. And this little girl? Who was she to his love? They seemed so close. He didn't like that at all. But then again, maybe she'd be a nice addition to his herd. She was lovely to look at, her burnished brown skin tight and appealing, but she dimmed in comparison to his Sunshine.

He sighed and quietly exited the theater. He'd watch them in the lobby and plan for his time.

❖

Drew shivered as she watched Wy walk across the crowded lobby. Her skin was covered in goose bumps. Her stomach churned with acid and she felt like she was about to panic. This was too weird;

she wasn't given to panic attacks, only nightmares. Her waking life was fairly copacetic, and she didn't get thrown very often. Why was she suddenly feeling like she needed to grab Wy and run from the building? She shook off the feeling and focused on her sister.

Wy wanted to say good-bye to Charlie. She watched her walk right up to him as he served a cute girl her soda. *Dang, she sure is a confident kid. I would have been stumbling over myself at her age in that situation.* Drew felt a flash of pride for her.

Her phone buzzed in her pocket, distracting her.

Hey, sexy. I missed you this morning. I hope I'll be seeing you tonight? Let me know. XO

She couldn't keep from smiling at the message. When she looked back to the counter for Wy, she was gone. The panicked feeling rushed back and she scanned the room. She found her near the exit talking to some strange man. *No way.* She knew better than that. Drew hurried over to them, but the man slipped out the door before she reached them.

"Who was that?" Drew said.

"Huh? Who?"

"That man. Who was he?"

"I don't know, some weirdo. He just grabbed me when I walked past and told me how beautiful my skin was. Creepy. I told him where to get off and he hit the door."

"That's not okay, Wy. He could be out to harm someone. Let's tell the manager."

"No, Drew! Please! I'll be so embarrassed! Please!"

"We have to. What if he comes back and grabs some other girl? We have to let them know," Drew insisted, thinking about the bizarre crawling sensation she'd felt. *And those crazy texts...*

"Well, can we tell them quietly? He didn't hurt me, only freaked me out."

"That's fine by me, be we have to report him. Come on, you can ask Charlie who we should talk to."

"No! Not Charlie. Let's ask the ticket salesperson."

Drew understood then that Wy was embarrassed this had happened. She needed to make her see why it was important.

"Okay. Listen. This man had no right to stop you, absolutely no right to touch you, and it's up to us to stand up and speak out. If you had been younger or more gullible, something really bad could have happened. I'm glad it didn't and he left, but next time it could be different. If we tell the management that he was here and what he did, they'll tell the employees to watch for him, and we might prevent a bad thing. You get why that's important, right?" Drew stared at her, trying to gauge whether she really got it.

"Yeah, I get it, but I don't want Charlie to know it was me, if that's okay."

"Sure it is. Come on."

They asked the ticket counter person and were directed to the manager. It took them a few minutes to tell her what had occurred. She was grateful and even gave them vouchers for a future movie day with popcorn and a soda.

"I'm glad you convinced me to tell them. It made me feel better and how cool to get a free movie," Wy said as they left the building.

"I know, right? We told them to keep people safe, but it's nice to get a reward. Let's go eat, huh? You still up for burritos?"

"Heck yeah. I can't wait."

They were pulling their helmets on when Drew noticed an older model sedan cruising slowly through the parking lot. She stopped and stared at the driver, sure it would be the man again, but it turned out to be an old fellow just driving cautiously.

She didn't like this new hyper vigilant feeling. It was a one-off and she needed to let it go, but it was really bugging her. She slid into the saddle and kicked the bike to life. When she felt Wy slide in behind her and tap her thigh, she headed away from the theater and the creepy mood.

They enjoyed their lunch, and after topping it off with Amy's Ice Cream, she dropped Wy at home. She should've gone in to say hello to her folks, but she was anxious to reconnect with Cicely, so she let a wave suffice.

Kashka was in a real stink when she returned home. He was meowing loudly and she knew the second she sat, he'd be all over her. As a consolation, she opened a can of his favorite food for him.

"Good boy, eat up. Mom's sorry she's been gone so much. I promise I'll stay home tonight. Hopefully we'll have company."

She called Cicely.

"Hello, gorgeous. How was the movie date?" Cicely said.

"Boy, it's good to hear your voice. It was okay, some weirdness, but nothing big," she said.

"So what are your plans for the rest of the day? Want to come over for a swim?"

"Actually, I was hoping you might like to come here. I have a beautiful piece of salmon in the fridge that needs cooking today. I have some mean grill skills. What do you think?"

"That sounds great. What time shall I arrive?"

"Anytime. The sooner the better. I miss you."

"You're so sweet. Okay, let me get organized and I'll head over in about an hour. You're in Rosewood, right? What's your address?"

Drew didn't remember mentioning her neighborhood, but that was okay. Maybe she'd mentioned it at the festival.

"It's 2913 East Fourteenth. The green craftsman. I'll be waiting for you on the porch."

"You got a deal. Be there as soon as I can," Cicely said.

Drew headed back to her room for a quick shower. She wanted to take time to tidy up her room, too. She had left it in such a state the night before. As she rounded the corner and entered her room, she froze. Her stomach knotted as she looked around. *Nothing* was out of place. *That's not right. How could that be? I know I tossed shorts from my drawer all over the place.* Someone had been in her house. Drew shivered as the idea of such an invasion of privacy washed over her. This was her place. She was safe here. How dare someone break in and…clean her room?

This was too weird. She ran to the front door to check the lock. It was still dead bolted. The only extra keys to her place were with her folks. *Maybe Mom came by and did me a good turn?* She called her to check.

"Hi, Drew. Thank you for taking Wynika out. She loves spending time with you. So does your mother, by the way."

"Hi, Mom. This is going to sound strange, but did you happen to come by the house last night or this morning?"

"Well, of course I did. Didn't you see my note? I put it right on the refrigerator. I needed to get your blue quilt. The one Grandma Jean made? It was time to have it cleaned."

Drew almost collapsed with relief. Mystery solved. Her mom would never change her ways when it came to keeping Drew on schedule with chores. Thank heavens. Those stupid texts and the incident with her sister must have gotten under her skin more than she'd realized. "I missed it. I'm glad it was you. I could tell someone had been here and it freaked me out a little."

"My goodness. I sure didn't mean to upset you. I should've called. I know you've asked me to. I'm sorry, honey."

"It's all good. Thanks for the cleaning."

"Anytime baby. I want you to have that quilt for your lifetime. That will only happen if it gets proper care."

"Yeah, I know. But thanks for tidying up."

There was a pause on the line. Drew wondered if her mom was counting to ten like she had when she was a kid.

"You're welcome, dear. When are your father and I going to get a real visit from you?"

"Soon, Mom. I promise."

"Good. Why don't you come for lunch tomorrow? We can go to that Mexican place you love."

"I'll let you know. I may have plans."

"May have? A date? Oh, that would be nice."

"Yes, Mom. A date. I have one in an hour, so I better go jump in the shower. I'll call you if I can make it to lunch, okay?"

"Okay, honey. Have fun."

"Bye, Mom."

She tossed the phone onto her bed and stripped down to her underwear before heading to the bathroom. The shower felt fantastic. She dried off and pulled on some comfy shorts and a Beerland T-shirt. She considered dressing up a little, but she was going to grill, and this was home. She didn't want Cicely to get a false impression of her style. Shorts and T-shirts were her go-to outfits. If that made Cicely uncomfortable, it was best to find out now.

She grabbed a cold beer from the fridge, smiling at her mom's verbose note. It didn't mention the sad state of her room, so that was good. She made her way to the porch and dropped down in her favorite rocker. Kashka immediately settled in her lap. She stroked his silky fur as she waited for Cicely to arrive.

As she took her last sip, a yellow Mini Cooper, top down, pulled in with Cicely behind the wheel. Drew stood to greet her, and Kashka meowed at her for dumping him from her lap. She soothed him with a pat, and he jumped onto the porch railing to view the new arrival.

Cicely was wearing a yellow and orange sundress, her lips tinted to match the orange. *I want to kiss those lips.* Drew walked down the steps. Her nerves kicked in. *Will this be easy or awkward?* She smiled as Cicely stepped out of her car. "Hi, beautiful," she said, hoping to collect that kiss.

"Hey, sexy," Cicely said. She stepped into Drew's arms and kissed her soundly.

Drew sighed, feeling her knots unravel. This would be okay.

"Come on in. Can I get you a drink?"

"Sure, what have you got?"

"I made some sangria. Do you like it?"

"I do. Thank you. So, introduce me to your cat."

Drew laughed. "Cicely, Kashka. Kashka, Cicely."

"What a handsome fellow you are, Kashka," she said.

Kashka, with his typical sauciness, purred loudly and rubbed himself against her offered hand.

"I think he likes me," Cicely said.

"How could he not? Just know that he now considers you his and won't hesitate to jump in your lap. I hope that's okay with you."

"Perfectly okay. I love cats."

Drew led the way to her kitchen and poured them each a glass of sangria. She watched as Cicely took her first sip. *God, she's even sexy when she's drinking. I want to be that sangria.*

Cicely moved the glass away from her mouth and smiled at Drew. "What? Why are you looking at me like that?"

"You're so sexy. Watching you sip that drink is making me hot."

"Oh yeah?" She raised an eyebrow as she took another sip.

Her lips glistened with the sweet wine, and Drew could barely hold back from kissing them clean. She took a deep pull of her own drink to shake herself out of her stupor. *I've got all night, and I need to grill. Get a grip.*

"So, I take it the sangria is to your satisfaction?"

"Absolutely. What are you making to go with the salmon?"

"I was thinking just a salad and bread. Does that sound good?"

"It does. How can I help?"

Drew hadn't thought about them cooking together, but it sounded like a good idea. It would be fun to move around her small kitchen with Cicely.

"How about if I wash the greens and you work your magic with them? I have some fresh strawberries and some toasted pecans I was going to throw in. Here, take this bowl and I'll hand you stuff. While you're doing that, I'll get the grill going and heat up the bread."

"Great, do you have any tarragon?"

"I'm not sure. Let me check. What are you going to use it for?"

"I thought I'd make an herb dressing to toss with the salad," Cicely said.

"Really? Cool. I was going to pull out the bottle of vinaigrette, but a fresh dressing sounds better. Here's the spice cabinet. Knock yourself out," Drew said.

She watched as Cicely made herself at home in her kitchen. *This feels nice. I like this.* She pulled the greens out of the fridge and washed them. She dried them in her spinner and handed it off to Cicely. She put the berries and nuts beside the greens.

"Okay, if you've got this under control, I'm going to step out back for a minute."

"Sure thing. You do your thing with the grill. I'm good here."

Drew walked out to the deck and lit the grill. While the coals heated, she watched Cicely through the sliding door. *This is surreal. I've never felt so content with another person in my space. Not even Pres. I wonder if she feels this?* She watched as Kashka sashayed in and rubbed against Cicely's legs. She said something to him, but Drew couldn't figure out what. Then she squatted down and rubbed her cheek against his furry face. *Kashi sure feels it.*

What about her issues with trust? Am I going to be able to deal with that? What if she kicks me out of her life with no warning? She started feeling apprehensive. *What would it take for that to happen?*

Cicely looked up at her. Drew rocked back with the power of that look. She moved toward the door and in minutes, had Cicely in her arms. Her skin was as soft as velvet beneath her lips as she moved them up the smooth column of her neck. She felt Cicely's nipples harden against her.

"You need to stop doing that, never," Cicely said.

"Never it is," Drew said as she reached Cicely's full luscious mouth. She kissed her deeply and was rewarded by an equally deep welcome. She turned until she could feel the counter behind her and leaned back against it, off balancing Cicely. She fell forward against Drew, their lips never parting.

The intensity of feelings that rushed through Drew was overwhelming. *This feels so right. Why does it scare the heck out of me?* She broke the embrace and gave herself a little distance.

"Where are you going? I was enjoying that," Cicely said.

Drew reached for the platter on the counter.

"Salmon. I need to put it on the grill."

"Oh? Okay. I guess eating is the point, huh?"

"Here, grab your drink. Come sit outside with me," Drew said.

They went out and Cicely sat on the wicker love seat. Drew arranged the salmon on the grill and joined her.

"How's your sangria? Are you ready for a refill?"

"It's wonderful, but I'm fine. Tell me why you broke up our little make out session?"

Waves of anxiety washed over Drew. *Don't screw this up.*

"I don't know. I thought maybe we should slow things down. We've got this chemistry thing happening, but I'm not sure we want the same things. I know you want light and easy. I thought I could do that, but I'm not sure now. I mean we had a wonderful night last night, and tonight feels the same, but are we going to build something, or is this playing around?"

"I thought we already agreed we would take it slow and casual."

"I know, but how casual? Should I expect to see you on a regular basis, or am I here for this weekend only?"

"Do you *want* to expect to see me?"

"Of course I do. I want to count on that."

"Can we say for now we can count on it? Would that be okay? I told you I won't disappear. That's all I can promise today."

"I guess it has to be. I'm nervous. That's all."

"Me, too." Cicely squeezed her hand and gave her a gentle smile. "Now, can we talk about dinner?"

"Sure, let me get the fish and we'll eat."

"That sounds good. I'll refill our glasses."

Drew followed Cicely in and served the salmon. She'd marinated it in a soy, brown sugar, and honey glaze. Last night's dinner had been extraordinary, and she wanted her simple meal to be memorable.

She watched as she took her first bite. Cicely closed her eyes and tipped her head back, then moaned with appreciation. *That's a good sign. I think she likes it.*

"Taste okay?"

Cicely nodded and continued to moan as she ate.

Drew smiled. *I did it. It might be simple, but it's good, and she's enjoying it.*

Cicely took a sip of her drink and gave Drew a dazzling smile.

"Oh my God, how did you make it taste like that? It's so delicious."

"Aw, it's just a little marinade I threw on. I'm glad you like it. Wait till you taste the dessert," she said.

"Dessert? What's for dessert?"

"Ah, ah, ah, you have to wait and find out. The one thing I will tell you, it's the perfect dessert for this meal. Simple, but delicious."

"Intriguing. How's the salad?"

"It's fantastic. I love that dressing you made. So, tell me about your work. Do you enjoy being a social worker?"

"I love helping people. Sometimes it's hard, but the successes outweigh the disappointments. There's nothing like helping someone through the system."

"They're lucky to have people like you helping them. You said you don't work with kids though, right?"

"Yeah, too hard. I work with indigent folks. It's tough when you have to accept that they don't want to give up their street life. Some of them want to live homeless, since they can't imagine any other way to live anymore. It used to make me feel like I'd failed when I couldn't get them to move into transitional housing," Cicely said.

"I can see that. I've often imagined walking away from life and living on the land. You know, just me and nature. It has its appeal."

"You're joking. There's nothing at all appealing about freezing, or not being able to bathe or brush your teeth, and forget about proper meals or clean clothing. I couldn't do it. No way. I'd last about a day and a half before I'd begin to come unglued."

"True, I guess, but bathing and keeping clean and warm aren't conditional to traditional housing. I mean, if you know how, you can live off the land and still be clean and healthy."

Cicely gave her a hard stare. *She thinks I'm crazy. Why did I say that?*

"Maybe in some places, but certainly not in downtown Austin. It's not a utopian wilderness, you know. The people I deal with live a mean, hard life on the streets. One of my clients died of exposure last winter. That's real, Drew. That's not some survivalist fantasy. People die on the street all the time. When one of my clients would rather risk that than move into a nice clean apartment, it breaks my heart."

"I'm sorry. I'm sure it's hard. I was thinking about it from my personal point of view. I love being in the wilderness, and you're right, it's completely different from living homeless in a city."

"Do you really think you could go out into the Amazon and live off the land? You think you'd be okay in that sort of existence? I can't even imagine doing something like that."

"I think I could. I've been back country camping many times, and I love it. I guess the biggest thing would be knowing the terrain. The hazards of the Amazon would require a lot of research, but I could absolutely drive out into one of the wilderness areas around here and go off grid for as long as I wanted. As long as I had a source of water, and fuel for a fire, I'd be fine. Something about it strikes me as being really perfect."

"Well, you're stronger than me, then. I could never do it," Cicely said.

"I wouldn't choose it now, though. I mean, I have my family. And my job, I love my job. I'm quite content with my life, now. But there have been times that the idea of living off grid gave me the will to keep going. Knowing that when I was old enough, I could leave and be in control of my life helped me."

"You mean when you were younger? In care?"

"Yeah, then and those first few years with my parents. I have these nightmares. Waking up screaming is pretty normal for me. When I was a kid, it was so intense. My folks put me on a heavy dose of medication to help me sleep. It was so disorienting. I walked around in a fog all the time. The lack of control was so confining. I hated life back then. Thinking about running away and living off the land kept me sane," Drew said.

She felt so exposed and wondered if this was it. Would this be the moment that she lost Cicely? She was being open and honest. That should count for something, but she was afraid. She'd always been too strange for anyone. This was why she never ventured into relationship territory.

Anonymous gratification was much simpler and held less threat of pain. She could be someone complete, someone who knew who they were then she could walk away after a few hours, or the next morning. This new reality, this honest landscape Cicely wanted to create, was leaving her laid bare, her weaknesses and faults in the forefront.

Apparently, her emotions were clear on her face, as suddenly Cicely was beside her, wrapping her arms around her.

"No one but you knows how it feels to be you, Drew. I can't imagine how painful your early life had to be. I know a little about you now, and what I know, I like. You're not going to lose me for being vulnerable. It's a good thing, and it's worth it. Being open about your insecurities is scary. This kind of sharing is what I need. I just have to figure out what you need and we'll be okay," she said.

"What I need? I only need to know you're here. I need you to hold me and let me hold you. That's all."

"Yeah?"

"Yeah."

"Well, how about letting me hold you in your bed? Would that work for you?"

Drew pulled back and looked into Cicely's deep brown eyes. "That works great for me."

She stood and led Cicely to her room. In silence, they undressed and lay side-by-side on her bed. The warm, heated energy between them was intoxicating. She felt such a deep sense of contentment as they came together. She felt so connected and anchored in the now. It was a draught she could drink for eternity, given the chance. *I want that chance. I really want it.*

Sleep must have washed over her, because the next thing she knew, Cicely was shaking her, straddled across her body. The look on her face told Drew she'd been having a nightmare again.

"Thank God. Thank God, you're awake. Drew, you were screaming. It was so terrible, and then you went still and quiet. You... you stopped breathing. It seemed like forever. I was about to slap you, when you finally opened your eyes. It made me feel so helpless, just like last night."

"I'm sorry. I'm so sorry." She pulled Cicely to her, running a gentling hand up and down her back. "It happened last night?"

Cicely nodded. "We haven't really had a chance to talk about it, and it felt somehow...invasive, to bring it up this morning."

Drew nodded and sighed. "It happens to me sometimes. The breathing thing. I don't know why, or how long it usually lasts, but I know it's sometimes a component of my nightmares. I'm sorry you had to see that."

"Don't. Don't say sorry. If it's something you experience on a regular basis, then it's something I should know about. Have you talked to a doctor about it? I mean, now, as an adult?"

"I haven't in a while. The last therapist I saw kind of shrugged it off. He said it was a residual of the trauma that caused me to lose my memory, and there really wasn't much I could do about it if I wasn't willing to be medicated."

"That's crazy. There are so many therapy options out there for this kind of thing. Have you tried to recover your memory with hypnosis? You know, regression therapy?" Cicely said.

"I've been offered the option. I'm not sure I want to remember the stuff of my nightmares." She looked down, feeling embarrassed at her fears. "What if I can't forget them again? What if, instead of just messing with my sleep, they mess with my waking life as well?"

"Oh, Drew, I think you'd be surprised how many good things can come from understanding your past. I've helped so many people deal with things like this. Not anyone I've been intimate with, but clients. They've usually been decompensating due to self-medicating with alcohol or drugs. It's amazing how clarity can give you peace," Cicely said.

"I don't know. I can never remember anything when I wake up. I can get up in the morning, pet my cat, and start my day happy. If I find out the source of my dreams, it may turn out to be something that takes that from me. Is it worth the risk?"

"Well, is this worth it? Whatever you're experiencing in your dreams is so horrible it makes you stop breathing. That's not okay. You might not have been affected by it yet, but eventually it's going to start taking a toll on your health."

"It's not something I'm ready to deal with. I…can't."

"Why not? It's the past, Drew. It's over, whatever it was. If you ferret it out, you can see it with mature eyes. What terrified you at twelve might not have that power at twenty-six. Seriously, I want you to think about it. Kallie is an excellent psychiatrist. She could help you deal with this."

"Kallie? Your friend from the festival?"

"Yes. I've never met a better therapist. I'd trust her with anything. Think about it, okay? I can talk to her about you, see what she says?"

"No, not yet. I promise I'll think about it, but let me decide when, okay?"

Cicely looked disappointed. Drew hoped she could accept that she needed to move forward in her own time. Pushing her into something she wasn't ready for wouldn't work. "Please understand why I have to be ready for that."

Cicely's shoulders relaxed, though she didn't lose one jot of concern from her expression. "Okay. I won't say anything. It's your life and your decision."

Drew smiled in relief. "Thank you. Come down here and let me hold you again. I don't have more than one episode a night according to my mom."

Cicely relaxed into her, her head resting on Drew's chest.

Drew held her, reveling in the feeling of her breath against her skin. Before long, Cicely drifted into a deep, untroubled sleep.

Drew watched the gentle rise and fall of her chest, and tenderness filled her. *She cares about me. She wants me to understand my past so it won't haunt me. Maybe I should find out what's lurking in there.* She watched Cicely sleep until her own eyes began to close. *I want to sleep that peacefully beside her.*

CHAPTER SIX

He watched the strange woman walk up to the porch. Why had she come here? What was this about? Then he saw Sunshine take her in her arms. He felt their embrace like a blow to his gut. It was all he could do not to double over with the pain of it. *Why?* She was his. Did she forget him? Had her life away from him driven the memories of what they'd shared from her? At least it was a woman.

No real threat to them, of this he was sure, but the warmth evident in their embrace was painful, nonetheless. Seeing anyone standing in for him was painful. When they entered the house, he left his place of concealment and casually walked down the block past her house. He looked at the license number on the silly little car and made a mental note. He would find out all he could about this new person. If she tried to get between them, he would do what was necessary.

He continued down the tree-shaded road toward his car. After checking that he was unobserved, he climbed behind the wheel and turned on the monitor of the listening device he had placed in her house the day before. He'd had a hard time choosing between listening and watching, but seeing had won. He spent half the day watching her move about her tidy little house, playing with that wretched cat, his only tricky moment coming when she'd walked out to sit on her porch. He'd been stuck lying on the roof of the house across from hers for nearly an hour. But he'd used the time well. He had so many pictures now he would be able to complete their second album.

He reached across the seat and fingered the worn leather surface of an old photo album, its tatty, yellowed surface rough beneath his calloused hand. He inhaled deeply, the earthy scent of the book surrounding him like a welcome blanket. Soon, now. Very soon.

He stroked the book one last time before he started his car. Time to add another doe to his herd. He drove to the northeastern side of town, to the areas showing more wear and economic depression. When he gathered he always sought the vulnerable, the ones who wouldn't be missed.

He had scouted a good gathering place earlier, a park, shaded with live oak and in need of upkeep. He had observed the comings and goings of various young people, well into the night. He had selected a small, dark girl, not more than sixteen by the look of her. He watched her for several days, taking note of how often she visited the park. Sometimes she came with a group of others, but more often she was on her own. He'd followed her back to her campsite once, to satisfy his belief that she belonged to no one.

She had a habit of spending an hour or so on the rusty old swing at dusk, making her way back to her place after the fall of full night. If he found her alone tonight, he would gather her.

He parked his car under the concealing limbs of a large tree and settled in to watch. His wait wasn't long. She came bobbing up the sidewalk after about half an hour. She went directly to the swing and sat, but seemed distracted, watching the sidewalk on the other side of the park.

He gripped the door handle and eased the latch free, wanting to give no warning of his approach. Before he could slip out, she stood and began waving toward the far sidewalk. He froze. Who was coming?

It was a young man, looking deliberately disheveled. He sat on the swing next to hers, and they talked. Before long, they had joined hands and were swinging in unison. What was happening? This wasn't a part of the routine. Where had this man come from? He gritted his teeth in frustration. Sometimes it happened this way. Sometimes he had to abort his plan. Gathering was risky. Everything he could control, he needed to. Today would be a fruitless day. He watched them as they slowed and stopped. The young man popped up and offered his hand to the girl. She acquiesced, and together they walked off the way the man had come.

He needed to make a different choice. Clearly, this one would be missed if she disappeared. He waited until they were out of sight before reclosing his door and cruising for other likely gathering places.

Chapter Seven

Cicely waved as she drove away from Drew's house. Last night had been interesting. Drew's insecurities actually reassured her. Being that open about her fears showed her determination to be honest. Cicely liked that. *But I'm not sure I can handle the nightmare thing. That shit is scary and she's not ready to deal with it. I'm not sure how long I can go before that makes me bolt. What happened to make her lose her memory? Gotta call Kallie about that.*

She told herself it wouldn't be dishonest if she asked some simple questions. She could relate it to a client, not to Drew. She just needed some general information, and Kallie always clarified things like this for her. She wouldn't bat an eye at the question. *And I'll feel better knowing exactly what Drew's dealing with.*

She glanced at her watch. She had time to run by the store and grab some things to give to Edwina. She was the first client she had had at the Mental Health Public Defender's Office. She was one of those who could have easily been a success, but who had no desire to give up life on the street.

Still, she's a success in some ways. She isn't abusing drugs or alcohol. She makes it to her scheduled appointments with her probation officer, and most importantly, she's stayed out of trouble. No more trips to the Travis County Jail.

She pulled up at a local market and went directly to the pharmacy section. She filled a hand basket with toiletries she knew Edwina could use. She tossed in a four-pack of wool socks and some protein bars. Edwina would be happy to see her, but the gifts were more for Cicely than her.

No matter how many times she told herself that this was what Edwina wanted, she still felt guilty at not being able to change her living circumstances. But overall, it was easier now, accepting the desire of those who wanted to remain homeless. She had also gotten much better at convincing them that transitional housing was a better solution.

Cicely drove to the Drag and parked near the Co-op. Edwina slept in the alley behind the famous store. There was a transient community that floated between this place and the northern edge of the campus area. She found her sitting in the shade of a live oak.

"Hey, Edwina. How are you doing today?"

"What? Oh, it's you again. I'm good. How are you? Got a boyfriend yet?" Edwina said.

"Now, I told you, I won't be getting a boyfriend. I like girls. I have a new girlfriend, though," Cicely said. She smiled warmly at her. She looked in pretty good shape. Her shoes were worn, but no holes showed, and she looked like she'd been eating regularly.

"I brought you some things. Just little stuff. Here." She handed the bag to Edwina, who brightened at the gift.

"Well, that's awfully nice, C. I appreciate you bringing me things. You know you don't have to, but it's nice to know you still care."

"I do care, Edwina. Tell me what you've been up to lately."

"Aw, well, I been working over at that place, you know, that Casa place. They give me a steady bit of money to help with serving meals and cleaning up. It's a nice place. Lots of kids and ladies there. They keep on trying to get me to stay there, but I can't leave my stuff," Edwina said.

Cicely was glad to hear she was working with the Women and Children's shelter. They would be sure she was given health care and use of the facilities if she needed them. *I need to call and thank them for that.* It wasn't typical for a shelter to offer assistance and income to indigent people who were averse to moving off the street. The director probably saw the same qualities in Edwina that Cicely herself saw.

"So tell me about your friends, Edwina," Cicely said. She sat on the wall beside her and listened to all of Edwina's stories. She made sure there were no issues she needed help with before saying good-bye and heading to her office.

She sat at her desk, checking her messages. The lawyer she worked with had left her case notes on a new client they would meet on Tuesday morning. He was a fifty-six-year-old man currently incarcerated for misdemeanor assault. It looked like he would be a good candidate for their program. She read the notes and prepared her file for the next day.

She opened the files on her other clients and made note of upcoming trial dates and appointments. One of her functions was to act as a liaison between the attorney of record and the client service representatives. She made sure things were woven together to give the client the best outcome. If there was a time conflict, she would reschedule things so nothing was missed or neglected. It took careful planning, and she never failed to double-check her scheduling on Sundays. She took great pride in the work they were doing. It mattered. She mattered. She made a difference in the lives of so many people, and that gave her a great sense of self-worth. *I could have been one of these lost souls. The distance between me successful and me homeless was as thin as a thread.* She'd been lucky, and giving back was an absolute.

As she was finishing the last file, her phone rang.

"Hello?" she said.

"Cicely? Hey, girl. What have you been up to? I expected to hear from you yesterday," Kallie said.

"Hey, Kal. I'm doing so good. I spent the weekend with Drew."

"What? You're kidding. Is that a good thing or a bad thing?"

"A very good thing. I really like her," Cicely said

"Really? Wow, that's huge for you. What convinced you to take a chance on her?"

"There's something between us that's special. I don't know what it is exactly, but something about her, about us, works."

"That's great to hear. I'm so glad for you. I know how hard that is for you. So dish. Tell me about her."

"It's complicated. I mean, she's a park ranger, outdoorsy and all. She likes simple things. She has a cat," Cicely said.

"That doesn't sound complicated."

"Yeah, I guess you're right. I'm not used to having this kind of thing happen to me. It's so weird."

"Huh? I thought all you lesbians brought the U-Haul to the second date."

"Ha, very funny. You know that's not reality."

"I know. I just think it's funny that it's happened to you. Are you really okay with this? I mean, you have such high standards and all. Is she going to live up to your expectations?"

"I hope so. She's already told me she's terrified that I'll boot her out of my life. I wish I didn't come off that way. I only want honesty. Is that so bad?"

"No, it's not bad at all. It's just a lot to ask when you're newly getting to know someone. It's instinctual to keep your faults and fears hidden. That goes back to the nature of the species. The main thing to remember is that if she does have something she's holding back, it's not about you. It's a defense mechanism. Be open to understanding her, okay?"

"She's not holding back as far as I can tell. She's been very open. I think we're going to be okay," Cicely said.

"Good. It sounds like a healthy beginning for both of you. What does the future hold? Are you going to keep things light for a while?" Kallie said.

"Yeah, I think we're going to play it by ear. She's going to be working until late tonight, but plans to come over after."

"Awesome. It sounds like it's as special to her as it is to you. That's a good sign."

"Yeah. Hey, can I ask you a question? It's unrelated," Cicely said.

"Sure you can," Kallie said.

"Okay, I have a new client. He's in his mid-twenties, and charged with misdemeanor assault."

"Yes, how can I help?"

"Well, he can't remember his life before adolescence. I mean nothing. He was in foster care from twelve to eighteen, and homeless since then."

"Has he been evaluated? I'm sure he has if he was in care for so long. Any history of drug abuse?"

"He was diagnosed with dissociative amnesia at thirteen. But what exactly does that mean? How can it affect him at this age?"

"Really? Wow, that's very rare. It's usually a temporary condition. There's almost always a violently traumatic root cause. The subject appears alert, but can't remember anything of their past, not even their name. It's an extremely rare diagnosis. I'd love to interview him, if possible. It'd be fascinating to explore the circumstances of his condition."

"I'll check and see if he's willing. Our first meeting is tomorrow. How about a late lunch?"

"Let's make it an early dinner. I've got so much to do today. What I'd give for more hours in a day," Kallie said.

"I know what you mean. Okay then, I'll let you go," Cicely said.

"Right, dinner at Gueros, six o'clock?"

"Absolutely."

"And, Cice? I'm so glad about Drew. I've got a really good feeling about the two of you."

"Thank you. See you." She smiled as she hung up the phone. *So do I, and that scares me.*

She pulled up her search engine and read case files of dissociative amnesia. She needed to know as much as she could about Drew's condition. *And what about dreams that make you stop breathing? What's that about?*

She read so much her head ached, but she'd found nothing to explain the frightening dreams. Everything she read described the condition as temporary. It also made it seem as though those suffering from it were unable to function in society in a normal way. None of those qualities described Drew. Aside from the nightmares, she seemed perfectly normal. In fact, if Drew hadn't told her about the amnesia, she'd never have guessed. *How hard it must be to not know where you came from.*

She laughed then, her own childhood coming back to her. Her parents. They had been such a happy family for so long. She remembered family vacations to Florida, her mom and dad laughing as she splashed in the clear green water. The cruise they'd taken to the western Caribbean. *Those memories are a part of me. Those good times help me when the bad times want to drown me. What if I didn't have them? Would I be more or less happy? Would I be more trusting? What if I could erase only the painful memories?* She shook her head. *No. I need all the parts of me to be who I am now. I wouldn't want to forget them. How does that affect Drew? Who would she be with her memories intact?*

It was five thirty. Time to head to the restaurant. Kallie was always early, so she needed to get a move on. She wanted to be home by nine, when Drew got off work.

Gueros was busy, as usual, but she saw Kallie right away and made her way to the table. The noise level was the one drawback to their favorite eatery. She leaned down and gave Kallie a quick kiss on the cheek and squeeze.

"I'm so glad you were up for dinner. I'm dying to hear all about Drew. Sit. I ordered you a margarita," Kallie said.

"Perfect. I'm starving, and a drink sounds divine," Cicely said. She dropped her bag into an unused chair and sat across from Kallie. "It's Sunday, so that means fish tacos, right?"

"That's right. I ordered some queso, too."

"Great. So what kept you so busy today? You don't see patients on Sundays. What was going on?"

"I had a consult with a family I've been counseling. I made an exception for them. Their fifteen-year-old is having some issues that require extra help. I know, I know, I shouldn't do that, but it's hard. You're one to talk. You were working today."

Cicely shook her head. Kallie made Sundays off limits for patients because she had a hard time saying no. Her boundaries were blurred when kids were involved, and she had to have hard and fast rules to keep from being exploited. They'd talked about this before.

"You know you have to have time for yourself. You'd give away every bit of yourself if I didn't remind you. Yeah, I was working, but that's super rare for me, and I've got time to make up from last week."

"You're right, but it was worth it today. The son was finally able to tell his folks about his drug problem. We got him into a clinic. That warranted an exception."

"Okay, I suppose it does. Just don't let yourself make a habit of it. You need to have some me time."

"I know. I already scheduled myself out of the office this Friday. That will make up for today. Anyway, enough about me, tell me about Drew," Kallie said.

"What do you want to know?"

"Everything. Start with what happened when she came to your apartment."

"We had such a good time. It was so easy being with her, but it set off all my alarms. You know what happened the last time something felt so right. But we talked it out and agreed to keep things slow and casual. She's nervous about it though."

"Why is she nervous?"

"I'm not sure she likes the fluid relationship style I've asked for. She wants to have some sense of where it's going, even if we take it slow. It bugs her that I can't be on that level."

"Did you tell her about Jacki?"

"No, it didn't come up."

"Cice, I'm not sure that's being very fair to her."

"I know. I'll tell her, but not yet. I want to be sure of her first."

"That's not how this works. Look, I met Preston the same night, we've had a few dates and had a great time together. Now, I don't know everything about him, but what I know, I trust. So we'll go out again until we decide if we fit for something long-term or not."

"She's okay with things on my terms."

"Really? She gets the need for background checks and all of that?"

"Well, I didn't tell her about that. I think I can, though. She'd understand that my fears are beyond my control."

"*Not* beyond your control," Kallie said. "You've got the power to change the way you react. Nothing has been important enough to you yet to let go of your fears. That's not quite the same thing."

"But—"

"No buts. You know what I'm saying is true. If it weren't, you'd have to do the same kind of routine with me, and all of your clients, and your coworkers. Nope. I can't let that slide, kiddo. You can control your reactions. You know you can. You're choosing not to, because you're not there yet. But you have to take responsibility. You know that."

The words felt like blows, but Cicely knew this was what she had coming. Kallie always made her own it. She was right, of course, but sometimes she wished Kallie wasn't quite so good at reading her.

"You're right. Okay, not beyond my control, but very much a thing for me. Now, do you want to hear what happened? Or are we going to go on with my little free counseling session?"

"Ouch. You know I wouldn't say it if I didn't love you, Cice."

"I know. I'm sorry. Sometimes it's hard. Okay, so let's get back to Friday, huh?"

"Yeah, spill."

"She was so amazing, Kal. Really amazing. It was about as perfect as I can imagine. We fit. Every touch was the right touch, every kiss, like magic.

"Sounds like you really like her."

"A lot."

"When will you see her again?"

"Tonight, after dinner. She's coming over when she's done at work. I'm so ridiculously happy," Cicely said.

"Wow, I like that. Let's keep that going, okay?"

"Yeah. I'm good with that. So what about you? Tell me about Pres?"

"Well, if you want to know the truth, he's pretty great," Kallie said. "He's different for me, but I like him and we hit it off at the festival. We've gone to dinner and a movie. I'm looking forward to seeing more of him."

"I expect you to keep me up to date," Cicely said.

"You know it." They pinky swore and moved on to other topics.

When the entrees arrived, Cicely tried to stay focused in the moment, but she kept looking at her watch. Normally, she was an in-the-moment person. But right now, all she could think about was being somewhere else.

CHAPTER EIGHT

Two weeks later, Drew was beyond tired. It had been an unusually grueling day. She had spent the majority of her time leading a rowdy group of twelve-year-olds on a four-mile nature hike. She liked working with the kids on most days, but today's group was really a challenge. They didn't want to be out in the park, and they made it her fault that they were there at all. *Hey, I'm not your mom, and I didn't sign you up for this, brat.* She'd had to bite her tongue on several occasions to keep from letting them know how she felt. Some days this job sucked.

Now she was back at headquarters working on the tedious inventory forms. Luckily, she didn't have days like this very often. Truman knew her strengths were best suited to the wilderness areas and patrolling, and not hanging out with people. She generally had one or two days a month like this.

Thank God this one is almost over. I can't wait to get out of here and back to Cicely. She smiled, remembering the past few weeks. It had been so fantastic to wake up with Cicely in her arms more days than not. Today they'd shared a quick breakfast before they'd each run off to work. *I get to see her in less than two hours.*

She pulled up the next form, an allocation of fuel resources. *Great.* Now she had to figure out where, exactly, the log book for the gas pump had wandered off to. The crew was pretty good about replacing it, but every once in a while someone spaced out and drove out on patrol with the log. That must be what happened today. *It sure isn't anywhere in this office.*

She went to the radio room and sent out a call for the logbook. Best to find it now, even though someone else would have to deal with the allocation form at this point. Shouldn't be long before she heard something. *Damn, I'm so ready to go. Cicely will be waiting for me.*

The memory of silky skin under her hit, and Drew gasped at the strength of it. She felt as if Cicely's body were pressed to hers, soft yet unyielding. She shook with a tremor of excitement. *I want to be in that memory forever. I want your skin pressed to mine, your lips and mine completing the circle of us.* She dropped down into the chair at the radio desk. *What's wrong with me? Why is this thing with Cicely so consuming? Is this normal?* It had only been a few weeks and she was knocked out with this kind of whole body memory.

She wondered if her intense reaction to the whole developing relationship had something to do with how shut down her mind was, if her amnesia and the consequent numbness of presence were being shocked by the deep electric introduction of Cicely. *Is that a good thing?* Her nightmares had certainly ramped up since they'd started seeing each other. Before Cicely, she'd reached a point where they were happening only about once a month, and now she'd had one every night since they met.

Maybe I need to see someone. I sure don't want my unconscious mind to sabotage whatever this is that's happening with Cicely. The last time she'd seen a therapist about her amnesia she'd been a freshman in college. It hadn't been a good experience. Not that the doctor didn't try, it was just that she'd been over the whole "drug yourself and move on" thing. She'd wanted resolution, not anesthesia. Now that she was an adult, maybe she could benefit from a therapeutic relationship. Cicely had mentioned that Kallie was a psychiatrist. *Maybe I should set something up with her. Would that be weird? Seeing Cicely's best friend for therapy?*

Drew wouldn't have to worry about that. A therapist of any note would easily separate her work from her personal life. Besides, whatever was happening in her head wasn't anything she expected to have to hide from Cicely. That would be a relationship bomb. Honesty was the frame of their beginning, and she knew she had to build on that. She liked Kallie and felt like they could build a good doctor patient relationship, so why not? She'd talk to Cicely about it tonight.

She pushed up from the chair and headed back to the next pile waiting on the desk. Her phone buzzed in her pocket, and she slipped it out as she scanned the paper in front of her. Vehicle inventory. That would be easy. She read Cicely's message.

Thinking about you. Missing the feel of you inside me.

The raw emotion in the words made her face flare and her body burn with desire. She turned the desk fan on her face and tried to focus on the work in front of her. She would happily lose herself in the luxury of Cicely, anytime, anyplace, but right now she needed to finish this day so she could get back to her.

Haven't stopped tasting you all day. I miss you. She sent the reply then tucked her phone away. It would be better to keep the temptation in her locker, but she couldn't. She finished the vehicle inventory form and started collecting the completed forms to give to Truman. Her time was nearly done, and if she could manage it, she'd sneak out a few minutes early.

"Done for the evening?" Truman said in acknowledgement of her knock.

"Yes, sir. I know it's early, but would it be okay with you if I call it a day?"

"No problem. Have a good one."

"Thanks. See you tomorrow."

He waved her out of the office, and Drew practically skipped to the locker room. She loved how easy things could be sometimes. Truman knew what a rough time she'd had with her hikers, and he compensated by giving no flack at her wish to leave early. She had a good give-and-take relationship with him. Too bad Pres couldn't take a page from her book. He'd be so much happier if he could work with the man. He'd gotten better about being on time in the past few weeks. Dating Kallie seemed to be helping him appreciate nights off.

She skimmed out of her uniform shirt and pulled on her leather jacket. She kicked her locker closed, headed to the parking lot, and tossed the soiled shirt into the laundry bag on the way. She considered going home first to shower, but the thought of Cicely waiting made the decision for her. As she straddled her bike she pulled her phone out to text Cicely. There was an unknown number text on her display.

Not again. I'm going to have to call the phone company. This is getting ridiculous. She'd had two other messages in the last couple of weeks, and like the others, she'd blocked the number but saved the texts. She opened the message against her better judgment.

Where are you tonight? I've been waiting for hours. It's almost our time, Sunshine.

The nickname made her skin crawl. *Sunshine. Why does that make me freak?* She realized she was gripping the phone so tightly it was cutting into her palm, and every muscle in her body was tense and alert. *What the hell? It's some whacko trying to get a response.* She flipped to Cicely's contact and texted that she was on her way. She kicked the powerful bike into life and sped out of the parking lot.

The drive to the apartment was filled with confusing thoughts of the strange texts and the name, Sunshine. She had no conscious memory of anyone named Sunshine, but thinking about it now made her break out in gooseflesh.

When she arrived at Cicely's, she tried to forget about the text and be present, but it lingered. Cicely greeted her with a deep embrace and a fantastic kiss.

"Hi, baby. What's got your brow furrowed?" Cicely moved to the side but kept an arm around her.

"I don't know. The day wasn't my favorite, but it could have been worse. How about yours?"

"Good, it was good. I got a lot accomplished and had dinner with Kallie and Pres. He said to tell you hi. Are you hungry? I brought you some ribs, just in case."

"Yum, that sounds delicious." The weird texts had made her queasy, but she didn't want to decline Cicely's sweet offer.

"Great, come, sit. I'll grab some wine."

Drew watched as she poured two goblets of Chardonnay for them. The table was set with a single plate, napkin, and silverware. Cicely had even placed a peach colored rose across the plate. *So thoughtful.* "This is beautiful. Thank you."

"You make me feel romantic, so, roses."

"I like it. I'll remember to let you know how you make me feel after I take a shower."

"I like the sound of that."

"You don't mind me showering, do you? I wanted to get here as soon as I could."

"I don't mind a bit. In fact, I might join you."

Drew smiled, but she couldn't shake the things bothering her. Before they did anything else, she felt like she needed to bring up the texts and her reaction to the last one.

"Cice, there's something I need to talk about."

Cicely looked surprised, but open.

"Okay, I'm listening."

"So, a few weeks ago something strange happened. I got this weird text. I just deleted it and blew it off, but now there have been more. Tonight's made me feel…I don't know, creeped out."

"That happens sometimes, you know people fishing, wrong numbers and such. But they aren't usually creepy. Did you save the texts?"

"I saved most of them. It's so strange, even though they're from different numbers, they connect enough in context to make me feel like they're from the same person."

"Could I read them? Would that be okay?"

"Sure, here." Drew pulled up the saved texts and watched as Cicely read them.

She looked thoughtful as she handed the phone back to Drew. "Those are pretty creepy, all right. What do you think about them?"

"I don't know what to think. At first I thought it was random stuff, but there have been so many, and that last one? That one curled my hair. Something about it really freaked me out."

"Why? It's not as weird as the one before. What did the first one say?"

"I don't know, something like 'you're mine and it's our time' or something."

"The early ones are little threatening, but this last one seems less so."

"It's Sunshine. Something about the name Sunshine makes me feel unnerved."

"That's strange. I wonder why it triggers that reaction. Have you ever known someone named Sunshine, or been called that as a nickname?"

"Not that I can remember. Of course, there's that whole period of my life I can't remember. Maybe I knew someone back then."

"See? That's one of the reasons I think it's important to explore regression therapy. I think you'd feel better if you knew."

"I've been thinking about that, too. I think I might be ready to try something like that. Do you think Kallie is the right therapist for me? I mean, since you guys are so close?"

"I think she'd be perfect for you. You don't have to worry about her sharing anything with me, though. She's the utmost professional and would never breach your confidence."

"You know I wouldn't keep anything from you, right?"

"I want to believe that, but I also know that things come up in therapy that you have to process and deal with. When you're ready, I hope you'll share. I want you to get some help with those nightmares. Kallie is your best bet, as far as I'm concerned."

"Good, okay. I'll call her and set up an appointment."

"Great, I'll get your ribs."

Cicely set the rib plate in the center of the table and sat in the chair beside her.

Drew was happy Cicely liked to be so close. She had never been much on personal contact, but since the very first night it was like her soul craved Cicely's. When their skin touched, even in the smallest way, it was like coming home. She wanted this all the time. Every day. It was too soon to broach the subject with Cicely. She knew what she wanted, but she needed Cicely to get there in her own time.

She slid her free hand down and entwined her fingers with Cicely's while she ate.

Cicely was unusually quiet. She liked to talk about her day with her clients over dinner. *Did I freak her out with the texts?*

"Hey, are you okay? You're not very talkative tonight."

"I'm okay, just processing. If the texts are related to your past, why do you think whoever it is would send such weird messages? I mean, why not lay it out, let you know who they are and what they want."

"I don't know. I mean it could be some random weirdo, but to keep contacting me from different numbers? Seems like they must have some personal connection to me."

"Yeah, but what? And why are the messages threatening? I think you should call the cops."

"No way. That would be overreacting. This person hasn't ever approached me. They haven't asked to meet. I bet it's some punk messing with me."

"Texting you once or twice, maybe, but this? Texting from four different numbers? That's stalking and you need to take it seriously."

"Come on, it's not a big deal. I'm not worried, just creeped out."

"You understand how serious stalking is, right? It's a crime for a reason. These things can escalate if you don't stop them."

Pressure built in Drew's abdomen and her hands were clenched. She felt like Cicely was attacking her. *Isn't getting the freaking texts enough?* "Stop. Let's not talk about this anymore tonight. I'm freaked out about the texts, but I'm also grimy and worn out. Can we just finish dinner and relax?"

It was like pouring lighter fluid on hot coals. Cicely jumped up from the table and held her arms across her chest.

"You aren't dealing with this. How can you not take this seriously?"

"I am, I promise I am. I'm just exhausted. I can't think about calling the police tonight. Can't we talk about it tomorrow?"

"Talk about it? Seriously? You've got to *do* something about it, not talk about it."

"Okay, I'm sorry. Tomorrow I'll do something about it, I promise."

Cicely dropped back into her chair. Drew could tell she wasn't happy.

"Tomorrow, you promise?"

"I promise."

"I guess it'll have to do. Finish your ribs and go shower."

"Are you going to join me?" Drew gave her best hangdog expression, hoping to reach her.

It worked. Cicely couldn't help cracking the tiniest of grins. She punched Drew in the arm hard enough to bruise, just to be sure she knew the topic wasn't off the table. *I better get to the police station first thing.*

"Okay, you win, for now. I'm going to go get the shower set up for us. You take your plate to the kitchen and meet me there."

Drew watched her go, then hurried to clean up her dishes so she could join her. That was the closest they'd come to a fight. *It wasn't horrible. At least we reached a truce. I wonder if I'm going to pay for that after our shower?*

❖

She couldn't see anything. The darkness surrounding her was so absolute it was crippling. Her arms were pinned against her sides, the backs of her hands irritated by some rough surface. She tried to scream, but her throat was raw and tight. Sounds from above; scrape, thunk. Scrape, thunk. *Whatever she was lying on was unforgiving. Her shoulders and the back of her head ached with a fierce intensity, telling her she'd been lying here a long time. Her bladder was full to the point of bursting, and something stung in her forearm.*

"Please. Let me out. Please. I want out. I want light. Please. Please."

She wanted to shout, to beg, but no words would come. She kicked out with her sluggish foot, instantly rewarded with a sharp pain in her toes and a shower of something fine across her body. Dirt. It's dirt. You're buried. You're dead. *Panic flooded her, and she thrashed, trying to move, but only reinitiated the shower of silt. "I'm not dead. I'm alive. Somebody get me out. Please." She tasted earth in her mouth, ground her teeth on the grit. Then a larger shower of dirt fell into her face, blocking her nostrils and mouth. She coughed and choked, turning until her airway cleared slightly.* I'm going to suffocate. There's not enough air. I can't breathe! I can't breathe! *She felt her lungs laboring to draw in oxygen and feed her starving body, but there wasn't any.*

The panic dulled at the realization that what was happening wasn't going to stop. She felt her senses dull and her mind grow heavy with sleep. But she knew it wasn't sleep.

A breath. Wait. Wait. A breath. Wait. Wait. Wait. Nothing. Cold. Still. Empty. Dead.

Sharp pain across her cheek. Again. And she heard her then.

"Dammit, Drew, breathe. Breathe!" Cicely was shouting. Another slap across her face. She jerked her hand up to protect herself.

"Jesus Christ on a cracker, Drew. This is getting way too crazy. You weren't breathing again. I can't take this. I can't do it. This is going to kill me. You have to do something about this today. I won't. I just won't." Cicely wrapped her arms around her knees, tears streaming down her cheeks.

"Hey, it's not my fault. I can't control my sleeping mind. Jesus, I'm the one living it."

"I'm living it with you. I'm done with this."

"What do you expect me to do about it? Sleep on the couch?"

"Get some help, already. Seriously." Cicely jumped up from the bed and stormed out of the room.

Drew tossed off the coverlet and went after her. She was pacing in front of the sliding door to the balcony, the early morning light illuminating her smooth skin. She could feel the heat radiating from her and knew the best thing to do was to let her walk it out. She slid onto the couch and tried to clear the fog from her mind. *God, let me wake up before you go off on me again.* Snippets of the dream came together, and Drew realized she could remember the bulk of her dream. This was the first time that had happened. She wanted to talk to Cicely about it, but she had to wait until she was settled down a little. Granted, she was a little irritated that Cicely was freaking out rather than being gentle, the way she had been before, but she cut her some slack. It must be crazy scary to have someone not breathing in bed next to you.

Cicely was muttering as she walked, the whole line of her body taut. Drew wasn't sure if she was angry or frightened. Probably both, and she was going to wear out the carpet if she didn't stop pacing soon. Finally, she dropped her hands to her sides and looked at Drew. There were tears streaking her cheeks, and it broke Drew's heart to see them. She held out her arms, hoping Cice had reached a place where they could come together. The relief she felt as Cicely came to her and eased down into her arms was palpable. *Thank God.* She wrapped her in her arms and held her. She could feel the rapid pace of Cicely's heart against her chest.

"I'm so sorry, Cice. I—"

"No, don't say you're sorry. It's not something you can control. I know that. It's just so upsetting and scary. It took me more than three minutes to wake you this time. What's going to happen if that time increases? What are we going to do?"

"I'm going to see Kallie as soon as she can get me in. Maybe she can give me a prescription to help in the meantime."

"You don't want to be medicated, and I support that. I just want a way to wake you easier."

"Well, this was an unusual nightmare for me."

"How? It seemed the same to me."

"I remembered this one." The cold, empty feeling that overwhelmed the end of her dream came back to her. Her heart raced in remembered panic.

"Oh, wow. Tell me what you remember. No, wait. Let me get a journal. Let's write it down. You can take it to Kallie when you see her. It'll be helpful." She got up and went to the bedroom, returning with a leather bound book.

"Okay, now," she said.

Drew's throat tightened, and she had to cough before she could begin. Residual anxiety from the dream still rattled her, but she was going to share this.

"I was in absolute darkness, and I couldn't move. It was uncomfortable, rough and confining. I could hear a strange scraping sound, and then dirt was falling on me. I couldn't breathe." Drew stared at their intertwined fingers, the enormity of what she was thinking overwhelming. "I think I was buried alive."

Cicely had stopped writing as she spoke, and her grip tightened on Drew's hand. A sense of safety infused Drew and she continued. "I couldn't breathe, and it was so cold. I remember the taste of the dirt and how it felt hitting my face. It was so real." Drew brushed at her face, feeling the grit of dirt in her mouth and nose.

Cicely slid closer to her, and rubbed her hand up and down her back. "Oh, Drew. That's so terribly frightening. No wonder you stop breathing. This has to mean something. Kallie'll be able to help you identify what it might be connected to, I'm sure of it."

"I'm scared, Cicely. I don't like feeling this way."

"Of course you don't, baby. We're going to help you get past whatever made you feel buried. I promise you that."

"Would you go with me? When I see her?"

"You'd want me there?"

"Of course I would. I'd feel much better if you were with me."

"Of course I'll go with you, but Kallie might want to see you alone."

"But you'll be waiting for me, right? I mean, if I need you, you'll be close by?"

"Yes, of course I will."

"Good. I think I can face anything if you're beside me."

"I think you should call her right now."

Drew checked the time and figured it was acceptable to call, even though it was early. "Okay, let's do this." Drew punched in the number as Cicely dictated and tried to calm the butterflies in her stomach. She'd talked to so many therapists in her youth, she was a little gun-shy, but knowing Kallie helped.

"Hello?" Kallie answered on the second ring.

"Hi, Kallie. It's Drew Chambliss."

"Hi, Drew. What's up? Everything okay?"

"Yes and no. I need a therapist and I was hoping you'd take me on."

There was a long silence on the other end of the line. Drew tried not to get even more nervous.

"Does Cicely know you're calling me?"

"Yes, she's right here beside me. She's the one who suggested you."

"Okay. I'll have to look at my schedule and see when I could work you in."

"It's kind of serious. I mean, I know you're really busy all the time, but I'm in a bad place."

"Drew, I understand it feels that way, but there's an established routine to becoming a patient."

"I understand. If you could try to fit me in as soon as possible, I'd really appreciate it." Drew watched Cicely as they spoke, her face mirroring the tension humming through Drew's body.

"Good. So we're clear, are you in danger of hurting yourself or anyone else?"

"Oh, no way."

"You're certain? We don't want to take any chances if you or anyone else is at risk."

"No, it's nothing like that. It's more like my unconscious mind is trying to hurt me."

"Elaborate, please."

"I have these nightmares. They've been getting worse. When I have one, I kind of stop breathing."

"Kind of stop breathing?"

"I stop breathing. It's freaking Cicely out. And the nightmares are happening a lot more often."

"That's very upsetting, and very dangerous. How often are you having these episodes?"

"It used to be about once every few weeks, but now they're coming every night."

"Okay, here's what you're going to do. You're going to go to an urgent care center and get yourself checked out. Go now. Don't wait. Make sure you tell them about what's happening and let them check for any medical issues that could be causing this. When you're finished there, I want you to call me and we'll talk a bit about what they discover. Okay?"

"I've been to the doctor before. They've always said it isn't medical." Drew felt old frustrations rising and tried to keep them at bay.

"I get that, but since you're contacting me in a kind of emergency situation, there are protocols I need to follow, and this is one of them. Do it for me, and I'll talk to you after."

Drew sighed internally, but accepted Kallie's reasoning. "Thanks, Kallie. We'll go right now." *They're not going to find anything. Whatever happens to me is because of my childhood.* Frustration welled up in her, but she pushed it down. This needed to happen or she might lose Cicely. *I have to face my fears and deal. I can't lose her.*

CHAPTER NINE

He carried the sack up the steep rocky hillside to the nearly invisible cabin tucked in among the scrub oak. He pulled out his keys and snapped open the shiny padlock on the rusted, brown hasp that barred entrance to his hideaway. He was proud of the two-roomed cabin built into the hillside, with the northern end covered with earth and sod. It made the building nearly invisible to the casual observer.

The room within was dimly lit by the four slit windows on each opposing wall. They were only four inches wide, but two feet high and gave him more than enough light to get around. He placed the bag on the rough-hewn table. It was cool out, but plenty warm in the cabin. No need for the hearth fire. He opened the grate on the cast iron stove and lit the kindling inside. He wanted some tea, and boiling water was necessary, as he lived off grid the way he always had. He filled the kettle from the barrel in the corner and placed it on the cooktop.

He took the lamp from its wall hook, snatched up a long twig, and lit it from the stove. He placed it at best advantage on the table and sat on the trestle bench. With shaking hands, he pulled at the leather thongs that secured the bag. He tipped the contents out onto the table. Six. He'd hoped to manage more, but six would have to do for now. He would need more soon, but for now, he needed to get the members of his fledgling herd fed.

He gripped the bags, then made his way out to the pen. He paused, listening for any errant sound in his peaceful kingdom. When he decided all was well, he climbed the remaining ten feet to the hilltop.

The cedar stand was ensnarled with prickly pear and bull nettle. He preferred to keep the pen overgrown and inhospitable. More likely to keep roaming hikers and such away. Knowing the place as well as he did, he found the path to the interior with ease.

Remnants of yesterday's meal glistened in their polyvinyl bags. He moved to the first stall and deftly removed the old bag and hung the new. He adjusted the valve to increase the flow, then moved to the second. Maybe he should take one of the girls out for a bit of exercise. No, too soon. He'd give them a few more days to settle in. Besides, it was still full light and it would be cruel to bring them out in daylight. Night was much better suited to his purpose, kinder. He took pride in his herd and treated them with the care they deserved.

He sat on the cool earth between the two stalls and breathed in the peace of this place. He loved it here. She would love it here. Sunshine needed a place like this. She was born to it. He couldn't believe how he'd lost track of her so much lately. She was hardly home at all these days. He'd tried to figure out where she was spending her time, but he'd not been able to follow her.

The park service place where she worked had far too many exits, and no place to stay hidden while waiting. His frustration left a sour taste in his mouth. Why was she being so difficult? He needed to get another phone soon so he could break the silence between them.

The thought of his kettle on the stove and a nice cup of tea ahead urged him up from his spot and down the hill to the cabin. Tomorrow. He would text her again tomorrow.

"Come on, Drew. Let's get going," Cicely said.

"Coming, I just have to grab my shoes."

Cicely was anxious to get to the urgent care center and get a clean bill of health for Drew. She was certain the breathing thing had no connection to a health problem, but the sooner they knew for sure, the sooner they could move on to therapy. She'd been tempted to call Kallie and discuss the dreams with her, but that wouldn't have been fair to Drew. She was beyond ready to get some resolution to the issue.

It's fucking scary. I don't want to deal with it anymore. She was confused, and didn't know what she wanted or what to do. She hated feeling so helpless. Drew finally came out of the bedroom and they headed to her car. They'd planned to go shopping for a helmet for Cicely today, but this was more important.

"Do you think we can stop for coffee on the way?" Drew said.

"I don't think coffee is a good idea for you until we're done with the medical stuff."

"Hmm, you're probably right, but you should have some, and we can save mine for later."

"It will get cold."

"I don't mind cold as long as it's good."

"Let's go to breakfast after, if you don't mind. I just want to get this over with."

"Okay. That's fine."

Cicely asked if Drew had any particular place she wanted to go, but they decided the closet option would work. Once they arrived, Drew filled in the paperwork, and they sat in the waiting area. The TV was tuned to some infomercial about a juicer. Drew sat as close as the chairs would allow and squeezed Cicely's hand.

"It's going to be fine. We need to know if there's something physically wrong with you."

"There won't be. There never is, and I can't stand doctors' offices. Too many bad memories."

"Well, this is important. Kallie wouldn't have sent us if it wasn't. While you're in the back I'll call her and see if she'll meet us for breakfast. She needs to know what an impact these dreams are having on both of us."

"You're sure that's a good idea? I mean, I don't want her to think I'm bucking her system."

"Screw that. I'll call because she's my friend. She'll tell me to back the hell off if it's inappropriate, because I'm hers."

"If you say so."

"I do. Look, there's the nurse. Go on back and get checked out. I'll be right here."

As soon as Drew had cleared the doorway, she called Kallie.

"Cice, hi."

"Hi, Kallie. I'm calling—"

"I know what you're calling about, and I'll tell you the same thing I told Drew. Make sure there's no medical cause and then call me back."

"We're at the clinic right now. She's with the doctor. I need you to know how serious this is."

"Anytime you stop breathing it's serious, but that doesn't mean emergency therapy."

"I know, but, Kallie it's happening every night, and it's getting harder to wake her all the time. It fucking scares me to death. Please help her, for my sake?"

"You know I'll do my best to help her, Cice, but that doesn't necessarily mean I'll see her today. You're the one who tells me not to give myself away. Why doesn't this qualify?"

"Because it's for me. I know I'm being a jerk, but I need this, Kallie. I need to know you're going to help me. Would you meet us for breakfast after we're done here? It will just be breakfast, not a formal session. Please?"

Kallie sighed loudly into the receiver. "Okay. Fine. I'll meet you guys for breakfast, but she still needs to set up regular counseling sessions."

"She will, I promise."

"Okay. Text me when and where and I'll meet you."

"Thank you. I'll never forget this."

"I'll never let you forget it. I better go get in the shower."

Cicely put her phone back in her pocket and waited for Drew to finish up.

Thank God for Kallie. If we don't get some serious help with this today, I might have to ask Drew to take a break. It's unnerving to see her lying there like that. I don't want to push her away. It's going to hurt both of us, but I can't do this. And what about calling the police about those texts? She needs to follow through on that.

Ice filled her veins as she waited. *What else is going to happen? What am I doing in the middle of all this craziness? I want to be with Drew, but I don't really know who she is. Why is this happening?* It was affecting her, too. She'd had trouble sleeping the past few nights. They'd have wonderful, tender sex and she'd fall into her typical post orgasmic sleep, but before the hour was up, she'd be wide-awake, staring into the dark, listening for the thrashing that always preceded the mock death. *And I haven't been disappointed once this week. We've had so many nights in a row of nightmares and death that I'm completely frazzled. We need to take a break. That doesn't mean an end, just space until this thing is handled. Surely that's good for Drew, too? So she can concentrate on her own stuff?*

She felt cold at the thought of losing Drew. They had so many right things together, and this one wrong thing was going to undo them. *Not undo. Stop letting that run through your head. Not undo, only a break.*

She cradled her head in her hands, weighing the pros and cons, trying to convince herself one way or the other. She heard something buzz on the seat beside her. It was Drew's phone.

Hmm, must have slipped out of her pocket. She picked it up and read the display. It was a text. *Not your business. Not your phone. Just put it in your bag.* She slipped it into her bag and looked at the unmoving door. What if they found something physical?

The door swung wide and Drew walked out. She couldn't read her expression. Was the news good or bad? She stood to greet her.

"How'd it go? Any news?"

"No, not really. They took some blood, but they basically gave me the all clear. The way they always do," Drew said.

"You did tell them what's been happening, right?"

"Sure I did. That was the whole point of this. It's all in my head, like we both knew it was. The doc encouraged me to do a sleep study, to map my brain activity. What do you think?"

"I think it's a good idea. They'd be able to pinpoint what happens physically and how it correlates to your brain. I like it. How do you set that up?"

"He gave me a referral for a place downtown. I'll call them later. For now, let's go eat."

"After you call the police."

"Huh?"

Anger sparked inside her. Drew knew exactly what she meant. *She doesn't want to deal with this. Why can't she see how important it is?* "You need to report those texts."

"Can't we have breakfast first? I'm starving."

"You're not taking this seriously. This shit is getting scary. I don't want to be tense all the time about who's texting you or whether you're going to go all Living Dead on me. Come on. The least you can do is be concerned. Whoever it is that's texting you needs to be stopped. I can't believe you want to go eat breakfast like none of this is happening."

"Okay, okay. I'll call right now."

"Good."

Drew made the call, and Cicely finally started to relax. She didn't understand why Drew seemed so unconcerned about the texts and the breathing thing. *Does she not see how upsetting it is? Isn't she concerned?* It made her wonder how deeply Drew felt anything. *Is she so cut off from her emotions that she doesn't register how frightening last night was? What does that say about her feelings for me? Can I trust those feelings?*

Drew hung up and shrugged. "They said I can bring in a log of the texts, but there's nothing they can really do except keep it on file. If it gets worse, I'm supposed to let them know. Can we please go eat now?"

Everything felt out of control, something Cicely had promised herself she'd never allow to happen in her life again, and she needed to talk it out, but after they talked with Kallie. If she didn't make sure that happened today, who knew if it ever would.

"Sounds good to me. I need to let Kallie know where to meet us. What sounds good?"

"Let's go to Biscuits and Groovy."

"Okay. I'll let her know and get her order."

The drive to the food truck gave Cicely time to calm down and try to see things from Drew's perspective. *She isn't a worrier by nature like me. Her childhood is a blank, so she's had to trust blindly. Maybe I'm expecting her to react the way I do. That's not fair.*

When they arrived, they grabbed a picnic table, and Drew went up to place their order. She was back with the fresh pressed coffee in a few minutes.

"I forgot to ask what Kallie would want to drink. I hope she likes coffee."

"Are you kidding? Who doesn't love coffee? What did you decide to get?"

"Just a biscuit and jam. I'm in the mood for something sweet. Besides, I don't want to eat too heavily since things might get upsetting later."

"Probably a good decision. There's Kallie." She motioned her over to their table.

"Good morning. Thanks for coming. I'm sorry to drag you out so early," Drew said.

Kallie waved her apologies away and sat down. After taking an appreciative sip of her coffee, she said, "Don't worry about it. Tell me what the clinic said."

"They didn't find anything wrong with me, but the doctor wants me to do a sleep study," Drew said.

"That's a good idea. How comfortable would you be if I asked you about your dreams?"

"You can ask me anything. I want your help, and I know from experience that therapy requires open, honest discussion."

Kallie looked from one to the other of them. Cicely realized she probably should have told her about Drew's past. She reached into her bag for her journal and felt something hard bump her hand. Drew's phone.

"Drew, here's your phone. It must have fallen out of your pocket."

Drew took the phone and looked at the display. Cicely noticed her pale as she read.

"Is it another one of those texts?"

"Yes." Drew held the phone to her.

The text was short and to the point, creepy. *You can't hide from me forever. I won't wait much longer.*

"Oh my God, Drew, you need to call the police again. This is bullshit."

"What is it?" Kallie said.

"This." Cicely passed the phone to her.

"Who's this from? What's this about?"

"It's some weirdo who's got my number and keeps sending me these texts."

"You should block their number," Kallie said.

"I do, each time. Whoever this is just gets a new phone. It's getting really annoying."

"It's more than just annoying, it's fucking scary," Cicely said.

"It's only text messages. They can't do anything about it. I'll change my number. The weirdo probably thinks I'm someone else."

Cicely wanted to shake her. *I would've changed my number after the second text. Jesus, what's wrong with her?* She bit down on the urge to tear into Drew, sure that the others could feel the waves of heat coming off her.

"So about those dreams?" Kallie brought them back to the point of their meeting.

As they ate, Drew told Kallie about her amnesia and her history with therapy.

"So, you can't remember anything? Not a place or even a face from your childhood?"

"No, nothing. It's a blank. I did remember my name six months after I was found wandering, but that's it."

"Your full name?"

"No, just Drew. I had the same pattern of nightmares when I was younger. My parents decided medication was the best help for me then."

"Did it help? I mean, did the nightmares subside?"

"I guess so. I know that until six weeks ago I was only having them about once a month."

"How do you account for the increase? Are you under more stress at work? What factor might have triggered their resurgence?"

Cicely caught Drew's sideways glance and felt uncomfortable. Their relationship started six weeks ago. *Am I the reason she's been having more nightmares? That's crazy. I'm the one pulling her out of them.*

"I don't think it's any external reason. Maybe I'm reaching a point in my life where I'm connecting more with my emotions. I feel things now. Maybe that's triggered them," Drew said.

Cicely could feel Drew shutting down. Her words became hollow and her voice dropped in tone. *What now? Come on, you have to give it all to her. Let her know how bizarre these dreams are.*

"Tell Kallie about last night's dream. She remembered her dream for the first time. We wrote it down in this journal."

She handed Kallie the journal. While she glanced over the recollections, Drew told her about what she'd felt and remembered.

"Dream interpretation is a shaky science. It's very subjective. Some will tell you that dreaming of being buried means you're feeling overwhelmed in your waking life. Some will tell you it signals that you're on the verge of making a mistake that will be used against you. All of that is psychobabble, if you ask me. What matters more to me are the feelings the dreams brought up in you."

"She stopped breathing for nearly three minutes. That's what that damn dream brought up in her."

Kallie continued without pausing. "You felt pain, discomfort, and suffocation to the point that you stopped breathing. That's where it gets real. I don't know why you had this dream. You don't know if this is the same dream repeating each night. For now, let's get you on a sleeping aid that can suppress the physical reaction. I want to set you up with some sessions starting this week. Hopefully, over time, we can find the root of your amnesia and that will help resolve the dreams. Okay?"

"That sounds good to me. I want to let go of whatever is causing this. I want to be free of it," Drew said.

Cicely sighed with relief. *This is what I needed to hear. Maybe I can handle it after all, if she's actively working on it.*

"Okay. I've made some time available on Thursday afternoon. I'll expect to see you at four fifteen."

"That works for me. Is it okay if Cicely comes with me?"

"I don't have a problem with that, but it would probably be best if she stays in the waiting area."

"Okay. Thank you, Kallie."

"You're welcome. In the meantime, you need to get a new phone number."

Cicely smiled at Kallie, silently thanking her for that reinforcement. "Let's go take care of that when we leave."

They enjoyed the last of their coffee, watching people come and go. When they left, Cicely and Drew went straight to the wireless store and took care of changing her number. Then they found the perfect helmet for Cicely, a glittery yellow one with an orange and red phoenix on the side.

"I'm so excited that we can go for a ride on your bike now. I can't wait."

"I'm glad you're excited. I am, too. I much prefer traveling with the wind in my face. Makes me feel alive. You want to go back to the apartment and get the bike? Today's a perfect day for riding. We can go out toward Marble Falls. Maybe check out Pace Bend Park?"

"That'll be fun. Let's go," Cicely said.

She was relieved that Drew was going to move forward with getting help, but had misgivings about the next few nights. Thursday was a start, but what if the medication didn't stop the dreams? What if she woke up to Drew not breathing again? She looked at Drew, who had the same happy smile and laidback attitude she always had. She showed no sign of last night's trauma. *How does she do that? I'm fried, and she's bouncing along like nothing happened. It makes me want to scream. Maybe I should get some therapy.*

She slid behind Drew on the bike and pulled on her new helmet. Tomorrow night she'd broach the subject of taking a break. It would be the best thing for both of them.

Chapter Ten

Guilt weighed on Drew as she pulled the bike into her driveway. She'd feigned sleep when Cicely left that morning. Thanks to being on the bike the night before, they hadn't been able to talk much, and Drew was glad for the reprieve. When they'd gone inside, there'd definitely been tension, but Drew hadn't felt up to another big discussion. Now she gladly headed home. Poor Kashka must be missing her. She'd put plenty of food and water down, but he wasn't a plant. She needed to talk to Cicely about that. If they were going to keep ending up at her place, she needed to bring Kashka along so he wouldn't feel neglected. And she needed to check in with her folks. She hadn't seen her mom and dad and Javon in months and hadn't seen Wy since the movie. Javon's graduation was in a couple of weeks, and she knew her mom would appreciate some help getting things planned for his party. *Damn, I'm a bad daughter and a worse sister.*

She'd been so caught up in her budding relationship with Cicely that she'd really dropped the ball. Tomorrow she'd make it up to them. She hurried up the porch steps and put her key into the lock, but the bolt wasn't turned. She froze. Had she been burgled? It wasn't like her to leave the door unlocked. She toed open the door and looked in. Kashka sat on the back of the couch licking a paw. He looked at her and gave a disinterested meow.

"Hey, Kashi, come here, fella." She held out her hand to him. He jumped down and sauntered over to her. After she gave him a good rubbing, he proceeded to let her know what a jerk she'd been. He meowed so loudly that she wondered if the neighbors could hear. He seemed to be his normal self.

"Come on, boy. I've got some tuna with your name on it."

The living room seemed as normal as ever, and nothing was visibly out of place. *I can't believe I left the door open.* She'd been in a rush to leave the other night, but it bothered her that she'd been so careless. The neighborhood had had a few break-ins, but things in those houses had been stolen, and everything in her place looked intact. *I'm lucky no one walked in and cleaned me out. Don't be stupid and do that again, idiot.* She went into her room and dropped her bag on the bed. Everything was normal, except it wasn't. It felt weird. There was a heavy feeling in the room. She was probably projecting that, though.

She mentally ran through the last time she'd been home. She'd finished at work and come home to feed Kashi and grab a shower before heading to Cicely's. She'd tossed her dirty clothes into the hamper by her bathroom and taken care of things. Then she'd dressed and had a cup of tea on the couch, loving on Kashi before heading out. She hadn't been in a hurry. In fact, she'd made a point of taking her time because she was worried about the cat.

Drew was disquieted by the unlocked door. She'd never done that before, and those creepy texts... *What if someone was in my house, but wasn't looking to steal from me?* She felt like she should call the police, but what did she have to show them? An unlocked door? They'd write her off as paranoid. She didn't have time to worry about it, anyway. Tonight Cicely was coming to her place, so she had to think about what she had in the kitchen to cook. There was tortellini and some nice basil pesto she'd picked up at the Fresh Market. That would do with a nice salad and wine. She poured herself a shot of tequila to shake the weirdness. Maybe watching the news would help. She flipped on the TV and dropped onto the couch. She tossed back the shot and watched the evening weatherman.

"Let me out. Please. I want out." The rough boards ripped at the skin on the sides of her hands. She couldn't move far enough away to keep the irritation at bay. He was up there. She knew he was. He was standing up there and he wouldn't let her out. She could hear him.

Why did he do this? She heard the dirt crashing down on the board above her head, silt filtering in and peppering her face.

"Please. Walt, let me out. I'll be good." More dirt pounding down, dampening the sound of his activity. He wasn't going to let her out. She started to panic, screaming out to him. She screamed until her throat was raw. She shook the confining walls as best she could and only succeeded in showering more dirt on herself. Then she kicked out, her foot sluggish. Dirt clumped down now, filling her mouth and nose. She was choking. No air—

Drew sat up, drenched in sweat, knowing she'd had another breathing incident. Her heart pounded, and she felt tears on her cheeks. At least now she knew she would eventually wake herself up, but that was small comfort when she realized this was the first nightmare she'd had that wasn't in the middle of the night. Kashka was perched on the arm of the couch, watching her. *I wonder how long you've been there, buddy. Why didn't you wake me up?*

Damn, it was after four, Cicely would be there in about an hour. She went to her room, stripped, and tossed her clothes in the hamper on her way to the shower. She turned the water as hot as she could stand it and let the stream soothe away the remnants of her nightmare. *Walt.* The name popped into her mind. There was someone in her dream named Walt. *Who is he and what is he to me? Is he the creep that buried me?* She grabbed her loofah and scrubbed at the imaginary dirt she still felt on her skin. Why now? Why hadn't these shadow memories worked their way up when she was younger? Back then, she'd been a mess of emotions. Now she felt secure and stable; life was beginning for her. Why did this have to come up now? It was already impacting her relationship with Cicely. She had to get this shit under control.

She dried and dressed, thinking about what else she could do to resolve these memories. She headed to the kitchen to start dinner. When she reached to pull open the fridge, she saw a note, much like the ones her mom left her so often. This one wasn't from her, though.

You are mine, Sunshine. I'm coming for you.

She clapped a hand over her mouth to keep in the shout that threatened. *Shit. I knew someone had been in here. Shit. Shit, shit, shit.*

She frantically raced to her room, grabbed her phone and called the police, before calling Cicely and then her mom. Cicely's phone line went to voice mail, but her mom answered.

"Hi, darling. How are you doing?"

"Mom. Mom, someone's been in my house."

"What are you talking about, baby?"

"It's on the refrigerator. Mom, can you come over? Please?"

"I'm on my way, Drew. Lock yourself in and I'll be there as soon as I can."

Drew dropped the phone and crumpled into a chair. *Why is this happening?* Her phone rang and she scooped it up.

"Drew? What's up?"

It was Cicely. Relief rushed through her, unbidden. "Cicely. Someone has been in the house. Don't come over. It's not safe."

"What are you talking about?"

"My house. Someone's been in my house. The police are on the way, and I want you to stay away. If...if he's still around, I want to know you're safe. But I needed to hear your voice."

"Don't be silly, of course I won't stay away. I'll be there as soon as I can. I just got out of the shower. Ten minutes and I'll be on my way. Don't leave there without me."

"No, please. Just stay at the apartment."

"Wel—"

Drew hung up and ran to the garage for Kashi's carrier. He fussed mightily at being ushered into the small box, but she wasn't taking any chances. She wouldn't leave him here. She saw the red and white flashes of a patrol car and went out to meet the officer. Her mom drove up as they were climbing the porch steps. They waited for her.

"Drew? What's going on?"

"I told you, Mom. Someone's been in the house."

The officer went through the rooms and returned.

"The house is clear, ma'am. Do you want to show me that note now?"

"It's in the kitchen."

"What note, honey?"

"The note. On the fridge."

"Ma'am? Can you lead the way, please?"

Drew showed the officer the note on the refrigerator.

"And you're certain no one else might have put it there? One of your friends pranking you?"

"No, no one would do that, and besides, they don't call me Sunshine. That's from the texts."

"Texts, ma'am?"

"Yes, I reported them this morning, but I haven't been in to log them officially yet. I've been getting these weird texts. Now this. He's been in my house."

"Could I have a look at those texts, please?"

Drew handed him her phone.

"They're all flagged. They're from different numbers, but they're all from that guy."

"How long has this been happening? Have you reported the texts before today?"

"It's been about a month and a half. No, I didn't report it. I figured it was some creep messing around."

"Well, now you know it's not. This is stalking, and you need to get it on file so you have some way to protect yourself. Stalking is a third degree felony here. From today forward, you need to report every instance of contact. Do you think this might be someone you know? An ex or a coworker?"

"Not an ex, no, and I don't think it could be any of the guys from work. We're a pretty tight crew. I've never gotten a bad vibe from any of them, other than harmless teasing."

"Has anything unusual happened in the time since you've received the texts? Strange calls? The feeling of being watched? Have you noticed anyone out of the ordinary?"

"No—wait, there was a guy in the theater."

"Yes? Go on, please."

"Well, I got a creepy feeling, you know, goose bumps and stuff? Then I saw a man holding my sister by the arm. He took off when I headed over, but it bugged me."

"Can you describe him?"

"Um, he was around forty, best guess. Thin and scruffy looking."

"His height? Race?"

"He was average height, and white. Pasty looking, like he needed to get out in the sun."

"Did you report this at the time?"

"I spoke to the theater manager, but not the police. I mean, I got a weird feeling, but he didn't break any laws."

"Have you seen him or anyone who could have been him since?"

"No."

"Okay, I have a pamphlet on other steps you should take to make sure you're safe. Do you have a safe place you can go tonight? I'll have a safety officer contact you in the morning to run a check of your home security. It's not uncommon for these fellows to threaten family members and pets. You really need to be aware of your surroundings at all times."

Fear chilled Drew from her head to her feet. The officer was clear that this was serious. *I don't want this in my life. What about Cicely? How can I keep this from touching her? What if she's in danger too?*

Drew's mom wrapped an arm tight around her. "You can deal with this in the morning."

As the officer finished writing up his notes, there was a knock on the door. Drew jumped. The officer motioned toward the door, and at her nod, went to answer it.

"May I help you?" he said.

"I'm here to see Drew." Cicely's voice was clear and firm.

Panic filled Drew. *Why did she come? I can't deal with this right now.* "Cice? It's okay, Officer. She's my girlfriend."

Cicely walked cautiously into the room and nodded at the officer.

Drew's mom stood up, smiling brightly at Cicely. "Hi, I'm Jeanne, Drew's mom."

"Hello, I'm Cicely Jones. It's nice to meet you."

"Same here. I've been wondering what's kept Drew so busy. Now I know," her mother said.

"Excuse me, ma'am. We have all we need here. If you'll forward those texts to the number on this card, along with a log of when and where you were when you received them? The safety officer will call you tomorrow. Until we can get something more concrete, we won't be able to stop him, so if anything happens, call us right away. Please be safe, and call if anything else happens."

Drew shivered as the reason they were all gathered really hit her. Someone had been in her house. Someone was actually stalking her. She couldn't stay here. Wouldn't.

"I have my things packed and Kashi's in the carrier. We can't stay here. Mom, can we go?"

"Of course we can. You don't even have to ask."

"Drew? Aren't you going to stay with me?" Cicely asked.

Drew motioned to the porch and she and Cicely stepped outside.

"I can't handle anymore tension tonight. Not tonight. I asked you not to come for a reason. I need to focus on getting a grip, and I can't do that with you depending on me right now." Cicely looked like she'd been struck. *I might lose her, but I can't be with her right now. If she's not with me, she'll be safe.*

"But...well, I just figured we'd work this out together."

"I can't."

"What? Why are you doing this?"

"I have to get things under control. Please understand."

"I understand you're shutting me out."

"I don't have a choice. I'll call you."

"Drew? Help me understand."

"I can't." Drew turned away, unable to face the hurt in Cicely's eyes, and called to her mom. "Can we go? I don't want to be here anymore."

"Sure we can. Let's go."

Drew locked the house up, triple-checking the locks, and then followed her mom to the car. Cicely stood watching them on the porch. *She's pissed. I should go talk to her.* But something kept her from going back to the porch. Her mom started the car, but Drew put a hand to her wrist.

"Wait. Don't go yet. I want to make sure she gets to her car."

Cicely stared at her for a long time before finally walking to her car and squealing off. *Yep, she's pissed. But at least she's safe.* She sighed. "Okay, let's go."

The quiet stillness of the car was what Drew needed. She knew she'd hurt Cicely, but something about the night made her want to curl up and hide, and she couldn't do that when she was with her. They had to talk everything out, all the time, and she wasn't ready to analyze her feelings. The dream, the texts, the message. They were all connected. Somehow they were all a part of the same thing. She didn't understand the way it all fit together, but she knew it in her bones.

How can I talk rationally about something that's so nebulous? I know these things are a part of me. I know it. This is something I should be able to connect to, but my mind isn't letting me. If I went home with Cice, she'd want to drag it all out, and I don't have it all yet. Then she'd be freaked and scared when I dream later. And I know that's going to happen, too. I want it to. I want to understand that dream. I can't yet, but it's mine, and I need to figure it out before anybody else tries to dissect it.

Drew was edgy, filled with anxiety about the way she left things with Cicely. She chewed at her fingernails .She was also worried about her family. The officer said stalkers sometimes threatened family, too. If she was with her family, she could protect them. And if Cicely wasn't around her, maybe the stalker wouldn't know about her, and she'd be safer. *But what if he does know about her?* She didn't know what to do, and had never felt so helpless.

"You're sure quiet over there. You want to talk about it?"

"I don't know, Mom."

"Well, Cicely is beautiful and seems to be a lovely person. Why haven't we met her?"

"Mom."

"It's a simple question, Drew. She's obviously important to you. I'd thought you'd have wanted her to meet your family."

"I do, Mom. Seriously. It's still kind of new and stuff. I was going to ask to bring her to dinner next weekend, but now. Well, now I don't even know if she'll want to see me again."

"You lost me. What do you mean?"

"I mean, tonight. I sort of shut her out, if you didn't notice. That didn't go over well."

"But, honey, your house was broken into. And that scary message? It's normal to want to be with your family."

"Yeah, I guess. It's just that Cicely and I were kind of starting to feel like something. You know?"

"Oh, you are serious about her. Good for you, honey. You can clear up any hard feelings tomorrow. I'm sure she'll understand."

"I'm not, but I hope you're right."

"Trust your mother on this. If she's right for you and you're right for her, all of this will come to nothing."

Drew leaned her head against the window. *I don't know about that. Things have been weird between us all day. I'm sure there was a discussion on her agenda for tonight, maybe even a fight. Now I've bailed on her.* The break-in was upsetting, but she'd chosen her parents partially to avoid a confrontation with Cicely. *I'm so messed up.*

She sighed and tried to tamp down the panicky feeling inside. Her life had been so normal, so settled. Now, it felt like she was trapped, a feeling she was coming to realize she knew all too well.

CHAPTER ELEVEN

What the hell? Cicely couldn't grasp what had just happened. Okay, so Drew was freaked out because someone had been in her house. Okay. That was creepy and freak worthy. But to shut her out like that? Why?

She had been totally messed up by the dream last night, as well as the texts, and Drew brushing them off. But she'd planned for them to talk it out, to face what was happening, maybe even take a break while Drew worked stuff out. *And now I'm hurt because she shut me out. I wanted a break, but on my own terms. I'm such an idiot.* Drew shut her out completely, and Cicely hadn't felt this hurt since her parents had thrown her out. *This feels so like that.* The tap turned from open and loving to cold and empty in seconds. She swiped the angry tears off her face. *Why does that happen to me? Am I not worthy of love and trust? Is that it? Is there something about me that makes people turn away from me? Did Drew think she couldn't count on me?*

The warning blare of a horn let her know she needed to focus on driving. She was going way too fast. She slowed and pulled into a parking lot. *Get it together. You're bigger than this. Don't let her win.* But rationally she knew Drew wasn't trying to win anything. Why would she do this? She went back over the scene in her head, looking for some clue, some reason Drew had pushed her away. Was it because her mom was there? Was that it? Did she think her mom would object to their relationship? She sure seemed friendly and kind, but Drew had asked her not to come. *Was she mad because I showed up? But she seemed relieved to see me. It doesn't make sense.*

Desperate for some solace, she called Kallie. She would help her get a hold on what had happened.

"Hi, Cice. What's up?"

Cicely started to speak, but choked up and nothing but sobs came out.

"Oh no. Come over, now."

She managed an okay and hung up. She headed straight out to Kallie's place and did her best to calm down on the way. Kallie would help her gain some perspective on what had happened. Kallie was waiting for her on the porch and held out her arms to her. Cicely felt her heart leap to have such a constant in her life. She folded into Kallie, letting her warm embrace soften the hard ache of pain in her heart.

"Come on in the house, sweetie. Let's get you settled." She led them into her austere modern living room. The black streamlined couch was much more comfy than it looked.

"There, you relax and I'll get us some wine. Then we'll talk." Kallie tossed a fleece blanket to her. She wrapped it around her body and pulled her legs up under her.

Kallie was back in a minute and handed her a balloon goblet of deep red wine. She sipped and allowed it to soothe her wounded nerves.

"So, tell me."

"I don't understand what happened. Drew basically pushed me away."

"What? You're kidding, right? You guys were so connected yesterday. What happened between then and now to change that?"

"It was the break-in. I'm sure that was it."

"Break-in?"

"Drew left this morning when I went to work. She had some things she had to do at the park, but expected to go home around four. Apparently, when she got home she found someone had been in the house while she was gone. There was a message like those texts on her refrigerator."

"Oh no, that's creepy."

"Yeah, it was, but I mean, she called me and told me what had happened. I pretty much grabbed my things and headed over to her."

"And?"

"Well, she asked me to wait at the apartment, not to come, but I went anyway. I got there, and the police officer was finishing up, so I sat with Drew and her mom. She held my hand. But when she was ready to go, she told me she couldn't handle being with me, said she needed to go to her mom's house. Said she needed to be home. I thought *I* was home. I'm such a fool. I've gone and done it again, Kallie. I've let myself in for a world of pain by letting her into my heart."

"Now hold on. That's not what I'm hearing. Let's look a little deeper at this. You showed up, when she asked you not to. Clearly, Drew was very upset by what happened. Is it possible that she was acting this way to shield you from her emotions? She knows how upsetting her dreams have been for you. Maybe she couldn't be who you expected her to be in that moment."

"But, Kal, it was so cold. So final. I don't understand."

"I can't tell you what she was thinking, honey, but it doesn't sound at all like Drew. She must have had a reason. You need to give her a chance to explain. And maybe you need to stop and check your own emotions, too."

"I'm not sure I can. I hurt so bad, Kal. I want to be with her, helping her feel better, but instead I'm here licking my wounds. I don't know what I'm doing."

"You're feeling, and that's good."

Cicely felt empathy for Drew, but being pushed away hurt. She just wanted to cry. "She's been getting those texts the whole time we've been dating. Why didn't she do something about them sooner? I think she pushed me away tonight because I was pushing her to take them seriously. She avoids conflict and I meet it head-on. Damn, Kallie, what am I going to do?"

"You're going to give her space to handle this stuff. You're going to remember how Drew has made you feel in the past six weeks, excluding today."

Cicely didn't want to think about that. How she felt before today was what made today hurt so bad. She wanted today not to have happened. "It doesn't matter how she made me feel before. All I can think about is how she treated me tonight."

"Really? I know you're upset, but I want you to try to separate that anger and hurt from all the other feelings you've had while being with Drew. I want you to box those emotions off for just a little while. Can you do that?"

"I don't want to do that."

"Will you try? Please?"

Cicely dug her nails into her palms, trying to do as Kallie asked. She tried to cut off her current feelings and reflect on the feelings of yesterday. It was no use. Today hurt too much. Maybe she could do this exercise tomorrow.

"Kal, I can't do it. Not tonight. It's all too real right now."

"I get it, so what'll it be? *Fried Green Tomatoes*? *Steel Magnolias*? *Stella*?"

"Oh, let's watch *Stella*. I need to get my groove back."

"You got it. Popcorn?"

"Sure."

They settled in on the couch and watched the classic, Kallie lending a warm comforting presence to Cicely. *This is nice. I've missed our girl's night in. If only Drew was here with us. Would she like that?* The thought of never knowing the answer added a fresh sting of pain to Cicely's battered heart. She snuggled deeper into her blanket.

The next thing she knew, Kallie was gently shaking her awake. She was groggy and disoriented.

"Come on, let's get you settled in the guest room. I don't want you driving home so late."

"What time is it? I can't believe I fell asleep."

"It's a little past eleven. The movie ended a while ago, but you were sleeping so deeply, I didn't want to wake you. I finished some notes for tomorrow and took a shower, but now I'm ready for sleep myself. You're good with staying over, right?"

"Yeah, thanks. My apartment's going to feel awfully lonely for a while."

"Maybe, maybe not, but for now, let's get to bed."

She led the way to the room that was like a second home to Cicely. She even had a nightshirt tucked into the bottom dresser drawer.

"Is my toothbrush still in the bathroom?"

"Where else would it be? Go on. Get some rest. I'm planning to be up around six. Does that work for you?"

"I have to be in court tomorrow morning at nine, so I'll probably get up and head home around then. I won't wake you if you're still sleeping."

"Don't worry about that. I'll be awake, I'm sure."

"Kal?"

"Huh?"

"Is anything going to ever go right in my life?"

"That's up to you, kiddo. You've had a good stretch of everything right lately. This is just a bump, and I know you can get to the other side. You only have to let yourself."

Cicely shook her head. It didn't feel that way. She felt empty, hollow. Like a huge piece of her had been carved out and tossed to the side. Maybe she was overreacting, but she didn't have faith in that. She had trusted Drew with her heart and she felt crushed.

She said good night and closed the door as Kallie went down the hall to her room.

Her nightshirt was a reminder of her life before Drew. It had no hint of her scent, no whisper of her touch. It was safe, but strangely, it didn't comfort her. She wanted to wallow in the essence of Drew. To lay her head on the pillow Drew had slept on that morning. Find her toothbrush in the cup beside her own. *What are you feeling right now, Drew? Why am I not holding you while you dream, creepy or not? Why did you push me away when all I want is to be with you?* It had to be freaking her out to have had the stalker guy in her house. Drew must be terrified. *Are you trying to protect me by keeping me away?*

She finished getting ready for the night and climbed into the cool sheets that reminded her of nothing but loneliness. Her head hit the pillow, and she turned into it, crying silent tears for what had been. Tomorrow she'd deal with what to do about Drew. Tonight was for grieving. She gave in to it completely, knowing that with the sun she would find resolve to wake up and face whatever came. *I have to make her understand she doesn't need to protect me. Pushing me away isn't the answer.* She hugged her pillow as she fell asleep, imagining she was hugging Drew.

Chapter Twelve

He'd watched as she moved around the house, waiting for her to find it. She needed to find it. He wanted to share that moment with her. Instead of going into the kitchen, she watched TV.

The past few days, she had been missing. He'd managed not to panic, since he knew she wouldn't leave the cat alone too long. It was such a rush to see her riding up that afternoon. He wanted her to go straight to the kitchen and find his message, then he could've burst in and they could've started their forever. But it didn't happen. Instead she sat there watching TV and he sat waiting for his moment.

His frustration grew the longer he waited. It was beyond time for her to be with him. She would struggle, at first, but he would win her over. He knew he would.

He waited, impatient and brooding over her disappointing behavior. Why did she fail to understand the importance of his messages? She'd never once replied. She was playing hard to get, clearly angry that he had left her alone for so long. *I couldn't help it, Sunshine. I was in prison, and they hid you from me, but I'm here now. You've got to go in the kitchen. Go. It's time.*

The sound of a barking dog distracted him. The beast was beyond the fence at the base of the tree he was in. If it gave him away, he'd be in real trouble. Damn thing. He looked once more at her. Still sleeping. *Time to move.* He could listen from the car and still get to her.

Carefully, he shimmied down to the street and moved casually to the corner where he'd parked. When he'd climbed in behind the wheel, he noticed the curious glances of some neighbors.

Crap, he'd have to move the car. He drove down the street and around the block, hoping to return after a short while. For now, he'd have to be satisfied with listening.

For a long time, there was nothing but quiet coming over his headphones. Then there was murmuring, like voices on the other side of a door. It rose in volume, still no distinct words, then screaming. He ripped the headphones off. What was happening? He listened again. It was quiet, then a noise like someone startled. He heard her talking to the cat, her voice full of sleep. *Must have been a dream.* The soft rustle of movement and footsteps. Then, distinctly, the sound of the shower being turned on.

He caressed the photo album, his fingers tracing a well-worn pattern in the leather. His own breathing became erratic as he imagined her slipping out of her clothing and into the stream of water. His other hand ran the length of his member, its stiffening a sure sign of his timing. He would have her. They would be together. He pleasured himself to the sounds of her ablutions. So good. So, so good. Nothing compared to her. Even the fantasy of her was worth the time and effort it took to claim her. She was his.

The water stilled and he distinctly heard her sharp intake of breath. This was it. The moment. He turned the key in the ignition and...

Bang, bang bang!

He jumped, turning to face the window. An angry red face peered back at him.

"Hey, scumbag. This is a family neighborhood. Take your weenie wanking back to your own place. I've already called the police, so if you don't want trouble, you better get on out of here."

He jerked the car into gear and tried to pull away from the curb, and the man hit his window again.

"And I have your license plate and your picture, you pervert. Stay away from here."

He did his best to keep his face averted as he drove away. *Damn all nosy neighbors to hell.* Even though he was sure he'd missed his chance, he circled back past her house. There was a police cruiser with flashers outside, and the silly little car was there. He pounded his fist against the armrest. Would he never get a break? Didn't these idiots realize they were keeping them apart? They were meant to be. She would surely have no doubts now, having seen his message.

He needed to find a way of getting her attention away from the prying eyes and troubling actions of her "friends." He knew they weren't really friends to her. They were space fillers, taking his place. They were troublesome and unnecessary. *Time to cut them loose, Sunshine.*

He had no option now but to drive on. There was no possibility of reconnecting with her now. He drove to the outskirts of her neighborhood and pulled into a drive-thru restaurant. He needed to think. To figure out a better plan. He would eat and think.

What to do? How can I lure her away from those she feels bonded to? How can I remind her of what we had, what we will have? Maybe if he waited inside her home? No, what if she wasn't alone? He wouldn't want his dealing with an irritating interloper to come between them and frighten her.

He hit on an idea, and quickly figured out it was the best way to go. He would plan everything carefully, overlooking no possible obstacle. He wouldn't fail. Satisfied, he started the car. When he turned to exit the parking lot, his headlights illuminated a car. It looked like the same silly car he'd seen at her home so often. Could he be so lucky? He drove to the other end of the lot and reparked, watching the car. If it was the tall woman, he could follow her. Find out where Sunshine might be spending her nights away from him.

The car sat there for five or so minutes, then started up and pulled toward the exit. He followed, careful to stay unnoticed. The driver headed toward the west end of town, oblivious to him. He noted the landmarks as they passed. The university exits, the old highway, then she exited and headed up West Slaughter Road. An appropriate street for his mood. He followed as she drove into a neighborhood and pulled into the driveway of a modern home, all glass and limestone.

He continued down the street, but watched as she left the car and walked into the arms of some completely unknown woman. It was definitely the tall woman, though. He was struck again by the rich glowing quality of her ebony skin. She was beautiful. Worthy. How attached was Sunshine to this woman? If he could arrange things his way, she would be a fine addition to his burgeoning herd. *A fine addition indeed.* He felt himself stiffen at the thought. He could imagine what her breaking sessions would be like. She would be tamed, as they all were in the end, but the ride would be wild and satisfying.

Mind made up, he found a good place to stake out the house and watch for her exit. Cutting and collecting for the herd was so much easier than his careful stalking of Sunshine. He didn't worry about the variables with cutting. He simply isolated his choice and collected them.

He sat for hours, watching the house. Finally, the lights were extinguished and he realized she wasn't leaving tonight. He looked at his watch. Twelve fifteen. He would be back at five and be ready. When she left, he would follow and work on collecting her.

The predawn light was comforting. He felt in his bones that this would work. She would be an easy acquisition. He had to take the normal precautions, but he would have her.

She came out of the house a few minutes before six and climbed into the little car. He released his parking brake and let the car inch forward. When she accelerated out of the driveway and down the street, he was right behind her. He followed, noting the light traffic at this hour. When she slowed at the light to turn on Slaughter, he bumped the back end of her car. Then he fell forward, allowing his head to strike the steering wheel.

As he predicted she stopped and exited her car, coming toward him. He was ready. He saw no other vehicles in the area. He slipped the Taser gun into his jacket pocket and opened his door. He stumbled out, feigning a more serious injury and went around to the back of his car. He fell against his trunk, snicking the latch open as he fell. She was there in seconds.

"Are you okay? Hey, what's wrong?"

She gripped him by the upper arm, trying to steady him. He stumbled back and away, throwing the trunk open and pulling the Taser out. He fired in a quick motion, striking her on the left side, midway up her torso. She screamed reflexively and began the drop he knew was coming. Before she could fall all the way to the ground, he stopped the current and slipped his arms under her. With a twist, he rolled her into the trunk. He grabbed the bottle of laced juice and poured some in her mouth. She coughed and choked, but he made sure she'd gotten enough down to keep her disoriented. He slammed it closed and looked around again. The whole maneuver took less than two minutes. He was clear and no one the wiser. *So easy.*

CHAPTER THIRTEEN

Drew agonized over the way she'd parted with Cicely. *Why did I do that?* But she knew exactly why she'd done it. She'd been afraid. Scared for herself, and even more frightened that the weirdness in her life would drive Cicely away. How could she fix it? Would Cicely even consider fixing it? *Doubt it. You blew it.* Pushing her away had been selfish. *But I was protecting her, wasn't I?* She knew that wasn't entirely true. She didn't want to deal with Cicely confronting her about the texts and her blasé attitude about them. She hadn't taken them seriously enough, and now she was paying for it.

She should call her. At least make an effort to build a bridge. Cice knew how crazy her dreams had become, she had to know that was messing with Drew's sense of security. Maybe she'd understand. She'd leave a message if Cicely wouldn't take her call. And she'd call Kallie's office, too. She still wanted to get help with her dream situation, but Kallie might not be receptive to seeing her anymore. She could always call Dr. Balke's office. They knew her and might be able to fit her in.

She called Cicely first, the call going straight to voice mail.

"Hi, Cicely. I know you probably don't want to hear my voice right now, but I had to call. I'm so sorry about last night. Call me."

She choked up on the last words, wanting to tell Cicely what she really felt. How much she loved her, but she couldn't do that. Not under these circumstances. She had to overcome her fears to be any good as a partner. That would take some serious work, and it was beyond time to get started.

She called Kallie's practice next and was put on hold for an eternity. Finally, the receptionist came back on the line.

"Ms. Chambliss? Dr. Heidt is with a patient right now. She has confirmed your appointment for Thursday at four fifteen. Does that still work for you?"

"Yes, that's fine. I just wanted to make sure she'd still see me."

"She hasn't indicated otherwise. If that changes, I will call you well in advance of your appointment."

"Okay."

So that was something. Kallie would still help. She wished it was Thursday. She needed to do something to keep from worrying about things she couldn't change right now. Maybe Wy would be up for a movie. She pushed herself up from the couch and went up to Wy's room.

"Hey, kiddo. Want to go see a movie?"

"Huh? Um…no, thanks."

"Really? I thought you'd jump at the idea. I'm sure there's something you'd like to see at Charlie's theater."

"No way. I'm totally not interested in Charlie anymore. Besides, Javon said he'd take me down to Waterloo to get some ice cream. He'll be back from practice in an hour and I want to go."

"Oh, okay. What happened with Charlie? I thought he was all that."

"I don't want to talk about it, okay? It's been over, like, forever."

Drew could see talking about it upset her. What happened? She'd been so out of touch with Wy in the past six weeks. They hadn't spent any time together at all. She could tell Wy was upset with her, too. She dropped onto the bed beside her.

"Okay. I'm sorry I didn't know. Tell me what's going on in your life these days."

"Like you even care. You're all 'I'm too busy' or 'I have to work.' You don't have time to mess with a kid like me. Go away, Drew."

That stung. She'd really neglected Wy. And she hadn't shared the reason why with her. She hadn't even introduced Wy and Javon to Cicely. Much less invited them to do anything with them. *Shit.* Now that she didn't have Cicely, she had time for Wy. No wonder the kid was hurting.

"Wy, I'm really sorry. I've been a pretty rotten sister lately. I didn't mean to make you feel bad. I've been so wrapped up in my own life, I haven't been keeping up with yours. That's not okay. I don't want to be the absent sister. You're important to me."

"If I'm so important, how come you haven't even texted me in a month? Huh? What, you think my life's been on hold while you got all busy with some chick?"

"No, not at all. Listen, I've been in a place I've never experienced before. Yes, I've been getting busy with some chick, but she's a chick I'd like to build a future with, you know?"

"Hmm." Wy crossed her arms over her chest.

"With this girl, I've felt things I've never let myself feel before. Not just physical things, but emotional things. She's important to me, Wy, but not more important than you."

"Well, how come you disappeared? I mean, you don't even return my phone calls. I miss you, Drew."

"I miss you, too. I guess I figured you and me were solid. Nothing could shake us. And getting to know Cicely, that's her name, Cicely... well, getting to know her took a lot of time. She needed to know she mattered to me."

"I need to know that, too."

"I know you do. I'm sorry if I made you forget. You're my sister, and you'll always be my sister. You and me. We're forever. I want to get to forever with Cicely, too."

"You can't get there if you leave us behind."

"You're right. I can't. I need all of you. Can you forgive me?" Drew opened her arms, hoping she'd struck the right chord. Wy climbed into her lap, just like she had when she was six. Drew wrapped her arms around her and rocked her.

"I love you, Wynika. You will always matter to me. I hope we can get Cicely into this embrace with us. Then we can all be a family."

"She'd be lucky to be in our family. We rock. When am I going to get to meet her?"

Drew felt the fear from earlier pushing at the edges of the tender moment. Would they ever get to meet her? Drew sure hoped so, but only time would tell. "I'm not sure. She's kind of mad at me right now."

"Huh? Why? What did you do?"

"She was kind of upset that I didn't want to see her last night. She wanted me to come home with her, not here."

"But this is your family. You needed to be with us after what happened. 'Sides, you had such a wicked bad dream last night, you didn't need to be around anyone but us."

"I did, huh? I didn't remember it. How much did Mom tell you about last night?"

"Everything. She knows I'm not a little kid anymore. Not like some people."

"Hey, I know you're growing up, but you'll always be my kid sister, okay? So do you want to ask me anything about what happened?"

"Yeah. Who broke into your house? Why'd they write that message? Are you in danger?"

"I don't have the answer to the first two questions, other than maybe they were trying to scare me. I'd like to think I'm not in danger, but with something like this, I'm not taking any chances."

"You promise?"

"I promise."

Wy started crying then, hot tears falling on to Drew's shoulder as she held her. Her heart warmed as the love they'd always shared was renewed and strengthened. Wy was her touchstone and she was Wy's rock. They were good for each other.

"It's okay, I promise. I'm not going to let anything happen to me. You'd kill me if I did."

"You're righter than you know. I would kill you, and Mom and Javon would help me. Even Dad would help."

Drew chuckled. This was the Wy she'd been missing.

"Dad would never help you guys kill me. He counts on me to help him with the yard work."

Wy punched her arm.

"Ow, that hurt."

"You deserve a little hurt."

"Okay, I give. So what happened with Charlie? Seriously, I want to know what I've been missing."

"That boy's too immature for me. He thought he could get away with going with me and Sherrie Thurman at the same time. No way,

I don't play like that. If he wants to get straight with me he's gonna have to do some growing up. No girl deserves to be disrespected like that. Soon as I found out, I texted Sherrie and we both dropped him like a bad habit."

Drew smiled inwardly at the grown-up phrasing. "He didn't know who he was messing with. Good for you, Wy. I'm proud of you for standing up for yourself. No girl should be treated like that."

"Yep. He's been all hangdog, trying to get back with me. Javon even asked me if he needed to have a talk with him. I told him no. This is my business and I can sort it out."

"Right on. You really are growing up."

"Yes I am."

"You really don't want to go to a movie? We could go to Barton Creek. Maybe Jay would want to come too."

"I told you, he's taking me to Waterloo. There's this boy named Buster who works at the Amy's there. Javon says he idolizes him. He's kind of cute and stuff, so…"

"Ah, got it. You don't really need a boring big sister hanging around, huh?"

"You're not boring, just old."

"Thanks."

"Don't mention it."

"So are we good?"

"Yeah, for now. But don't let that happen again, okay?"

Drew could see there was still a little pain in the veiled request.

"No worries. You won't have to wonder where I am. I'll be living here for now. Me and Kashi."

"He's a brat."

"Kashi?"

"Yeah. He dragged my earbuds from my desk all the way downstairs to the den. I wasted twenty minutes looking for those dang things."

"Sorry."

"Sure you are. He's cute, though. Came and curled up on my bed when he realized I was mad at him. I think he's in my bathroom now, playing with the faucet."

"Good to know. I'm going to go see if Mom needs any help with anything."

Drew headed down to the kitchen where her mother was hard at work pitting cherries. Bad time to show up.

"Hey, Mom. Need some help with that?"

"Oh, what a savior. If you'll finish the pitting, I'll start on a crust and we can have cherry pie for dessert tonight."

"Great. I love cherry pie."

"Hence my juice stained fingers."

Drew sat at the table and her mother slid the bowl of cherries her way. It was mindless work, and she did love the finished product. They worked in pleasant silence.

The front door slammed, and Drew jumped. Her heart pounded in her chest.

"Hey, it's probably Javon. You're fine, honey," her mother said.

"I'm sorry. I'm a little edgy right now."

"Of course you are. You're going to be okay, though."

Drew poured the cherries into her mom's beautiful crust. Javon walked into the room, snagging a cherry from the pie shell.

"Mom, Drew, how's it going?"

"Hey, Jay. It's good, how about you? Good practice today?"

"Oh yeah. I rocked it. Threw some beautiful spirals to some greedy boys on the turf."

"When's your next practice? I'd love to come watch." Drew meant it, too. Watching Javon move his team down the field was like watching a ballet and a strategic battle combined. He was a great leader. Football had been his passion for years. His idol was Peyton Manning and Drew wouldn't be at all surprised to watch him play at that level before too long.

"Did you decide on which school you're signing with?"

"Nah, I'm letting them suffer. I want the best education I can get. Can't play football forever, you know?"

"That's good, I'm glad you're weighing your options. Personally, I like Cardinal red, cool gray, and black."

"Stanford's still in the running. I'll let you know what I decide. Might stay right here in Austin."

"The Horns would be lucky to have you."

"Thanks. Are you doing okay? I mean, after yesterday?"

Drew felt the cloud of anxiety settle back around her. She'd been able to distract herself from it by helping her mom. *I need to figure out what to do about all of this.* "Yeah, I'm freaked, but I'll be okay."

"Well, good then. I got your back, if you need anything. I mean that."

"Thanks."

"I'm going to hit the shower. I'm taking Wy to get ice cream in a while. Is that okay with you, Mom?"

"Of course, dear. Just be safe."

"Always. Later, Drew."

"Later."

"And, Jay? Be home by six for dinner. We haven't all been together for a meal in weeks. I want to look at all my beautiful children tonight."

"Yes, ma'am. Drew, you can come watch practice any Saturday."

"Sounds good. You guys have fun today."

When Jay had gone upstairs, Drew and her mother started cleaning up the pie preparation area.

"Drew? How are you really doing? You had the worst dream I've ever heard last night. I mean, your scream woke everyone. By the time I made it to your room, you seemed to be sleeping again, so I didn't wake you."

Drew felt terrible to have awoken the whole house. "I'm sorry, Mom. I didn't realize."

"Of course you didn't, honey. But it hasn't been that bad since you were fourteen. What's changed?"

"It's probably the stress from last night, though the dreams have been more frequent. I even had one during a nap yesterday. And Cicely says I stop breathing during the end of them."

"What? That's scary, Drew. What does your psychologist say?"

"I haven't seen anyone in a while. I've been doing well with everything until recently. It's only been the last six weeks."

"Six weeks? So right about the time you started seeing Cicely?"

"Yeah, I guess. But it's also the same time the weird texts started, so it may be more connected to that."

"Oh, honey, I really don't like that you haven't talked to a therapist about this. I know you were at odds with some of your early practitioners, but you really need someone to help you through this."

"I know, Mom. I'm seeing someone on Thursday."

"You're not going alone, are you? What about the person who was in your house? How are we going to be sure you're safe?"

"I'll be careful. I can't stop living my life because some creep is trying to scare me."

"Well, they've scared me, and I'm not sure I like the idea of you being on your own until the police catch him."

"We don't know that they ever will. For now, I'd like to stay here, with you guys, if that's okay?"

"Good. That makes me feel better, and of course it's okay. I think it might be a good idea for you to always have someone with you, at least for a while."

"If I can, I will. It might not always be possible, but if not, I'll be extra careful."

"Are you sure? I think you should consider anything you have to do alone off the table for now."

"Mom. Seriously, how can I do that? I have to go to work."

"I think you could take some time away, under the circumstances."

Drew thought about that. It was true that someone was stalking her. She needed to take that seriously, like Cicely urged her to. *Where did I put that pamphlet on stalking?* "I'll think about it. You might be right."

"Good. So, tell me about Cicely. She's gorgeous, as I'm sure you noticed. Tell me what she's like."

"Oh, Mom, she's amazing. I really connect with her. We fit together so seamlessly. There have been a few bumps. She's all about honesty. Everything that comes up has to be dealt with openly and instantly. That's been a challenge, but it's worked. Until now."

"Why until now?"

"Well, I pushed her away last night. I'm sure you noticed."

"Heavens, you needed your mom. Nothing wrong with that."

"Yes, but there's more to it than that. I knew we were going to have a confrontation last night, and I think part of why I chose here over her place was to avoid that. I'm sure that's what upset her."

"A confrontation? What about?"

"The whole stalker thing. She was pretty upset that I wasn't taking it seriously. She had to push me to call the police yesterday morning about the texts. I know she was a little mad all day."

"I swear, sometimes I wonder that you and your father aren't blood related. You're exactly like him when it comes to being cautious and avoiding confrontations. You need to work on that. Stop running away when you think things are going to be unpleasant."

"I know, you're right. When I talk to her I'll apologize."

"You need to do that, the sooner the better. And ask her if she'd like to come stay with us, too. She's more than welcome."

"I called her, but her phone must be off. My call went straight to voice mail."

"Listen, honey, if Cicely is the girl you want in your life, one call to voice mail isn't going to be enough. I think you should go over to her house and talk it out. I'll take you there."

"She had to work today."

"She comes home eventually, right? Do you know where her office is?"

"Yes and yes. But I can't just show up at her office. I'll sort this out, Mom. Don't worry. She may need a day or two to get over being angry at me."

"I wouldn't leave it a day. Not if you want to heal the injury. That kind of miscommunication and anger festers the longer you leave it."

"I get it, Mom. Thanks." Drew loaded the last spoon into the dishwasher and left the kitchen. She knew her mom was right, but she was going to give Cicely time to calm down. She knew her, and knew that yesterday would take a while to get over. She'd call her again tomorrow.

She also needed to figure out what to do about her home. Would she ever feel safe there again? The adult, responsible part of her told her to go home, get new locks, get an alarm system installed. Get past the fear and move on. But the part of her that was instinct, the truest part of herself, urged caution.

Someone had set that up to scare her, and they'd succeeded. Why? What was their reasoning? Drew had never had any enemies. There were no crazy exes or messed up friendships that could lead to this kind of thing. Was it someone from her childhood, like she suspected? Someone she had no memory of? How had they found her, and did that mean that when she did finally go home, they'd be watching for her?

She looked all over for the pamphlet, but couldn't find it. She needed to talk to someone about this kind of behavior and what she should do to protect herself. First things first, she'd check out what people said about this kind of thing online. Sometimes reading about other people's experiences could help. They'd probably have steps listed she could take.

She was blown away by the number of resources that popped up on her first search. She read the first three, and immediately felt better about being cautious. This kind of thing happened to a lot of people, and all the sites advised trusting your instincts. They advised her to move as soon as possible and do her best to keep her information private.

At least my new number seems secure, since there haven't been texts since I changed it. But move? I love that house. Why should I run away because someone's being a jerk? She closed the laptop in frustration. *Because I want to live without fear. I need to suck it up and do it. And make sure I do it in a way that whoever this is can't figure out where I'm going.*

She went back down to the living room. Her mother was on the couch reading a book.

"Hey, Mom?"

"Yes, love?"

"I need to move my stuff out of the house. Do you think dad and Javon could help with that? And I need to find a place to store my things until I can find a new place."

"A new place? Do you really think you have to move?"

"I do. It's what's most advised in these types of situations. Besides, I don't know how comfortable I'll feel back in the house. As much as I like it, I can probably find somewhere I like even more."

"Well, of course you're welcome to stay here as long as you need, honey. I'm sure your dad and Javon will help you move. We still have that storage unit downtown. You can keep your furniture there until you're ready to get settled in a new place."

"Thanks." Drew's voice quavered, and her mom looked up.

"Come here, honey." She held her arms out and Drew sank into them. "I can't imagine how hard this is. You know you're safe here with us. We'd never let anything hurt you."

"I know, Mom. It's so overwhelming. I mean, first this guy sends crazy texts, then he breaks in, then I screwed up with Cicely. Now I'm finding out just how real and scary it is to have a stalker. I feel like I've been hit by a huge wave and I'm rolling in the surf, trying to find my footing. I don't know what to do but cry right now."

"Crying's underrated. You should always cry when the mood strikes you, baby. You go ahead and let it go. I'm here."

Drew did let go, her fear of losing Cicely, her fear of the stalker, and the sadness at uprooting her life. The wash of heated tears felt cathartic as they fell. She cried until she had no tears left to shed. Still, her mother held her. She ran a gentle hand up and down Drew's back and made soothing noises that felt familiar.

Drew felt her tension slipping away. "What are those sounds?"

"Hmm? Oh, just sounds, to comfort you."

"They feel familiar."

"They should. I used them with you night after night when you first became my daughter. When the nightmares came. We would sit and rock and I'd make these silly sounds."

"I like them. Thank you, Mom. I love you."

"I love you, too, darling. When Dad gets back from the store, we'll all sit down and figure out how to get you moved. You don't worry about a thing, okay? Take care of you."

"Okay. You're the best."

"I know. Now let's do something fun to take your mind off of all of this."

"Like what?"

"Let's go shopping. We can pick out something new for your new house."

Drew felt the love her mother was sending with this offer. She was exactly the tonic she'd needed to feel better about things.

"That sounds like fun. I'll go shower."

"I'll be right here when you're ready to go."

Drew got in the shower and let the hot water slide over her. She imagined her fear, confusion, and loneliness flowing down the drain with the soap bubbles. She missed Cicely, and she missed the calm routine of her everyday life. *Why can't my life just be...normal?*

CHAPTER FOURTEEN

Cicely's first awareness was of the fierce pain in her head and a distinct lack of oxygen. She had to consciously tell herself to breathe. She felt like not focusing completely on the motion of her lungs would cause her to stop breathing entirely. And her heart. Why was her heart beating so fast? She felt sick, needed to throw up desperately.

She tried to sit up, but found she couldn't remember how to make herself do that. *What the hell is going on?*

With no more time to think, she turned her head to the side and puked. The motion in her gut caused a wave of agony to roll across her entire being. The smell of her bile made her retch again. She needed to get up, move away from the stench of it, but her body simply wouldn't cooperate. She was shaking uncontrollably. Shutting out the offending smell, she tried to remember where she was.

It was no use; she couldn't remember anything, and everything hurt. *This isn't happening. This is a dream.*

Eventually, she adjusted to the pain, anticipating the waves before they arrived, and she could think about something else. She realized that beyond the revolving pain there were points that stood out. Something stung like a burn on her side and there was a strange sensation on her left forearm. She started to take in her surroundings. Everything was dark. She could sense no light of any type around her. *Where am I?*

She tried to move again, but it was futile. The effort was exhausting, and she found herself drifting off. She gave in and let sleep take her. *Let me wake up in my bed, please, sweet Lord.*

She drifted back into sleep but wasn't there long. A crashing sound startled her back into full awareness. The pain was still there, but less intense. Her back and arm were more in the forefront than the general pain she felt earlier. There were sounds in the darkness, shuffling steps and the scrape of something heavy being moved. Then light exploded around her, blinding her.

The new affront was like a dagger through the head. She jerked, trying to bring a hand up to shield her eyes, but she still had no control over her movements.

"Just be still, now. You don't want to hurt yourself." The voice wasn't one she knew. Rough and definitely masculine. *Am I in a hospital? Is that a doctor? I must have been in a wreck or something.* That would explain the various points of pain and her general lack of coherence. She must have been hit by another car. *I remember leaving Kallie's house. It had to have happened then.*

Cicely prided herself in being a cooperative patient. She knew that was the best way to get things handled and get back to her life. She stilled as best she could and waited. The hard surface she was lying on must be a backboard. The discomfort in her arm, an intravenous drip. The voice would explain what was happening if she were patient.

"Good. That's better. I'm going to move you a little, so I can clean up your mess, okay?"

She tried to reply, but her mouth wasn't cooperating either. She tried a nod. It must have been enough, as she felt him grab either side of her backboard and slide her down, away from the vomit from before.

I wish he'd turn the light down. I can't see anything. But I guess that's better than pitch-black. She could hear him moving, grunting with the effort of cleaning. She tried to clear her throat again, to speak, but had no luck. Then a soft warmth touched her face, and she was gently wiped clean of her offending sickness.

"I know you can't speak, you probably shouldn't even try. You're safe, and nothing will hurt you. I'm in charge of your care and feeding. As long as you cooperate, you'll not suffer. The moment you choose to do other than you're directed, you'll get the Taser."

What the hell? Suffer? Care and feeding? What the hell is going on here? She knew how to do as she was told. Her parents had instilled that in her long ago. They may not be a part of her life anymore, but the lessons they taught her would always be a part of her. She needed to listen so she could figure out where she was and what was happening.

"I'm going to put you back in your box so you can rest and recover from your reaping. In time, I'll start working with you, teaching you all you need to know."

There was a touch then, one that made her more afraid than she had been yet. A hand, brushing her side, right above her hip and running down the length of her thigh. Her bare, unclothed thigh. *Why am I exposed? Hospital gown?* But she knew in her heart this had nothing to do with healthcare. She tried to assess if she was wearing any form of covering, and felt sick at the realization that she was completely naked.

The hand stopped at her knee and ran back up, caressing and kneading her skin.

"My, but you're beautiful. So supple and smooth. You're quite a prize, my dear. I won't leave you too long. You'll be fine. You have a constant drip of nutrients, and should the need arise before I return, there is an absorbent pad under you. Just let nature take its course. I won't mind cleaning you one little bit. Not one bit. In fact, it would be a pleasure."

She wanted to scream at him, demand that he let her up, but she couldn't move anything. Something was restraining her, but it wasn't physical. She felt no straps or anything tying her down, she just couldn't get her body to move.

She felt him move, and the board slid back to its original position. Then, what appeared to be a second board came down, blocking the bright light and closing in on her space. And the blackness was back. Now she knew it was a deliberate removal of light, one that would probably be her reality until she figured out how to get out of this mess.

She had to figure out if her inability to move was temporary or something else. She couldn't get free if she couldn't even move. She fought to move her head, to blink, anything, but she was completely incapacitated. How could that be? She still had sensation, she'd felt his filthy hand, but she was paralyzed.

Would her breathing be compromised? She remembered how she had to consciously make herself breathe when she first awoke. That was better now. Maybe whatever he'd given her to cause this was wearing off.

She could do nothing in her current state but wait. And think. She should be thinking about how to get away, but her mind was filled with Drew. Their time together over the past six weeks, and the confusing events of…was it only yesterday? How long had she been in this stygian prison? Would Drew know something had happened to her? Or Kallie? Surely she would check up on her. They would be looking for her. *Right?*

Drew. Her crooked smile. The rakish way she wore her hair, her honey brown eyes. Her hands, short-fingered and powerful, so perfect for loving her. *Drew. I need you.*

She wanted to cry for the pain she felt when Drew turned away from her. For the joy she had felt when she came back that very first night. For the passion they'd shared so easily. *We never had a chance to have makeup sex. I want that. Please, God, please find me.*

He pushed the box into place. The rails he'd installed for ease of access needed to be greased. The round room had access doors every few yards. Each door contained a specially designed chute with a pulley and rail system which held a tray topped by a coffin sized steel box. He could slide each box out of the recessed chute with very little effort. After the new one was back in place he moved to the next door and swung it open. The stench was almost overwhelming. Damn. This one was either sick, or dying. Maybe both. He hated it when things like this happened. He turned the crank to draw the box upward. When he could see the box lid clearly, he pulled the handle at the base and brought it full out in the open.

The plastic tubing that snaked from the upper portion of the box looked fine. No kinks or breaks that he could see. He had checked the fluid levels above ground before entering the room, and all the bags were as they should be. When he first dug the corral he'd had a problem with the tubing snagging on protrusions he couldn't see, but he'd fixed that with an earth auger he'd borrowed from a former client who worked in well digging.

Gingerly, he pried the lid off the box. Clearly, the woman inside was beyond help. Such a waste. Now he'd need another redhead. He looked carefully over the evidence in the box. She must have pulled the catheter free somehow. Could have even been an accident. Whatever, she'd regained the use of her muscles when the flow of nutrients and chemicals waned. The box showed her struggle to free herself from her prison.

Stupid. Stupid. Stupid. He'd been such an idiot. His pursuit of Sunshine had cost this poor woman her life. He'd stayed away much longer than he should have. *You have to keep to the schedule. If you fail to care and feed your herd, you're going to lose them and you know it.* He'd prided himself in the careful tending of his herd until now. He'd never left them alone more than a day until this week. He loved the time he spent grooming them. The careful bathing of their supple bodies gave him such pleasure.

He dropped down on his chair, rubbing his face and trying to come to terms with this loss. She had been a favorite of his. So compliant and receptive. Nothing to do but get on with it at this point. He stood and walked to the far wall where he'd installed an offal chute. It led to a secondary chamber with a furnace. He opened the trap door and wheeled her to it. Without ceremony, he dumped the contents down the chute. Once she was gone, he got busy trying to save her box. Someone new would take her place, and it would be better to reuse her box than to have to build a new one. He was angry with himself for failing the herd. They depended on him for everything. He knew he needed to check the others, but dread weighed on him. He didn't want to find another corpse.

When he'd washed and sanitized the metal box, he placed a new body board inside. It was as ready as he could make it. He had no further excuse to avoid the rest of the herd. One by one, he brought them up. They were all in good shape, reacting well to confinement. He bathed each one, took them through their paces to varying degrees, and re-stabled them. The fact that not one other girl in his quickly growing herd showed any sign of neglect restored his confidence in his work. *When I leave, I need to keep better track of time. I can't let this happen again.*

He wanted to head back to the house as soon as possible. He needed to know if Sunshine had returned, but he was tired and needed a good night's sleep. He climbed the incline to the recessed door and left the corral. It was time to go see Sunshine.

CHAPTER FIFTEEN

Drew left another message for Cicely and disconnected. Why hadn't she given some sign that she'd received them? *I know she was upset and hurt, but this is extreme. Has she really decided to boot me from her life?* Pain like a knife, cut through her. *Have I lost her forever? No. That's not acceptable. Not without some conversation, some closure.* She needed to see her, to look into her eyes and know, one way or another, if they were finished.

"Drew?" her mother called from downstairs.

She tucked her phone away and called back. "Coming."

Today was the day they were moving her out of her house. She'd been able to talk to her landlord and explain the situation. He'd been sympathetic and released her from her lease without penalty.

Her dad had organized a moving crew to get her things packed and moved out. She and her mother would go to the storage facility and sort out which boxes she would take to the house and which would stay there. It felt good to be moving forward. The police advised that she not return to the house. She couldn't anyway. She felt violated every time she thought of it, and without knowing who the hell her stalker was, she wouldn't feel safe there anytime soon.

Javon, Preston, and Wy were helping pack and load. Dad had gotten several of his students to assist, and things should be moving along. *I'm so lucky to have such great people in my life.* With the thought came an echo of the pain of missing Cicely. Sometimes it was enough to stop her in her tracks, knowing what they'd had and fearing it was lost.

This afternoon she would go to her appointment with Kallie. Maybe she could help her understand what Cicely was thinking. *Stop. You're going to Kallie to deal with your issues, not to dig for information about Cicely.* But she knew, should the opportunity arise, she would ask. She had to.

She joined her mother at the car and they headed to the storage place. It would be a busy day and Drew was looking forward to having it done.

"Honey? Are you feeling okay about all of this?"

"I'm okay with it. I'm dealing. I want closure on so many levels. I loved living in that house, you know? It was perfect for me. But I've accepted it's not going to ever feel that way again. I'm just glad I have you, and everyone."

"What about Cicely? Have you heard back from her yet?"

"No." She couldn't hide the pain in her voice, and her mother picked up on it immediately.

"Oh, love, she'll come around. Just give her time. She'll realize this thing that happened between you was all about the stalker. She'll realize you wanted to keep her safe."

"I hope you're right." *I hope I get the chance to find out what she's feeling.*

"Trust your mother."

Drew smiled, but it was a false, superficial smile. *You have no idea what you're talking about, Mom. You don't know her.* She felt like the walls around her were too close and she was suffocating. She had to stop thinking about Cicely for the moment. She needed to be present and she couldn't be if she let herself sink into the spiral of those feelings.

They spent the next several hours sorting boxes and stacking things in the large unit her parents leased. Drew was alternately excited about the reality of creating her life in a new place and fearful that the stalker might already be watching. *Will I ever not feel like someone's in the shadows watching? Will I ever feel safe again?*

On the last run, her dad picked up a couple of pizzas and a variety of beverages. They all sat around the truck and enjoyed the feast. Drew tossed her empty soda can into the recycling bin nearby. She needed to think about getting back to the house so she could shower and get ready for her appointment.

"Drew? Mom said you need a ride to the house. I have to get back, too. Let's take Mom's car and go," Javon said.

"Sounds good. Thanks, Jay."

The ride to the house was quick and relatively peaceful. Javon talked excitedly about his plans on the way.

"I really want to go to Stanford. I mean, that's a school that can stretch my mind. I want to go into aeronautics, and their program is stellar."

"Aeronautics? Wow, that's awesome. I thought you wanted to go into medicine."

"I did before, but not anymore. I love the idea of commercial orbital travel. It's going to happen, you know. By the time I'm forty, people will travel from place to place supersonically. I'm going to be a part of that."

"I can't even imagine that. How could that be possible?"

"Ha. It's more than possible. It's in development now. Virgin Galactic, baby."

Drew had to laugh with Javon and share his excitement. He had such dreams and she knew he'd work to make them a reality. *Will I be around to see it?* An internal voice she'd been trying to ignore wondered if her family would be safer if she were far away. It was too painful to contemplate fully.

When they reached the house, Drew made her way to her room and showered. She wanted to arrive early at Kallie's, so she'd have time to fill in the paperwork they'd need. She grabbed her helmet and headed to her bike. A wave of sadness hit as she remembered the last ride she'd taken. Cicely had been wrapped around her, laughing in her ear as the wind whipped at them. They'd had such a great day. Would she ever have that magical connection of spirit that she and Cicely shared effortlessly with anyone again?

She shook it off, thanking her father and Pres for getting the bike from the old house to her folks' place. She was lucky. She'd been able to leave the house the night of the break-in and not return because of the people who loved her. Now she could get on her bike and take the first step toward overcoming whatever was in her past that caused the nightmares. Possibly figure who the stalker was, and maybe, just maybe, she'd be able to repair the damage she'd done to her relationship with Cicely. Maybe she could have it all. *Or maybe the nightmares of my past will take away my future.* The thought was crushing.

The bike roared to life under her and she sped down the street. The route was easy, but traffic made it a pain. The roadways in Austin were so full of cars at all hours that getting from one place to another was agony. She had too much time in her head when she sat in stop-and-go traffic, and the lanes were too narrow to split them. Despite her plan to be there early, she made it to the office with only a few extra minutes.

When she entered the cool, modern building, the receptionist greeted her by name.

"Ms. Chambliss, hello. I have your patient information sheet right here. Dr. Heidt will be with you shortly."

Drew thanked her and took the clipboard. She sat and began filling in her history. She knew there'd be no way to finish it before she was called, but she did her best. She was only halfway through when the receptionist called her.

"You can come on back now. Keep the clipboard with you and you can go over it with Dr. Heidt. You can finish up after your session."

She led the way down the hall to a room lit with recessed lighting and floor to ceiling windows. It was a comfortable room. The wood was light grain and reflective, the ceiling painted varying shades of blue with a large skylight. One wall had lines of green and yellow, crossed like a grove of bamboo. She felt like she'd walked into nature. The seating was warm wood with generous cushions in a matching green. There was no desk or table in the space.

"Hello, Drew," Kallie said.

Drew turned toward the door. Kallie looked very different here, in her workspace, than she had at breakfast or on the other occasions they had been together. She wore black linen slacks and a tailored shirt in pale green. Her demeanor was also notably different. She carried herself with a professional air that hadn't been detectable before. Was this typical? Or was it in reaction to her separation from Cicely?

"Dr. Heidt. Thank you for seeing me."

"Oh, please, call me Kallie. We're friends, right?"

"Well, I guess so. I just figured you'd want this to stay on professional terms."

"Of course, the counseling will be on those terms, but we can't undo the fact that we know each other. So, Kallie, please."

"Okay, Kallie." Drew felt herself relax, knowing things were going to progress in a friendly way. She didn't think she could have a therapeutic relationship with Kallie if they back-stepped on their friendship.

"Sit down. Make yourself comfortable." Kallie sat on one of the chairs and pointed to the other. Drew sank down into the cushion, comforted by its yielding surface.

"I know you haven't completed your paperwork yet, but let's go over your history in therapy. Not in depth, but give me a general idea of what you've experienced and how I can best help you," Kallie said.

"My first introduction to therapy was around age twelve. I…I was found running down a country highway. I didn't know anything about myself. Not my name, not where I was from or where I'd been. Nothing."

"I see. And what did you learn in those earliest sessions? Did you feel they helped you?"

"Well, I'm not sure. They didn't help me figure out who I was, but I guess they helped me cope with the not knowing."

"Did you feel good? Talking about what had happened? Did it make you feel safe?"

"Yes, in some ways. Mostly it was the consistency. The fact that each time I went, Dr. Balke was there. I started building an identity based on those experiences."

"And did you ever have a breakthrough? Any flashes from your past?"

"No. Not for the first year or more. I was in a group home at the time. It was stressful. Dr. Balke gave me medication, for the anxiety… and for the nightmares."

"Ah, the nightmares. Have you always had them? I mean as far back as you can remember?"

"Yes, absolutely. They were frequent when I was first in care. At least one a night until I was fourteen."

"And by that time were you with your family?"

"Yes, my parents adopted me when I was thirteen. So they had to deal with my episodes for the most part. They tried to limit the medication, for the sake of my health, but by the time I was in high school, they had to give in. The toll they took on my waking life and theirs was too much."

"I want to request your records from Dr. Balke. Would that be okay with you?"

"Of course. I want your help. Anything you need from me, I'll agree to."

"Are you sure? I mean, with the personal connection we have, and the situation with you and Cicely, am I really the right person to help you?"

"What? I trust you, Kallie. I trust that in this place, in this room, you'll look at me as a patient in need of care and do your best for me."

"And that's exactly right. I wanted to double-check before we proceed. I would never do anything to compromise your care. I'm glad you trust me and I'll make sure that trust isn't misplaced."

"Then please, go ahead and get anything you need from Dr. Balke."

"Great. I'll have a consent form for you to sign up front. For now, let's talk a little about your dreams."

"Okay."

"What feelings do you have when you have these dreams? Are you fearful? Anxious?"

"I always feel terror, but I don't usually know why. I always feel like someone's been either chasing me or choking me."

"And why do you say usually? Is it because of what you remembered the night before we last saw each other?"

"Yes, that was the first time I had a clear memory of anything. Usually it's just feelings."

"Tell me again about that dream. The one from last Saturday."

Drew told her about the dream of being buried alive. Kallie asked her what she felt, how it smelled, what she heard, what made her afraid. Suddenly, she felt like she had been slammed back into her dream. The sensations she felt during them came back with an intensity she didn't expect. She felt the rough surface around her, the hard board and full feeling of her bladder. It was like she was back in the dream. Her heart started racing, and panic threatened to engulf her.

"It's okay, you're safe and you're awake. You're in my office and there's plenty of air. No one can hurt you. Listen to my voice and try to relax. You're safe, Drew. You're here, in my office."

Kallie's voice was like a cool cloth on a fevered head. It soothed her and helped her get a grip. She slowly came back to awareness of the room around her. The black earthy darkness slipped away into her subconscious again.

"Are you okay?"

"Yes, I'm better, now."

"That was pretty intense. I want you to consider trying something with me, okay?"

"Okay."

"When we next meet, I want to start with bringing you into a semi-hypnotic state. How would you feel about that?"

"How would you do that? Would it be dangerous?"

"Not at all. I would give you some truth serum—"

"What? Truth serum? Why would you do that?"

"Drew, it's just how you would name the medication. It's sodium amytal. It's often used to induce such states during psychotherapy. You'd be perfectly safe, I promise."

"What would happen then?"

"I'd talk to you during the time you were in this state about the dream and what events in your past might have precipitated them. We would work through a healthy reaction and coping strategy. I think it's the best way to get to the root of your dreams."

"Are you sure? I mean, we haven't talked a lot yet. What if there's more to it than that?"

"I know how the dreams are affecting you. The sleep disturbances, apnea. I think we both suspect those are related to some trauma you've repressed. This therapy will give us results that could end those issues for you."

"I'm nervous. I'm not sure it's a good idea. Not yet. Maybe I should do that sleep study thing?"

"Of course you should. That would be helpful in mapping your brain activity. In the meantime, will you think about what I've said?"

"I will."

"You have to be ready to accept and manage your past if we open you to it. I'll help you as best I can, but the weight of the work will be yours."

"I'm ready for the work, I promise you. Before the other night… well, before the break-in at my house, I think the dreams were starting to tear Cicely and me apart. I think if that hadn't happened, we might still be together."

Drew could see that mentioning Cicely had made Kallie uncomfortable. She couldn't help it, though. Working through this stuff was a direct result of her relationship with Cicely. If she wanted to move forward with her, she had to work on her issues. Kallie had to help her. She had to.

"I need you to help me. Don't you see? I can't lose her. She means so much to me. Please."

"Drew, whether or not you and Cicely find your way back to each other has nothing to do with this therapy. Would I like to see that happen? Yes. I think you're the best thing that's ever happened to Cice. But she has her own issues to work through. Let's focus on you, for you, huh?"

Drew resigned herself to the fact that Kallie was going to be neutral in this. That was for the best, she knew, but she was her only link to Cicely right now, and it hurt.

"How about you talk to me about what happened the other night. When you got to your house, what made you suspect someone had been there?"

Drew told Kallie about the door being open, falling asleep on the couch and the dream she experienced, then finding the message in her kitchen.

"So you experienced the dream during the day. Are you sure there's no chance you could have written the message to yourself?"

"What do you mean?"

"I mean, sometimes, when we're stressed, our minds dissociate from our conscious self. Kind of like what caused your amnesia. Is it possible you had a mini fugue where you unconsciously wrote that message? Maybe the fear of your past and your relationship with Cicely were too much for you to overcome. Maybe you sent your subconscious self on a mission to destroy your relationship?"

"You're shitting me, right? Why would I want to destroy the only thing that ever made me feel whole? Why? Besides, what about the texts? Surely I didn't buy disposable phones and text myself. I'm pretty confident that it wasn't me."

"Good. I'm glad you're sure. The mind can be pretty strong when it comes to self-defense. It's not all that uncommon for a person to be self-defeating when they fear the breakup of a relationship."

"I'm sure it wasn't me. Can we move on?"

"Of course. Talk to me about what your first memories are. What is the earliest thing you can recall?"

They continued to talk for the rest of the hour, and when she was ready to leave, Drew felt better about things. She trusted Kallie to do her best to help her. She only had to open herself to healing.

As she rose to leave, she had to ask. "Kallie? Is she okay?"

"Cicely?"

"Yes. I miss her so much. It's killing me."

"I haven't talked to her since Tuesday. She was pretty upset, but I know that comes from caring. She's just not ready to see that herself. She'll come around."

"Would you...I mean, could you tell her I'm sorry if my texts are bugging her. I can't help sending them. Tell her I miss her and I'm working on myself so we can be together, okay?"

"How often have you been texting her?"

"Once a day since Sunday, so she'll know."

"And she hadn't sent you a flaming response to keep your skinny ass off her phone?"

"No."

"That's not like her. I guess she's getting something out of keeping you in limbo. I'll call her tonight to check on her. I'm sorry this is all happening. Keep thinking about the assisted hypnotherapy. I really think it's the best option."

"I will. Thank you."

Kallie surprised her by walking over and giving her a full embrace.

"You hang in there. She's worth it."

"I know. See you next week." Drew made an appointment, and she needed to think about the hypnosis. It was probably the best route, but it scared her. What guarantee did she have that what came up would be something she could handle? Hadn't her mind kept it locked away all these years for a reason? But at the same time, what was happening now, the dreams, the breathing issues, were keeping her from having what she truly wanted, a life with Cicely, a life without fear. *You know if you don't get this handled, she won't ever come back to you. Not ever. And then, maybe no one else will want you either.*

The weight of that realization was heavy. What she wanted was to have a forever with Cicely. She knew that with everything she was. Her happiness lay in the resolution of her past. That, and the reconciliation with Cicely. She decided she wasn't going to wait any longer. Cicely could be as angry as she wanted, but she couldn't just shut her out like this anymore. She'd wait at the apartment for her to come home. *She might avoid my calls and texts, but she can't avoid me if I'm determined.*

Chapter Sixteen

She wasn't home, but something was happening at her house. He drove past her place and watched as several young men and women carried boxes and furniture out of the house. They were moving her out. It was all he could do not to stop the car and rush over to find out where she was going. He knew that would never do. He had to stay hidden and follow to see where they would lead him.

He parked a block away and walked past them again. They were laughing and joking as they worked. It looked as if they had most of the house emptied, already. He entered the yard across the street, the empty house he had used so often as a base during his observation of Sunshine. He went around to the back of the house and propped the ladder he'd left there against the back wall.

In moments, he was on the roof and better able to follow the progress across the street. Yes, the house was emptying quickly. He watched as they moved her mattress into the back of the truck and closed the door. Several of them piled into the truck's cab and another vehicle. Others went back into the house. The truck moved out, followed by the SUV. He considered following them, but he was too far from his own car. Besides, there were still people inside and the larger furniture. They would return. He would be ready to follow when they came back.

He watched the moving figures traipsing back and forth in Sunshine's house. There. He knew that one. The girl who was at the theater with her. Why? How did they connect? It made no sense. How had this young girl become important to Sunshine? Was she someone she knew from her workplace?

He'd tracked her to her home and work via searches on the Internet. He'd found her only three months before, and he didn't really know or understand her life between the time he went to jail and the time he found her again. Maybe this girl had fallen into her life during that time. It didn't matter. What mattered was her future, and that would be with him. He would make sure of that.

He'd earned plenty of money in the two years since his release. He'd sold thirteen herds since then and had more than enough money to take care of her. He would start by taking her to his cabin and reacquainting her with life on the land. If need be, he'd use the corral and his new girl to break down her resistance, the girl his Sunshine had been using to fill her time away from him. When she was the docile wife he had groomed her to be, he could relocate them anywhere he chose.

Mexico. That was a country he loved. So many out-of-the-way places and so little in the way of interference from the government. Yes. He could settle in there, close but not too close to a tourist area. There he'd have more than enough girls to continue his work. He could set Sunshine up in a hacienda with his working corral not far. Then the breaking and sale of herds would proceed without the level of security he now employed. He would be free, and so would she. This was his dream. He would make it his reality.

He lost himself in the dream for a bit and was startled to see the truck pulling back up. The second vehicle wasn't far behind. He needed to get back to his car. He knew the general direction they would go and could lie in wait for them to pass.

He waited half an hour, growing anxious. Had they gone a different way? Had he missed his chance? But no, there was the truck, trudging down the road. He let both vehicles go by and then pulled out to follow.

The truck was slow, which made his task a challenge. He needed to be invisible to those in the cars. He moved beside them, passed the SUV and slipped between them for a bit. Then he turned into a parking lot and let them get ahead. He moved back out after two random vehicles passed. The journey took no more than twenty minutes, but he soon saw that the destination was no help to him. It was a large secured storage unit. He couldn't follow them in; that would be too obvious. Frustration and anger flashed through him. Why was he being thwarted like this? It wasn't supposed to happen this way.

He circled the block, looking for a good place to park. He finally parked on a side street, near the back wall of the complex. He got out of the car and made his way to the front entrance. He could go in and ask about a storage unit to buy some time. They'd have to unload and then, perhaps, they'd go to the place Sunshine was hiding. He needed to find her.

The office was closed, so he had no excuse to hang about the front of the place. He looked around, as if looking for a way to contact the caretaker. When he'd exhausted a reasonable amount of time, he walked to the next property, a closed doggie daycare. He found a bench in the shadows near the door and sat, watching the gates. This was a good spot. He'd bring his car to this parking lot and sit here with his phone out. If there was a security camera, all it would capture was a man making a phone call.

He waited and watched, hoping he was unnoticed. They seemed to be taking much longer to unload than they had to load, but finally, he saw the nose of the truck at the gate. He put his phone in his pocket and climbed into his car. When the two vehicles passed, he easily slid in place behind them. When the truck turned to the right and the SUV continued forward, he stayed with the SUV. More likely to be going to the final destination.

They drove into a neighborhood he was unfamiliar with. The houses were large, a mix of old and new. He suspected there would be security patrols in a place like this. He needed to keep his activities as limited as possible. No need to arouse suspicion. The house they pulled in front of was a two-story home, an older one, but it looked updated. He drove by and continued until he came to a neighborhood park.

If Sunshine was in that house, he would find out. He parked and pulled off his jacket. Without it, he was dressed for a run. Perfect. No one should look askance at him running by the park and down the streets here. He started at a slow jog, then bumped up to a nice pace. He lapped the park twice and, with a sheen of sweat showing, he slowed again to a jog and headed toward the house.

When he drew close to the home, he could hear laughter and shouting from the wide porch. He felt himself harden at the thought that it might be Sunshine laughing. Hoping he would be so lucky, he slowed even further. When the gate was beside him, he stopped and reached down as if to tie his shoe. He glanced at the house. There were six or seven young people on the porch, sitting in chairs and on the railing. None of them were his Sunshine. The young girl he'd seen her with was there, but not her.

Where are you? Why are you making this so difficult? He stretched his legs and ran on down the street. Clearly, Sunshine has some connection to this house. He had an address now. He could run some searches, find out who this house belonged to and sort out how they fit with Sunshine. He'd need to develop some type of plan to track her from this place. Eventually, she would surface. He needed to know all the parameters so he could finish this.

Cicely woke. She felt the same inability to move that she had before, but the intensity of it had lessened. She tried moving her feet and hands. She wanted to cry with relief when she felt her fingers respond. Then her foot jerked, not much, but movement. She tried turning her head. That was easier. Maybe the stuff he'd given her was wearing off. If only there was some light, some way to know where she was, if it were day or night. She tried to vocalize, and heard her own voice. Weak, but there. *I'm going to be okay.*

Then it hit her. She might be able to move a bit, but she was a long way from being okay. She needed to figure out a plan so she would be ready when he came back. If nothing else, she could listen to her environment, find out what sounds were normal and what signaled a change. She had no need to shut out any distractions, since the only one she could name was the sound of her own breathing.

At first she heard nothing. Absolutely no sound at all. How could that be? Where the hell was she that there were no road sounds? Her panic started to rise, but she shoved it down, willing herself to listen. Finally, she heard something, a motor or something kicking in. Whatever it was, it was either far away or very quiet. It sounded similar to a pool pump. There was no other sound she could determine, and soon the pump sound stopped. She was wrapped in silence again.

To keep herself alert she began to sing silently. She ran through every song she could remember and started again. Now she could nod her head in time to the internal beat. She tapped first one and then three fingers against the hard surface below her. *Fight, damn it, fight this shit. Make yourself strong. Beat this.*

The rhythmic tapping felt like freedom. She tapped harder and discovered her fingers made a sound if she reached a little to the side. She slid her hand back, not ready to give any signal that she had regained consciousness. What had he said? Something about nutrients? Think. Think. What was it? *A constant drip of nutrients...* She was hooked up to some kind of intravenous delivery system. Where was the needle? *In my arm. The irritation in my forearm.* She tried to move her left arm to her right side. She felt the movement and knew it wouldn't make it over her body. She was barely able to lift it at all. *Time. Work the mind to free the body, girl.*

She would make herself stronger than this nightmare. She would win, no matter the cost. He might be able to touch her body, but he could never touch her soul. She would make her freedom her only truth. That and Drew. Drew would be her truth. This creep would be a blip on her life screen and she would wipe all memory of him away.

She moved from tapping her fingers to bending her wrists, sluggishly at first, totally uncoordinated, but each repetition led to more determined movement. She could feel her body responding with greater vigor. She would be free. She added a point and flex of her feet.

The fear that this wouldn't be enough, that she wouldn't be able to affect an escape played with her emotions. She felt the hot tears slide down her face. *Drew, please come and find me. Please don't give up on me. I need you.* But reality was a harsh mistress and she knew Drew would have no way to know where she was.

She couldn't even piece together how she'd come to end up here. *Who is this guy? How did I become his target? Could it be the guy who broke into Drew's house? Did he take me to get to her? How am I going to get out of this and keep her safe at the same time?*

She pushed all other thoughts from her mind. What had happened? She remembered being upset with the way Drew had pushed her aside and gone home with her mom. She accepted now that Drew was probably avoiding a fight. *She'd ignored the real threat in those messages, and I was going to call her on it, big time. And I know she was afraid of how her nightmares were stressing me out. She probably thought I would break up with her that night because of those damn dreams. And the truth was, I was going to. But not now. I know how much I need her in my life, now. If I get my life back... Stop. No negative thoughts now. You will beat this. You'll endure, and at some point you'll be free and you will have your life. You must.*

They would be looking for her. Kallie would, Drew, too. She knew they wouldn't stop looking until they found her. There had to be some clue they could follow, something. She and Kallie talked almost every day. She'd know something was wrong fairly quickly.

In the meantime, she needed to do all she could to regain her strength.

Chapter Seventeen

D rew knocked on the door for the third time. If Cicely was inside, she wasn't answering. She turned away and headed back to the parking lot. Cicely's car wasn't in her usual slot, but that didn't necessarily mean she wasn't home. She could have left her car at work.

What am I supposed to do now? Why are you hiding from me? Don't do this, Cice. She was so in her own head that she walked right past her bike. She stopped and turned back. Something moved in the shadows and she jumped.

"Drew?"

It was Kallie.

"Jesus. You scared the crap out of me."

"What are you doing here?"

"Trying to get Cicely to talk to me. I'm miserable without her. Have you seen her?"

"Actually, no. And I'm getting concerned. She hasn't returned any of my texts or phone calls. That's really unusual. I haven't talked to her since Tuesday morning. She was supposed to meet me for dinner, but after…well, you know. I figured she needed some time alone."

"Do you think everything's okay? I just figured she was avoiding me."

"Have you been up to the apartment?"

"Yes, I knocked forever, but she didn't answer."

"I have a key. Let's go see."

They went back to the door and Kallie unlocked it.

"Look, maybe you should wait out here," Kallie said.

"What? Why?"

"If she's here it might be better if she sees me first. Then, if she's okay and wants to see you, you can come in."

That cut deep. Drew was sure Kallie was saying it to protect Cicely, but damn. It hurt.

"No way. I need to see her. If she wants me to leave, she can tell me herself. I'm not going to wait outside while you check to see if I'm welcome. I'm sure I'm not. But damn it, Kallie. I'm going inside."

She pushed past Kallie and walked into the apartment. Everything was too quiet. Cicely liked to have noise around her.

"She's not here," Drew said.

"How can you know that? We haven't even gotten past the front door."

"No music or TV. She would be playing something."

"She might be sleeping. Let's make sure."

They went in opposite directions, each checking for any sign of Cicely. When Drew entered the bedroom, her emotions almost knocked her over. The bed was as she left it Monday morning. She'd left after Cicely and had made the bed. She'd placed a rose on Cicely's pillow for her to discover that evening. It was still there, wilted and sad looking.

"Kallie."

"Huh?" Kallie called from the bathroom.

"She hasn't been here. Not since Monday."

"How do you know?" she said, coming to join Drew. "Wow. Did you leave that there?"

"I did. She wouldn't have left it there. If she was angry and came home to it, she'd have stripped it bare and tossed the petals. If she was hopeful, she'd have put it in a bud vase. She wouldn't just leave it. Hell, she'd have to move it just to sleep."

"You're right. Where can she be?"

"You said you spoke to her on Tuesday, right?"

"Yeah. She spent the night at my house. We had coffee together before she left to come home and get ready for work. She had court that morning."

"Well, I don't think she ever came back here. Did you leave at the same time?"

"No, she left about an hour before I had to go."

"And you didn't see any sign of her on your way to work?"

"I wouldn't have. She would go I-35 to her place. I go the other way, on Mopac."

"What should we do? It's been two days. Should we report her missing?"

"Probably. And I'll call her office. They'll know if she showed up for court. Maybe she just didn't want to be here, you know? Too many memories?"

"Possible, but why wouldn't she return your calls?"

"I don't know. Let me call."

Kallie called Cicely's office and found out that she hadn't been in since Monday. She'd missed her court appearance and they'd been trying to reach her as well.

"Okay, I'm freaking out now. Where is she?"

"We have to go to the police. Maybe she was in an accident."

They went to the main station on 8th street. The duty officer took their information and asked them to wait for an officer to come and speak with them. It wasn't a long wait. The officer led them to a room and had them sit at the table.

The officer was about Drew's age and intensely serious. She didn't smile or greet them. It made her flash back to her childhood.

"I understand you're here to report a missing person?"

"Yes, that's right," Kallie said.

Drew did her best to relax. Being in this building was no comfort. She remembered the night they'd brought her here, when the truck driver had found her on the highway. She'd been completely panicked and the same feeling swamped her now. She wanted to get up and run, to get away from whatever was causing her fear.

"Is there a problem, ma'am?" The officer had noticed her discomfort.

"No, just bad memories," Drew said. Acid filled her stomach and she tasted bile. *Won't do to throw up in here. Relax.*

The officer watched her for a moment and then turned back to the form on her clipboard.

She asked them lots of questions about Cicely. They told her everything they could. They didn't have her social security number, but Kallie offered to get it from her work place. It went quickly and before they knew it, the officer was handing a form to Kallie.

"I want you to fill out this form. Please be as specific as possible. I'll put this information into our database and see if anything is flagged. I'll be back in a few minutes. Please wait here," the officer said.

"This is so surreal. I can't believe we're here, doing this, right now," Kallie said.

"I know. It's all we can do, though. Maybe they know something, or can find something to help us find her." *God, I hope so.*

Drew couldn't even think about the possibility of not getting Cicely back. When she'd pushed her away, she had acted out of fear and insecurity, but she never imagined that it might be the last time she saw her. *Stop. That can't be the truth. You will see her again. You will have your forever. You will.*

The officer returned and sat down opposite them, again.

"Tell me again, what happened Monday night at your house?" she asked Drew.

"Monday? Someone broke into my house. They left a message on the fridge. My mom and Cicely came over, and we talked to the police," Drew said.

"And when you left, you went with your mother and Ms. Jones left in her vehicle?"

"That's right."

"You indicated earlier that you had some sort of falling out that night, right?"

"Well, not really a falling out. I mean, she expected me to go home with her, to the apartment, but I just couldn't. I needed to be with my family."

"And this upset her, right? Dr. Heidt, you stated that Ms. Jones was upset when she arrived at your home."

"Yes," Kallie said, "she was crying. She was hurt by what she perceived as Drew's rejection."

Drew felt horrible. She hadn't meant to hurt her; she was just afraid. She bit her lip hard enough to taste blood. *You idiot, this is all your fault.*

"Hurt enough to want to harm herself? Or to want to disappear?" the officer said.

"No. Absolutely not. Cicely is a very rational person. She was angry and hurt, but she would never do something like that."

"Perhaps she went home to her family. Have you reached out to them?"

"No, that can't be possible. She cut ties with them when she was seventeen. There's no way she'd go back there."

"Still, we have to check. Do you have their names and information?"

"No, I don't."

"Okay, I'll have them tracked down through her records. So, she left your home Tuesday morning around six?"

"Yes. She had to be in court at nine and wanted to go home and freshen up. She was fine when we had coffee. She wasn't angry anymore. Maybe a little hurt, but determined to be strong."

"We're treating this as a suspicious disappearance. I'm going to need each of you to come give a formal statement of your whereabouts Tuesday morning."

"What? Why?" they said.

"Just to eliminate you as suspects. If things went as you say they did, there's nothing for you to worry about. Come with me."

Drew's dread pulled at her like the strong current of a river. If she didn't make herself move, she was going to be swallowed up by it. She followed Kallie, but lagged farther and farther behind. Kallie noticed, finally, and stopped to wait for her.

"What's wrong?"

"Nothing," Drew said.

"Nope, that won't do. Tell me what you're feeling right now."

"Ladies? This way, please," the officer called ahead of them.

Drew nodded and picked up her pace. Talking to Kallie would have to wait.

She was shown into an interview room with a table and chairs.

"Sit there." The officer indicated one of the chairs. "I'll be right back."

Drew stared at the cinderblock walls, remembering them from before. Her heart pounded in her chest as the feelings from that time rushed at her. Fear, confusion, and what? Everything was strange to her. The noises and smells of the building, she could still feel how alien they had been to her. Why? What had made them so strange? It's not like the place was stinky or overly loud. In this room she could hear nothing but her own breathing. Why had it been so frightening when she was a kid?

"Ms. Chambliss?" A new officer was at the door.

"Yes."

The officer nodded and sat across from her.

"Could you go through the events of Monday night again for me?"

"Sure." Drew went over everything that had happened that night, answering questions she had answered twice before.

"And you didn't see Ms. Jones after that time?"

"No. I haven't seen her since Monday night."

"Now let's go over your movements on Tuesday morning."

Drew was angry they were acting as if she and Kallie had something to do with Cicely's disappearance. She wanted to scream at this man, demand that he get up and do something to find her. But she bit back her anger and answered his noxious questions. Yes, she had been at her parents' home. No, she hadn't left the house. Yes, her mom was home with her, as well as her younger sister. No, she didn't know of anyone who wanted to harm Ms. Jones. No, she had no reason to doubt Dr. Heidt's story. Yes, she trusted Dr. Heidt.

"It has to be him. The guy. The one who broke into my house and who's been texting me. It's the only thing that makes sense." Drew knew deep down it was true, even though she hated to admit it.

"Ma'am, sometimes these things don't make any sense."

"But you have to check. Please."

"Ms. Chambliss, we didn't get anything evidentiary at your house, other than the message."

"But the texts. Could you do something with the texts?"

"You forwarded them to the officer on your case, right?"

"I did."

"If there's anything we can get from them, I'm sure he's already working on that."

"But he's stalking me. All the information says it's likely he'd go after those I'm close to. Please, you have to take this seriously. You need to find this guy. What's he doing to Cicely? He's had her for two days."

"You don't know that's what happened. Stay calm. Let us do our job. Go home and wait until we have something we can report to you. And if you hear from the stalker again, let us know immediately. Obviously, if you hear from Ms. Jones, do the same."

Drew felt the energy that had consumed her fizzle into nothing. She had nothing. There wasn't anything she could do for Cicely. She dropped her head onto the table.

"I'm really sorry, ma'am, but there's nothing else to do right now."

"I have to get her back. I have to."

"I know you feel that way, and we're going to do all we can to make that happen. The best thing you can do right now is get some rest. Go home. Be with your family. If we get anything we'll get in touch."

He told her she was free to go. Her legs were shaky as she stood. She felt like she'd been doused in something thick and heavy, something that weighed her down and made it hard to move forward. Like her legs were stuck to the floor and a heavy weight was on her back.

Kallie was waiting in the front area. She looked grim.

"Did they tell you?"

"Tell me what?"

"They found her car. Less than a mile from my house. Her car was abandoned on the roadway, no sign of a struggle and no sign of Cicely."

Drew felt like her insides had turned to ice. What had happened? This wasn't real. It couldn't be real. She reached out to steady herself on the wall, then fell against it and slid down to the floor. She put her hands on her head and started rocking. *This isn't real.* Waves of grief hit her, forcing a broken wail from her body. She felt hands on her, lifting her. Kallie and the first officer, helping her to her feet. She had no power to move, much less keep herself upright. She felt a hard surface against her legs and was pressed into a chair.

Kallie was saying something, her lips were moving, but Drew couldn't hear her. Someone was screaming. All she could hear was the roar of pain in her heart. She felt warm contact from somewhere outside herself. Someone was hugging her. It was Kallie. She had wrapped her arms around her and was talking in a calm voice, rubbing her back.

Drew felt her panic recede, as the contact from Kallie became an anchor, something she could focus on. She felt herself begin to relax, her muscles becoming loose and limp. She lifted her arms and returned the embrace, the only way she could signal to Kallie that she was reaching her. Now she could feel the hot sting of tears on her face, the rough painful grind in her throat that told her the screaming had all been hers. She cried now, with feeling rather than blind panic.

"Good, let it go. You're okay, Drew. I'm here and it's all going to be okay," Kallie said.

She wanted to believe that. To feel that sure, but the loss was too strong right now. When she had Cicely back in her arms, then everything would be okay.

"I've called your mom. She's on her way. Everything is going to be okay."

"How…how did you call her?"

"I used your phone. I just asked it to call mom. She said she'd be here as soon as possible. Here, try to sip a little of this water. The officer is getting a blanket for you."

"I don't need a blanket. I'm okay."

"We both think it's a good idea to get you warmed up. You've had quite a shock and we want to be on the safe side."

Drew nodded and took a sip of the water. It felt good on her raw throat. She reached for the bottle and took another sip. Soon the officer returned and wrapped a fleece throw around her. The warmth did feel good. Maybe she needed the blanket after all.

"We can't give up, Drew. Cicely needs us to believe that everything will be okay, that she will come home to us. Please don't give up on her."

Drew didn't have a response to that. How could everything be okay? Cicely was gone. They had no clue where or how to start looking for her, and it was entirely possible she'd been targeted by

Drew's stalker. How could anything ever be right again? Couldn't Kallie understand that?

"I've called Texas EquuSsearch. Once the police give their consent, they'll help us with the logistics of starting a community effort to search for her. The police have assured me they're asking everyone who might have been in the area or seen anything. Please have faith. She needs that."

Drew wanted to say, yes, I have faith, but her heart didn't feel it. She felt like nothing would ever be right on the world again. The grief was like a solid weight holding her down. She couldn't say it, no matter how badly she wanted to.

"Drew?" Her mother rushed down the hall and sat beside her, holding her. "What's happened? Why is she like this?"

"It's Cicely. She's missing and probably was abducted," Kallie said.

"What? That's terrible. Was it the stalker? What can we do?"

"I don't think there's a whole lot we can do right now. The investigation has begun, but I have no idea how long it will be before they have any information they can give us. I called to request a search. We have to send them a form and a photograph. I'll do that as soon as I get back to my office," Kallie said.

"So for now, we just sit tight? Can we go home?"

"That's why I called you. Drew kind of came unglued for a minute. I don't think it's a good idea for her to be alone."

"I agree. Thank you for calling me. I'm Jeanne, by the way." She held her hand out to Kallie.

"Kallie Heidt. Nice to meet you."

"Will you keep us informed of anything you hear? I know Drew is going to be desperate for any information."

"Of course I will. I'll call as soon as I finish talking to EquuSearch. I'd like to talk with you further about the other night, Drew."

"I'd like that, too," Drew said.

"Good. I'll call. You guys go home. It will do you good to be out of here."

Drew leaned heavily on her mom as they walked to the car. She was so lucky she had her. What would her life have been without her parents? What would it be now, without Cicely? *Stop it. Don't give up on her.*

"They're going to find her, Drew. Don't even doubt it for a second."

Drew couldn't speak. It hurt to think about talking right now. All she wanted was to go to sleep and wake up when this was over. She wanted Cicely's arms holding her. She wanted her breath on her cheek. *Where are you?*

Her mom held the door while she slid in. Then reached across her to buckle her seat belt, just as she had done when Drew was a kid. Always making sure her baby was safe.

Nobody's making sure Cicely is safe. She had no answers, only a gaping hole in her heart that ached for Cicely's return.

"Honey, please talk to me about your feelings. I'm worried about you."

"I'm not feeling anything right now. I'm numb. What am I going to do without her, Mom?"

"You're not going to have to find out. They'll find her, Drew. I'm sure of it. Please stay focused on positive things, honey."

"There's nothing positive in any of this. I pushed her away because I was afraid. Hear me? I was afraid to have a fight, afraid she would break up with me, afraid that if she stayed close to me, she'd be in danger. And now, she's gone. It's all my fault, Mom. If I hadn't done that we would never have been apart. She'd have never been on that road at that time and he wouldn't have taken her. Don't you see? I'm to blame for this."

"You're not being rational. The only one to blame for this is whoever was involved in taking her. It could have happened at any point. You didn't make this happen, baby."

"Didn't I? If I'd been with her, he'd have taken me, not her."

"You don't know that and what you're doing is self-defeating. I know you're worried and you're angry. You have every right to be, but you have no right to assign yourself blame. This isn't your fault. Stop. Guilt does nothing to help the situation. What you need to be doing is thinking. Try and think about anyone you may have seen or noticed watching you two. Who could your stalker be? If he's the one who took Cicely, you have to think about where you might have known him. Was he maybe a classmate? Who is he? If this wasn't a totally random crime, then there's got to be something you can pin point."

"I don't know who he could be, Mom. I don't think anyone ever obsessed over me."

"I hate to say this, but you need to focus on trying, honey. I know how horrible this all is, but if Cicely's disappearance is connected to your stalker, you have to try."

Drew leaned her face against the glass. Despair swamped her, making every little snippet of memory seem irrelevant. *How can I make myself remember?*

Her mom took her home. She curled up on the couch with her phone in her hand. She wouldn't put it down again until she heard something.

Chapter Eighteen

She was thirsty. Her head ached and she needed something to drink. Whatever he had connected to her body was obviously not working. She panicked, wondering how long it would be before he returned and realized she was dying of dehydration. *I'm going to die in this dark prison. I'll never see Drew again, never hold her, touch her, kiss her. I'm going to die.*

She wanted to cry, to let her emotions go, but there was no point. It wouldn't bring Drew to her. It wouldn't even get the man to come back. She grasped for something to hold on to, to help her through this. If she was going to die, it needed to be on her terms. She wanted to leave this world with the best times of her life in mind, not with the fear and bitter agony of this prison. *Drew is my happiness. I can hold on to her.* She made herself forget her thirst and focus on the first time she saw her.

Dancing. Drew had been dancing, lost in the rhythm of the music, eyes closed. Her hair dark with sweat, her skin glistening. Cicely had slid in beside her and melted into the dance. It had been electric. And Drew had opened her eyes and looked at her as though she was the most beautiful thing she'd ever seen. Cicely had had to make some smart remark to get them moving again.

Their whole time together had been like that dance. Easy, rhythmic, organic. Except for the dreams, and Drew facing the threat of the stalker. How could she have considered letting Drew's dreams come between them? She knew now that she could never have let that happen. And to be so upset about the other night…

Yes, Drew had turned away from her, and it had hurt, but her reason for turning away? That wasn't Drew's fault. She owned that. She had created a wall in their relationship that was insurmountable. Her need for open communication and honesty was consuming. Not that she was wrong to expect that overall, but to make it more important than helping Drew work through her trauma? That was her fault. She had made it impossible for Drew to be vulnerable.

Now she did cry for the loss of their relationship. If she survived this ordeal, she would fix that. They would fix it together. She trusted Drew like she had never trusted anyone before, and she needed to tell her that. She had to let her know that nothing was so bad that they couldn't get passed it.

I love you, Drew. I will make it through this. I will.

She had no idea how long it had been since she woke desperately thirsty, but she heard something now. Something different from what she had heard before. The pump noise was there, but some other mechanical sound echoed through the obsidian tomb. Then she could hear the murmur of a voice. Bass tones. The man had returned. He was either talking to himself, or he had someone with him.

She expected that any moment he would do whatever it was he did to make her box rise and she would see him. But it didn't happen. The motor sound faded and she could hear him moving about, the sound of water. It made her thirst flare with a new intensity. Water. I need water. She started tapping as hard as she could on her box.

"Help me! Please, let me out!" she screamed, hoping he would hear her. She knew there was no way he would let her go, but if she could get his attention she hoped he would give her water.

The motor sound rose again, and she felt the sway and shift of her box. When the movement stopped, there was no sound. What was he waiting for? *Open the damned box.*

Light like a dagger struck her, blinding her. The pain in her head was unbearable. She shifted her head to the side, trying to get out of the light.

"You're not supposed to be awake, young lady."

"Screw you. Let me out of here."

"Now, now. Mind your manners. You wouldn't want me to send you back down so soon, now would you?"

Cicely panicked, fearing he might do just that. Her vision cleared, and she had her first look at her captor. He was a small man, scruffy, but with the look of strength in his lean muscled arms. His eyes were black, like coal and just as hard.

"Please, I need some water. Please." Her voice was harsh in her own ears.

"S'that so? You shouldn't be thirsty. In fact, you shouldn't be able to talk or move much at all. I'm going to give you some water, but first I need to make sure you're safe. I'm going to put these restraints on you so you can't hurt yourself." He held up several straps with Velcro fastenings. "When I know you're safe, I'll get you water, okay?"

She nodded, wishing she had the strength to fight him. She wanted desperately to hit, scratch, tear at him until he felt the pain his actions had caused her. *How could you? What gives you the right to imprison me?* But she had no strength, and knowing he would give her water soon was all she could hold on to.

He strapped her down to the board in her box, carefully checking each to make sure it was secure.

"Okay, then. I'll get the water." He walked out of her line of sight. She could hear him fiddling with something, then the unmistakable sound of running water.

Soon he was back, a small cup in hand.

"I'm going to let you have a few sips of this water, but not too much. That would make you puke and you might choke. So go slow, and stop when I say."

He held the straw to her parched lips and she drank. The water was warm and tasted like plastic, but she could have cried with how happy she was to have it. Her tongue had been like sandpaper in her mouth. Now she could feel the water soothing each part of her mouth. She held it there as long as she could and then swallowed, so grateful to have it.

"That's a good girl. You take another sip now, then we'll wait a bit."

She did as he asked, savoring the relief from thirst.

"I bet you're hungry, too, huh? Your line was supposed to take care of all of that. It's just as well. I was going to bring you up today.

Time for you to bathe and get some exercise. Most of my girls just lie there, compliant. That's how I like it. But I want you to have more of your senses about you. I might need your help, so I want to be able to talk with you."

Her help? *What kind of crazy is this guy?* And what did he mean when he said most of his girls? Were there other girls here? She would never help him keep women imprisoned. No way. But she might pretend to go along with him for a while until she could find her way out of this hell.

"Now, I usually do the bathing, you know, wash my herd, but I'm going to let you bathe yourself. I want you to learn to trust me, and that means I have to give a little trust in return. The shower is over there." He pointed to the far corner. "First, you'll need to eat so you can get your energy back. Then, when you're ready, you can go on over and get cleaned up. This here cable? This is going to guarantee that you don't try anything foolish while we get to know each other." He held up a plastic coated steel cable and a crimper. "For now, I'll give you twenty feet of slack. That can't get you into any trouble. If you're good, you'll get more freedom."

He wrapped the cable around her ankle and crimped the two parts together with some type of metal connector. He tugged on the ends, making sure they were fast. He walked to the end of the cable and she now saw a large, locking carabiner attached there. He pulled over a stepladder and snagged a line she hadn't noticed before. A cable that ran ten feet above the floor and for about twelve feet in either direction.

He was going to let her walk. She would get out of here; she knew it now. If she had freedom of movement, even to such a limited degree, she would find a way to free herself.

"There. Now, I'm going to get you some food. When I bring it to you, I'll loosen the straps. Then I'll leave you to your shower. Now, don't get any ideas in your pretty head. The door is magnetized. If you don't have the key, you won't get out. All you'll succeed in doing is pissing me off. You won't like me pissed off, trust me. When you're done with cleaning up, sit back on your bed. I'll know when you're there and I'll come back in. Know that I never enter this room without my stun gun. I am more than prepared to drop you where you stand if you abuse the privilege I'm giving you. If I have to resort to that, you'll be very sorry."

He left the room, but was back before she had a chance to look around much. He had some trail bars and raisins, as well as a banana. He set them at the foot of her board. Then he reached over and unfastened the top strap. She would be able to move her shoulders and arms now, after she wriggled her hands loose.

"There's a clean outfit and a towel over there. Use them. I'll be back." He left her alone, then, taking the ladder with him.

She worked at the straps until her hands were free, then sat up slowly. The world tilted and spun for a while, but soon things fell into place and she gained some perspective on the space she was in. It was a room about thirty feet in diameter. The ceiling was high, and rough, like the ceiling of a cave. Limestone. She knew the hill country was full of limestone caves. It wasn't damp, but it was cool. The floor was dirt, but packed.

She reached down and freed her legs. Gingerly, she moved them until her feet were dangling off the board she'd been tethered to. *Slow down; you're spinning again.* She gave herself time to settle before trying to stand. As she pushed off the board, she leaned heavily on it to keep her footing. The cable pulled at her ankle, making things that much more challenging.

She grabbed at the food he'd left her, chewing and swallowing the raisins as fast as her throat would allow. She glanced around for the cup. He'd left it near the far corner, where he'd indicated the shower was. She knew she wouldn't manage the trail bars without more water, so she peeled the banana and ate it slowly. She gagged at one point and nearly lost it, so she stopped and waited until the feeling passed.

When the banana was gone, she eyed the trail bars and the amount of space between her and the water source. She reached up and tugged on the cable. Sturdy. She could use it to help her balance as she maneuvered to the water. With nowhere to tuck the bars, she considered her options. Once she made it to the water, she wouldn't want to spend the energy to get back here, but she needed the protein in those bars.

She tossed first one and then the other into the path she would take to the water. She would kick them as she walked if she could. She straightened, ready to make an attempt. She was so off balance and wobbly she feared she'd fall over before she took more than a few steps. Using both hands, she pulled against her cable and found it helpful in staying on her feet. She shuffled slowly in the direction of water.

It took what seemed an eternity to reach the first bar. She knew now she'd never be able to kick it. She lowered herself until her fingers brushed the foil surface, then grabbed it and slowly pulled herself erect. This time she threw the bar with all her might. It thumped to the ground halfway to the water. She could do this.

After a long while and a few scary moments, she was able to make it to the water cup. She leaned against the small cabinet there. Only a few more steps and she'd be in the shower. When she entered the stall, she found a shower chair. She sat, grateful it was there. For a moment, she gave in to her fear and cried, her tears washing the sweat of her efforts from her face. She thought about the last shower she had taken with Drew. It had been their last morning together before things fell apart. Drew had the day off, but she woke with Cicely so they could share a shower. It had been so tender, so loving, having Drew wash her back, then slide her hands down and around until she was holding Cicely against her. They'd made love then, a sweet deep love that spoke all the things they had yet to say to each other. She needed that. She needed to hold on to that moment, that feeling, to get through this. She had to survive and get back to Drew. *I have to do this. I have to get free so I can find Drew and tell her I love her. She needs to know. I need her to know.*

She looked at the fixtures, trying to decide if there was a hot and cold. She reached out and twisted one and was doused in warm water. She held the cup up to the stream of water and filled it, then turned the shower off. She drank, refilled, and drank again. Now she could eat the bar. She tore at the foil packet with her teeth then filled her mouth with the nut and cereal mix.

She chewed and swallowed as slowly as she could, savoring the taste. She finished first one, then the other bar, stopping for more water in between. Sated, she looked at the soap. Castile soap. Peppermint.

He must intend her to use it for both her body and her hair. She wet her body and soaped everywhere. She rinsed and washed again, opening her mouth and drinking her fill as she rinsed.

When she was finished, she used the scratchy towel left on a hook near the stall. She dried and pulled on the shapeless dress that had been set out for her. No undergarments. She felt a twinge of nervousness at the thought of being uncovered that way, but she'd no other options, and this was a hell of a lot better than being completely naked.

There was no footwear visible, so she did without. If she made her way out of this mess, she'd have to be careful of her feet. Refreshed and finally almost back to her rational self, she decided now was the time to scout any weaknesses in the place.

She dragged her cable tether around the space to its fullest length. The exit must be up the ramp, tucked behind the shower stall. She couldn't see the top, and her leash didn't allow her to explore it. She looked at her board, still balanced where it had been. She followed the path it would take when the mechanism for moving it was engaged.

It was designed to slide the box horizontally into a wall niche. From there, the box would be lowered to a depth of six feet or so, the occupant still flat on the board. Why had it been so dark inside? There was ample light in the room she was in now. She could see the glint of plastic tubing snaking down the back wall of the chute. That was how he'd fed her, or not, as it turned out.

She walked until she was behind the board and leaned into the space she had recently occupied. Dark, empty space. She pulled back and noticed a latch on the facing of the niche entrance. She fiddled with it and a solid door slid noiselessly upward, closing the space completely. She pressed again and the door lowered, just as quietly.

This is beyond creepy. What in the hell is this place about? He had to have put some serious money into these mechanisms. Why?

She turned, looking carefully at the other walls of the room. Niches, many more. At least seven other tubes crawled into the abyss. Were there other women inside? Could she bring one of them up?

She looked at the ramp, wondering how long it had been since he left her. He'd warned her about trying anything. She needed to wait. Watch and learn what he was about when he returned. So far, he'd done nothing to injure her beyond the abduction. She needed it to stay that way so she could escape.

She walked to the other end of her chain and looked through the cabinet where he'd left the cup. Nothing useful. More soap, towels, tubes of lotion. She pulled at it, seeing if it was anchored. It scooted a bit away from the wall. She used more force and was able to get it far enough away that she could see behind it. There was nothing. She'd have to do this on her own, there would be no miraculous help hidden away. No superhero breaking in to save her. If she wanted to be free, she'd have to rely on herself.

All she could do at this moment was wait for an opportunity. She believed with all she had that one would come. She had to be ready to act.

CHAPTER NINETEEN

Drew winced as her pinched neck muscles relaxed. She sat up and pulled her phone up to check the display. Nothing. Her stomach was a cold knot of grief. Why had this happened? She started to throw the phone from her, as anger, hot and vicious, raced through her.

"Oh, you're awake. Come in the kitchen. I've baked some cookies, and you look like you need one," her mother said from the doorway.

"I don't need a cookie. I need to hear that they've found something, heard something, to bring Cicely back to me."

"I know that, honey, but in the meantime, a boost to your blood sugar won't hurt. Now get up and come into the kitchen."

Reluctantly, Drew rose and followed her mom to the kitchen. The warm smell of oatmeal cookies permeated the air. She knew that neither Wy nor Jay liked oatmeal cookies. They were chocolate chip fans all the way. Her mom had done this just for her. *She's doing her best to make me feel better.*

"Thanks, Mom. I love you."

"I love you, too, baby. I know how badly you've got to be hurting. Let's try to stay focused on a positive outcome, huh? The more we believe good things will happen, the more likely they will."

Drew wanted to scream at her, telling her nothing but hurt could come from this. That the chances of her ever seeing Cicely again were slim to none, but saying those things out loud would be her undoing. It didn't matter that the litany ran on and on in her head. She couldn't give voice to it or she would give it power.

She nodded and grabbed a cookie. When the flavor hit her tongue, it was every good memory she had. Every moment where she felt love, and gave love, every hurt kissed away was held in that simple circle of goodness. She felt tears slide down her cheeks as she chewed.

She felt her mom's arms circle her and the hug was what she needed. She leaned into her, letting her fears go, trying to find a thread that would lead to a happy thought. At least she had the love of her family. She could always count on that, unlike Cicely, who'd had to depend on herself for way too long.

Her phone buzzed in her hand, signaling a new text message. She pushed back and looked to see who it was from.

It was Kallie, asking if she could meet with her. She sent back an immediate yes. Kallie would be feeling as powerless as she was. Maybe together they could find something to help.

Great, meet me at the office in a half an hour. Don't worry if you're late. I'll be there.

"I'm going to go out for a while, Mom. I'll let you know if I'll be late once I see what's going on."

"Going out? Why? That stalker is still out there, honey. Where are you going?"

"To meet with Kallie."

"Well, I wish she would just come over here. I hate to think of you on that bike when you're so emotional."

"I'll be fine, Mom. I need to do this. Okay?"

"All right, but please be careful. Let me know when you get there, and when you leave. Okay?"

"I will."

Drew practically ran to the garage. She was so glad to have a direction, something else to focus on. She pulled on her helmet and headed to Kallie's office. She had no idea if they would come up with anything, but the effort would be cathartic, and she'd be able to talk to Kallie about Cicely. Kallie would understand the depth of her loss and the pain that was crippling her. If nothing more came of this than the opportunity to vent and share the love of Cicely, so be it.

She made it to the office with time to spare. Kallie had said not to worry if she was late, but she hoped being early wouldn't be a problem. She went into the office and spoke with the receptionist.

Kallie was seeing her last patient, so Drew sent her mom the text she'd asked for and waited. She couldn't help looking at her phone every few minutes, hoping time would speed up. It seemed an eternity before the door swung open and Kallie stood framed in the space.

"Come on in," she said.

Drew followed her back to her office. She sat on one of the comfy chairs. This was a good place. She knew if things resolved themselves the way she hoped that Kallie was the right person to help her unlock her mind. She would help without pushing.

"So, I thought it would be good to talk, okay?" Kallie said as she closed the door.

"Sure, of course."

"I'm not sure where to start, but I know you've got to be feeling some of what I feel. The helplessness."

"I can't help feeling it was all my fault. If I had only been stronger, she would have never been taken."

"You can't know that, Drew. We don't know for sure who took her or why. All we know is what happened before. How do you think I feel, knowing she was taken so close to my house? That I was the last one to see her? The reasons why aren't important. What I want you to think about is the break-in and how it might relate to Cicely's abduction."

"Of course it relates. It has to be that creepy stalker. He's taken her to get to me."

"If the person stalking you followed Cicely to my house. Why? Was he trying to eliminate his competition?"

"Don't say that. Please."

"But what if it's his motivation? I mean, we should at least think about who he could be."

"I know. I already gave the police everything I have. But, Kallie, we have no idea who he is."

"We don't, but somewhere in your head, you might have a clue."

"What? How could I?"

"Your dreams. The whole thing about their intensification after years of stable sleep patterns. Don't you wonder about how that coincided with the texts from this stranger? It makes sense to me."

"I...I'm not sure I understand. What exactly are you saying?"

"Think about it, Drew. You have such a severe trauma in your childhood that you have prolonged dissociative amnesia. You have a history of extreme night terrors, but with love and guidance from your adoptive parents you found stability. You built a life and the dreams receded. Not completely, but to a level much more compatible with mental health.

"Then, the texting starts and the dreams increase. So much so that you're now having them during diurnal naps. That signifies some trigger. Some association that your subconscious recognizes but your subjective mind doesn't see."

"But I associated the increase in dreams to my relationship with Cicely. They started at about the same time."

"But why? What's the trigger there? Did being with Cicely make you feel insecure? Were you afraid of a relationship with her?"

"No, not at all. I mean, I was nervous about her cut-and-dried rules on honesty and sharing absolutely everything, but I didn't have anything to hide. I knew that came from her fear of betrayal, and not from anything I projected. I just knew it was important to be true to her. I wasn't afraid."

"If that's true, then the trigger for your nightmares is something else. Why not the texts? What if the language of those texts is familiar to your lizard brain? What if it's something you've heard before?"

Drew felt her whole body go cold. How could that be? Could she have some visceral connection with the person who broke in her house? And if so, how certain could they be that this person was the one responsible for Cicely's disappearance?

"If you're right, what can we do? How can making that connection help? I don't remember my past at all. There's nothing I can do about that."

"I disagree. If you let me try regression therapy, maybe we could find something. Some small piece of information that could help us find her. Will you do it? Will you try? For Cicely's sake?"

Drew would do anything to help find Cicely. Anything at all. But she was afraid at the same time. The reasons she had been hesitant about the therapy were as valid as they had been. The difference now, though, could literally mean life or death.

She nodded. "Yes. I'll do anything that might help."

"Good, thank you."

"You'll be careful, right?"

"Of course I will, Drew."

"I'm trusting my life to you."

"I know. I'll be careful with it."

Kallie had her recline on the chaise while she got the injection ready. Drew tried her best not to be tense, but it was fruitless. Everything about life right now made her tense. She just had to get through this and hopefully find a way to get Cicely back.

"This is going to pinch a bit, but don't worry, you'll feel fine in a second."

"Am I going to panic? I mean, I'm anxious now. Is this going to magnify that feeling?"

"On the contrary, this will feel good. It will help you relax and let go of stress. That's why we use it. It lets you free yourself from fear. Okay, here we go."

In seconds, Drew began to feel happy. Warm and content without a care in the world. She could feel her face pulling into a grin. *I could get used to this feeling.*

"I want you to think about a peaceful place, somewhere you feel safe. Maybe it's a meadow, full of spring flowers and butterflies. This is the place you are now. Nothing can hurt you here. Are you with me in this place?"

"Yes. It's beautiful here."

"Good, I'm with you and you're safe. Watch the butterflies, Drew. They're so quick in their movements. Do you see them?"

"I do. They're so happy. They make me want to laugh."

"Then laugh, you can do whatever you want in your safe place."

Drew felt her belly shake with laughter, but the sound was far away.

"I want you to follow one of those butterflies. Do you see it?"

"Yes, I see it."

"Tell me which one you're watching. Is it the monarch? Or the yellow swallowtail?"

"The swallowtail. Look, it's there."

She knew she was pointing, hoping Kallie would see it, too.

"Yes, I see it. Let's follow it, okay?"

"But it's leaving the meadow. I don't want to leave."

"But we have to see where it's going. Don't worry, we can always return to the meadow. All we have to do is see it and we're there."

"Okay."

"Where is it going?"

"There. It's going up that hill."

"What does it see there?"

"I'm not sure. There are trees and bushes all around."

"Just keep following it."

"I don't want to. I don't like those trees."

"What are you feeling right now, Drew?"

"I'm afraid. I don't want to see what's up there."

"But we need to know, and we're safe. Nothing can hurt us. I'm with you."

"Okay. There's a cabin up there. The trees are thick around it."

"Fly over to the window. Let's see inside."

"It's dark in there. We can't see anything."

"Why is it dark? It's a bright sunny day."

"It just is. It's always dark in there."

"Look, the door is opening. Someone is coming outside. Who is it?"

"It's sunshine."

"Sunshine?"

"Yes, the little girl. She's coming outside to go feed them."

"How old is Sunshine?"

"Young. She's almost twelve."

"Is she happy?"

"No. She's very sad, and afraid."

"What's making her feel that way?"

"Walt. It's Walt. He's scary now, not like before."

"Let's think about before. What was Walt like before?"

"He was nice. He always brought her candy. He made her happy."

"What's changed? Why is she afraid now?"

"Because he hurt Daddy. He made him bleed. He hurt Mama, too. The rattlesnakes got her because Walt wouldn't help her."

"Is Walt with Sunshine?"

"Not now. He had to work. He leaves her here to feed them. She's afraid."

"Who is she feeding?"

"Them. Those underground people."

"Underground people?"

"Yes. He put them there. In the ground. They can't get out. He makes her feed them. He hurts them."

"Drew? Can you tell me more about the people? Has Sunshine seen the people?"

"Yes. She has to hold the hose when he washes them. They don't like it. That's when he hurts them. After he washes them, he hurts them. Then he puts them back in the ground."

"How does Sunshine feed them if they're underground?"

"Through the pipes. She puts the food in the pipes so they can eat. It smells where they are. She doesn't like it."

"What happens next? Does Sunshine have any friends? Does she go to school?"

"No, no school. Mama used to teach her, before, but now she feeds the people and stays in the cabin."

"Okay. Let's go back to the meadow. We can come back to watch Sunshine later, when she's older."

Gradually, the feeling of happiness faded and Drew became aware that she was lying on the chaise in Kallie's office. It was late, the sunlight fading to dusk in the window. She felt like a heavy weight had been lifted from her chest.

"How are you doing?" Kallie asks.

"I'm okay. That was really weird. I knew that kid and that cabin. I think that was me."

"I think so, too. I think we have a good idea what gave you the dissociative amnesia. Do you remember anything now from that time?"

"I remember everything we saw, and the feelings. I remember how Sunshine felt. How did that happen? Was it real?"

"We can't be sure, but the feelings were real. You felt fear. You believed that Walt had hurt your parents and the underground people. Do you remember how he looked? Could you describe him to me?"

Drew thought about it, but there was no mental image of him. The guy at the movie theater popped into her mind, but she couldn't match that guy with the one in her memories. *But then, it's been a long time. Maybe he looks different now?* "No, I just remember how I felt about him. What do we do now?"

"I think we should order some food, eat, and then try again. I want to bring you to the place that made you run away. I wouldn't normally do more than one session in a day, but if it can help us find Cice…"

"Okay." Drew wasn't sure she wanted to go back to that place. It felt like something unreal. She didn't know if she wanted to know what had made her run away. But if it could lead to something that helped find Cicely, she would do it. That was the single most important thing in her life. Finding Cicely.

They dined on Chinese delivery and spoke very little about the session. Drew wanted to ask what Kallie thought about what they'd discovered, but something held her back. She had called the officer who was working on her break-in to share the name Walt. It wasn't much, but it was something. He had responded that they would add that to the file and thanked her. She hoped they would run some kind of search, but it was only a first name.

"He finally reached Cicely's parents. Her father said she had made the choice to live as a sinner, so they weren't surprised if God made her suffer. Pretty heartless people."

Drew hurt for Cicely. Parents were supposed to love unconditionally. No wonder she had such trust issues.

She could remember everything about the session now, the cabin and its surroundings, but it felt like a movie she had seen, not something she'd experienced. Hopefully, going back into that state would give her more of a connection.

She pushed the foam container of food away, ready to get back into her psyche. "Are you ready to go back in?" she asked.

Kallie swallowed her last bite of Kung Pao chicken and nodded. "I'm ready if you are," she said.

Drew went back to the chaise and lay down. Kallie stopped halfway to the chair and was looking at her.

"What?"

"I think we should try voice guided relaxation. If it isn't working, we can always use more of the drug. I think now that you've had the experience, you'll be able to get to that state without medication."

"Okay, let's give it a try."

Kallie spoke in the same tone she had used before, and Drew felt the same sense of peaceful relaxation. She gave herself over to that peace.

"I want you to relax and be at peace. Think of your meadow, the flowers, the butterflies."

Drew saw the spring meadow in her mind, felt the same sense of happiness as before. She smiled and watched the flittering insects all around her.

"Now, let's follow our butterfly back to the cabin, okay?"

"Okay. There it is. See it?"

"Yes, I'm right here with you. Can you see the cabin?"

"Yes. The door is open. I'm on the porch." Drew's perspective flipped and she realized she was seeing out of her younger self's eyes now. She walked down the steps and further up the hill. "We're going up the hill now. This is where the underground people are."

"What do you see?"

"There are pipes sticking up out of the ground. Some are wider than others."

"How many pipes are there?"

"Twelve. There are twelve. A wide one and a narrow one for each of them."

"Why are we here? Do we have a task?"

"Yes. We have to put the soup in the narrow pipe. So they can eat."

"How? How do they eat the soup?"

"I pour it in. The bottom has an even narrower end with a cap. They pull off the cap and drink the soup."

"What is the wide pipe for?"

"Air. That's for the air. But something is wrong."

Drew felt her whole body stiffen as the memory washed over her.

"You're safe, Drew. Do you want to go back to the meadow?"

"No. I'm okay. There's something wrong though. One of the pipes is gone."

"Gone?"

"Yes. The air pipe for one of the underground people has been pulled up. It's lying on the dirt."

"How does that make you feel?"

"Afraid. He said if they were bad he would take their air away. Now he's done it. He took away her air. She's going to die."

"Where is he? Where is Walt?"

"Gone. He had to work. He must have taken the pipe before he left. That means she's already dead."

"What are we doing now? Now that we know he killed her?"

"I'm running. I'm running as fast as I can. But he catches me. He's so angry. He says he's going to teach me what happens if I don't behave."

"And? Does he hurt you?"

"He puts me underground. I'm in a wooden box. Rough wood. He closes the lid and locks it. He puts the food pipe in one hole and the air pipe in the other. I can hear the dirt. He's shoveling dirt on top of me. It's so cold and dark. Let me out! Walt! Please let me out, I'll be good."

"You're here with me, Drew. You're not underground. It's warm and safe here. You're fine."

"The dirt is coming down my air pipe. It's in my mouth! I can't breathe! I can't breathe!" Drew felt her body convulse with terror and she struggled to get air, but none would come. She could feel the cold grit of dirt in her mouth, filling it. Then pain rocketed across her face.

Her eyes flew open and she reflexively grasped her stinging cheek.

"I'm sorry. I'm sorry. I didn't know what to do. You weren't breathing, but you were fighting. Struggling against an imaginary foe. I had to wake you up. I'm sorry," Kallie said.

"It's okay. Really. I remember it now. He buried me, like all the others. But he let me out after an hour. He told me if I ever tried to run from him again he'd bury me and be done. I remember."

"Drew, I'm so sorry this happened to you. No wonder you blocked it out. There's no way a young child could cope with those memories. Are you sure you're okay now?"

"A bit shaky, I guess. But at least I know now why I have that dream. He really did that to me." Drew could feel the wood abrading her skin, smell the loamy scent of earth around her. Her heart raced and she could feel her chest tightening in terror. She took a deep breath and fought the sensations down.

"It seems like he did, but we still don't know who he is or where he is."

"That's true. His name is Walt, but I don't remember a last name. I can't remember his face. Why can't I remember what he looked like? Let's go back in, huh? Let's see if I can remember?"

"Not now. We both need a break. I want to be sure you're going to be okay before I put any more stress on you. Why don't you come and spend the night at my house, in case you have a nightmare?"

Drew thought about that. Her parents had years of experience dealing with her night terrors. Kallie was trying to be helpful, but she wouldn't be prepared if Drew had an episode.

"I've got a better idea. Why don't you come to my parents' house for the night? They know how to help me get out of these fugues. Besides, I'd feel better being with them tonight. And I don't like the idea of you being alone. Not after what happened to Cicely."

"I don't know..."

"Please?"

"Okay. Truthfully? I don't want to be alone in my house after this."

"Good. Let's go and try to forget about this for now. I'll lend you some sweats for the night."

"Great. Thanks."

They closed and locked the office. Kallie followed Drew to her folks' place in her car.

When they arrived, everyone was watching a movie, so they joined them. It was a good distraction from the day's revelations, although Drew couldn't stop thinking about what she'd learned about her past. After it was finished, Wy convinced them to play dominoes, and then Drew showed Kallie to the guest room and they retired for the night. With the whole family there, Drew decided she wasn't ready to discuss what she'd gone through in therapy, not yet. She felt raw inside, like the memories were being scraped out of her.

Drew slid her pajamas on and climbed into her bed. *I wonder what kind of terrors the night will bring. Cicely, I know you're out there. I'm coming to find you, I promise.* If it was the man from her childhood who had her, there was a good chance she was still alive.

Sleep was long in coming. Drew wondered if she was purposefully keeping herself awake to keep from dreaming. She got up and got herself a cup of chamomile tea. It had always been her fallback when sleep was difficult. She sipped and considered how knowing what had happened made her feel.

Before I knew what was in my past, I only knew fear. Now I know where that fear comes from. Maybe it won't trouble my sleep. Maybe I can finally be dream free.

Walt buried me to teach me a lesson, but obviously, I survived. And just as obviously, I got away from him. I don't know how, or what happened to him, but I escaped. Maybe those others escaped, too.

But somewhere inside she knew that wasn't the case. He might have pulled up their pipes, or something worse, but she knew they hadn't been as lucky as her. *What about Cicely? Is she in a hole like this? Is she going to be like them?* She felt the tightening in her chest as tears threatened. *I'm not going to believe that. You'll be lucky, Cicely. You'll come back to me.*

CHAPTER TWENTY

Cicely was restless now that her energy level was back up. She needed to be doing something to get herself free. At the very least, planning for his return. The only weapon she had available was the one he provided, her cable. If she could gather some of the slack, maybe she could loop it around his neck and strangle him.

That wouldn't work. He had his stun gun. He'd just buzz her and she'd flop over like last time. There had to be something else. He'd been gone for nearly two hours. She wondered what he was up to. Was he abducting another woman? Sleeping? Had he gone home to his wife and family? She had nothing but her own imagination to occupy her.

She leaned back on her board and tried to rest. Who knew what he'd ask of her when he returned. She was tempted, again, to open the other niches, but didn't want him to walk in and catch her at it. Better if he believed she simply showered and rested in his absence.

She heard him on the ramp before he appeared. He walked into the wide circular space and smiled at her. It made her stomach turn, but she did her best to smile back. *Keep him on friendly terms. Make him let his guard down.*

"Well now, aren't you as shiny as a new penny? You feeling better?"

Cicely nodded.

"Not gonna talk to me? That's not real friendly. I told you, the reason you're up and out of that box is so I can talk with you. If you're going to give me the silent treatment, there's no reason to keep you awake, hear?"

"Yes, I hear you. I don't have anything to say. Ask me something and I'll answer you."

"You work on being more civil, girl. Understand? I won't take no sass from you."

"Okay. What can I tell you? Why am I here?"

"You're here because I brought you here. I want you to tell me about your friend. You know, the park ranger."

Cicely tensed. Why did he want to know about Drew? Was this guy the stalker? "Why do you want to know about her? What's she to you?"

"She's an old friend of mine. We used to live together, you know, a while back."

Drew had never mentioned living with any man, other than her father. What was this guy talking about?

"She never lived with any man. You're lying to me. Why?"

He jerked toward her, his fist up. She'd pushed some kind of button. "Listen, you. I don't lie. She sure as hell lived with me. We were a family. She was going to be my wife, but things got complicated."

Drew? His wife? He was delusional. There was no way Drew would be any man's wife. Not if she had anything to say about it. "I think you have my friend confused with someone else. My friend would never marry a man. She's made to love women. She'll be a fine wife one day to some lucky girl."

"Bullcrap. She's just been keeping herself pure for me. She knows I could never forgive her for giving herself away to another man, but playing with another woman? That's just for fun. I don't mind a bit that she's done that. In fact, I'm pretty darn sure she's done that with you, right?"

Cicely didn't want to give him that satisfaction. He didn't have any right to know about her and Drew making love. His knowledge would only tarnish her memories. "No. You're wrong there, dude. We're friends. That's all."

"Sure you are. And are you made for loving women, too?"

"None of your business."

"I think it is my business. You belong to me, woman, and to me you will always be bonded. If you want to live and have some freedom, you'll speak only truth to me."

"I don't belong to anyone. I'm my own person. You can't undo that by chaining me up. I'm your prisoner, not your property."

"You just won't quit, will you? You better get straight with things, and fast. You're nothing, hear me? You're only what I allow you to be. Everything you knew before today? That shit's over. You'll do as I ask or you'll be dead. It's that simple."

"I'm not afraid of you. You can't unmake me."

"It's already done, sweetheart."

She ran at him, wanting to tear his eyes out, rip him, something. The shock of pain was quick and brutal, every muscle in her body cramping instantly. She felt herself go rigid and slam face-first on the dirt floor. He kicked her in the side, hard, as she twitched from the voltage of the stun gun.

"You'll learn. Hard or easy, you'll learn," he said. Then he turned and walked back up the ramp.

"Damn you, you bastard!" she screamed when she could. The pain of the electricity had stopped the moment he stopped administering it, but the pain of his kick and the impact with the ground were fresh and fierce. Her mouth was full of a combination of dirt and blood. She rolled to her side and spit the muck out.

She ran her tongue around her mouth, checking her teeth. They were all there and none seemed loose. She must have bitten her lip in the fall. Her side was on fire. That had been a cheap shot, to kick her when she was defenseless. *Bet he kicks puppies, too. Asshole.*

She couldn't stop the tears of pain and rage that coursed down her cheeks. She didn't even want to try right now. She wanted to wallow in her anger at the situation. *Who does he think he is? And what the hell was he talking about?* Drew, meant to be his wife? That was pure crap. What did he even know about her? Was this the person who had tormented her childhood?

Thinking about Drew hurt, too. She wanted to hold on to the anger, to cry in rage, but her emotions took over and grief filled her. *I won't ever hold you again. I won't ever feel the warmth of your kisses on my skin. The touch of your hand on my body.* She cried great wracking sobs, causing the dirt beneath her cheek to turn to mud. She cried until she felt like she had no more ability to create tears, and then she made herself stop.

Cut it out. You can't let him beat you so easily. Drew would want you to survive, no matter what. To do whatever it takes to stay alive so you can get back to her. Stop feeding yourself bull about never touching her. You want to touch her, more than anything. Hold on to that desire, that will. When everything else diminishes, hold on to Drew. She won't let you down. You have to survive for her.

She made herself sit up. The front of her dress was filthy. She brushed at the dirt. It wasn't important to her to be clean, but she had no way of knowing how long she would have to wear this outfit. She had to survive, and that meant she had to keep him from killing her. If she goaded him every time he came in, he would only act against her with more force. She needed to make herself bow to his will, if only outwardly. She had to gain some advantage over him, and that would only come with trust. Too bad she had such issues with trust. It would be a real challenge to convince him of her sincerity, but she had to try.

The next time he came in, she would give it her best performance. With a bit of luck, maybe she'd convince him.

He walked down to his car, shaking his head at the way the girl reacted to him. She needed to come to grips with her new life. Time is what it'd take. Time and the consistent reinforcement of his rules. She'd come around. He needed her to be somewhat cooperative if he was going to use her to help him get Sunshine.

She'll do as I say, or she'll be sorry. It's as simple as that.

In the meantime, he needed to get back to that house and check for signs of Sunshine. She had to surface soon. He was getting tired of waiting.

He needed to check his sites for possible buyers of his current herd, too. It was small, with the redhead's passing, but someone would bite. He'd intended to fill it out and keep them a bit longer, but now that he had the girl awake, he needed the others gone. It would be too hard to keep her in line and tend to them properly.

His buddy TJ let him use his computer setup for his transactions in exchange for a few rides with one of his broken girls. It was a good arrangement. He called TJ and got the code for the storage unit he had his setup in. He'd do his drive-by and then head to the unit.

When he reached the neighborhood where he'd followed the moving truck, it took him a few turns to get oriented. He finally found the right street and cruised slowly by the house in question. No activity. He stashed the car in the same parking area he had the last time and walked the few blocks to the house.

Where was she? This was getting aggravating, knowing she was connected to this house but not knowing how. He'd thought to bring a pack of smokes with him this time, so he felt it wouldn't appear strange if he leaned against the road sign and had one. He casually glanced at the house from time to time, hoping to catch sight of someone, but had no luck. He finally had to give up and head back to his car.

He was frustrated at this turn in his courting of Sunshine. He'd known it would be tricky to persuade her back into his life, but he'd never foreseen losing her. At least he knew where she worked. He could spend tomorrow at the park and follow her back to her new residence. He wished he had some skill with tracking devices. Then he could simply attach one to her bike and he'd always know where she was.

Things weren't going his way right now, but he knew it was only a matter of time. He'd find her and they'd be together the way they were meant to be.

He drove to East Austin to the rundown storage unit complex that TJ used. It was a clever way to keep his business away from prying eyes. TJ ran a porn hub that catered to unusual tastes. He sometimes made live streaming vids in the concrete room.

Walt never liked that sort of thing. He enjoyed girls. He was proud of the way he treated them and always tried to market his herds to folks who appreciated their fine care. He felt like the shit TJ wallowed in was nothing but filth. He wouldn't ever have one of his girls suffer those indignities.

When Walt paid his fair for the use of the computer system by letting TJ use one of his herd, he stayed right there to make sure TJ didn't abuse his girls. TJ gave him crap for it, called him a prude, but he held firm. His girls were trained and gentled. No reason to abuse them. He only sold to like-minded people, and tonight was time to find a buyer.

He entered the code in the gate and headed to the unit. TJ had reinforced the flimsy door, adding soundproofing and a Mag lock. Walt used the same code to open the door and went straight to the computers. When he pulled up his site, he loaded the thumb drive of videos onto the page and opened the auction. His regulars logged in almost as soon as he did. There were a few newbies, but they'd been through a rigorous vetting protocol before being admitted to the site. He paid his security guy well to make sure.

The bidding started quickly and rose in fury as his allotted window drew to a close. He was happy with the price he got for this group. A fair amount, deposited directly into his offshore account. He made arrangements with the buyer for delivery. The man, one of the newbies, would send a truck and two handlers for the girls this weekend. Good. He could focus on his personal life once they were away.

He shut down his site and logged in to his bank accounts. He watched the balance increase by six digits. Smiling, he transferred a reasonable sum to his local account. Maybe he would look into a tracking device. Perhaps his security guy could help him with that. He shot him an email inquiry and shut down the program. He'd check for a response later.

He hesitated. Going back to the cabin should be his plan now, but the temptation of driving by the house one last time was strong. He gave in to the draw and headed back to the car. It wouldn't be much of a detour, only a fifteen-minute delay. He might get a clue as to where she was. It was worth it.

The lights were all out except the landscape lighting and a single light in an upper room. The lateness of the hour gave him the opportunity to watch for a while. Everything was still and quiet, so he shifted the car into drive. As he eased his foot off the brake, a light flashed on in the front window. He stopped and slid the car back into park.

He could see movement in the window. He turned the ignition off and opened his door. He needed to get closer.

With stealthy movement, he crossed to the near sidewalk and through the front gate. He hid behind the ornamental shrubs and drew closer to the window. Soon he was close enough to see inside. Keeping to the shadows, he watched.

Someone was in the room just beyond this one, moving with purpose. A figure moved into the light, and he felt a deep satisfaction. Sunshine. *She's here, beyond the thin pane of glass.* He needed only to break the fragile surface to be close enough to touch her. He restrained the impulse to do just that. The house had other occupants, and staying hidden was an absolute necessity.

He smiled, knowing he was going to have her, very soon. He watched as she slid onto a couch, and sipped a mug of something. *Oh, Sunny, you're even more beautiful now than you were at ten. You melt me with your beauty.*

He didn't like what she'd done to her hair, but hair was easy to change. She'd be his long-haired love before long. He watched the simple movements of her hand, her lips, relishing the thought of those touches on his skin. He drifted in the fantasy, losing awareness of his surroundings.

The press of the bush he was standing behind brought him back to reality. He froze. If he hadn't come back, he'd have been at the window in a step. He tensed, realizing how close to exposure he'd come.

Just as he began to relax, a figure jumped into the window frame, causing him to stumble backward. The cat. The damn cat. It stared out at him with glowing green eyes, and he knew it had seen him. *Good thing cats can't talk.* He slunk back across the yard to the relative safety of his car.

He breathed a deep sigh of satisfaction as he settled into his seat. *She is here.* He would have her. He started the car and headed back to the cabin to prepare. He couldn't wait any longer.

Chapter Twenty-one

Drew woke early, anxious to do something more to find Cicely. She walked down the hall to the guest room, listening for any sign of wakefulness. All was quiet, so she assumed Kallie was still sleeping.

As she headed toward the stairs, she smelled bacon and knew her mom was up and cooking. When she reached the first floor, she heard soft laughter from the kitchen. Someone else was awake. She walked into the room and found Kallie at the wide breakfast bar, with her mom at the stovetop. Her father, Craig, was at the table.

"Good morning," she said.

"Good morning, dear. How did you sleep?" her mother asked.

"Actually, I slept well, once I finally fell asleep. No dreams. How about you, Kallie?"

"I tossed and turned. I couldn't stop imagining buried women."

"Sorry about that."

"No, don't be. Your remembering that incident helped you sleep. I'll be fine in a few days," Kallie said.

"Drew? What incident? Have you remembered something?" Craig said.

"Yes, Dad, I remembered a little about my life before you and Mom. It wasn't good."

"But still, this is a breakthrough. It has to be considered good, if you're remembering your past. Even if it's the bad stuff? Can you tell us about it?"

"The jury's still out on that, Mom, but if it helps us find some clue to getting Cicely back, I'm giving everything I have to remembering. I'll tell you all about it once I've processed it myself, if that's okay."

"Of course. Whenever you're ready."

"About that. I think the sooner we get started today, the easier it will be for you to reach the trance state."

"Okay. I'm good with trying right after breakfast. We can head to your office as soon as we're done."

"Can't you do it here? I mean, if you're okay with that, Drew. I'd feel better knowing you were close to home if anything comes up that upsets you. You can use the study," Craig said.

"Kallie? What do you think?"

"I don't see why that would be a problem. As long as you're comfortable, the location isn't significant. That said, if you require pharmaceutical assistance, we'll have to go to the office."

"I'd like to try doing it here. It's the safest place I know of. I think I'd be less likely to freak if I know my parents are here."

"Then it's settled. You'll try here and we'll be at hand in case you need us."

They ate breakfast in companionable silence, Drew pondering the new information she had and trying to figure out how to process it. *I have to do this. I have to remember everything I can about Walt. What he looked like, his full name, anything. If he has Cicely, I have to get her back.*

Her mother led the way to the study after they cleaned up the kitchen. She stopped at the door and took Drew's hands in her own.

"Honey, I know this goes without saying, but I love you. Nothing that you remember can change that. No matter what happened in the past, you are your own person. You're good, honorable, and beautiful. Hold on to that, okay?"

"I will, Mom. I love you, too."

Her mother pulled her into a hug, then kissed her cheek and walked back to the living room.

"You ready?" Kallie said.

"As ready as I'll ever be."

"Good. I want to record this, if that's okay. You may say something that can help the police find Cicely."

"That's a good idea. I'm fine with it."

"Okay, great. Pick a place to relax. I'll follow your lead."

Drew sat in her Dad's recliner and lifted the footrest. This had always been one of the most comfortable places she could think of.

Her dad had made it a point to spend time with her when things were overwhelming. He would sit at the desk and listen to her gripes. He never pressured her to make choices she didn't want to make. He always gave her a voice and the power to change the things that bothered her in her life. This was the perfect place to take this journey.

Kallie began the soft guidance to bring her to a semi-hypnotic state. She felt herself relax and go into herself. *I'm home. I'm safe. Nothing can hurt me here.*

She found herself in the cabin. It was dark and dank, the smell of damp earth heavy in the small room. She walked to the single table in the space and sat in the straight-backed wooden chair. There were papers on the table. Receipts of some type.

She moved them until she could make out what they were for. Bill of sale. He had sold something to someone called Gaylord. A herd of five fillies. Her skin grew cold and her insides turned to water, knowing exactly what that description meant. He'd sold the underground people.

She scanned down the form, looking for something. *What? What am I looking for?*

And then she saw it. A name. Walton Sample. A wave of emotions washed over her, threatening to drown her in their intensity. Fear, rage, grief, most of all terror. This was the man.

"Hey there, Sunshine. How're you doing today? I brought you some candy and a new book. Come on. Let's read it."

His face came back to her, sharp and clear. Stunned, Drew realized she *had* seen him recently. This was the man who stopped Wy in the theater, but he was older, more haggard. Harder looking, somehow. The creepy feeling and hypervigilance she'd felt then came rushing back. *He's been watching me, stalking me, and now he knows Wy.*

She fought against the memories, trying to force herself out of the trance state.

"You're okay. You're safe and nothing can hurt you."

The sound of Kallie's voice calmed her and she slid back into her past.

The panicked feeling faded and she felt the warmth of her early memories.

She remembered climbing up into his lap, the bare skin of her shoulders rubbing on his rough denim shirt, the cold metal of her overall buckles bumping her flesh. *I like Walt. Walt brings me good things. Walt makes me smile.*

"There's Mama. She's smiling at me and Walt. She likes him, too. And Papa. He's laughing. Walt makes him happy."

Flashes of memory, but somehow, the feelings shifted, became muted and darker. The warmth seeped out of them, and Drew stopped talking. She knew Kallie was there with her, but the rush of images and feelings were so intense, so real, that she couldn't articulate them. She had to experience them, even if she'd had to endure them once before.

The flashbacks came fast: Walt taking her and her Papa fishing in his truck, the sweet cold taste of the orange soda he packed in the ice chest, just for her.

Walt showing her how to use his buck knife.

Then, Walt was teaching her to drive his car.

Her Papa is watching, but he's not smiling now. He is angry with Walt for some reason. Walt and her papa are yelling at each other. Papa has his shotgun, pointed at Walt. Then, no more Walt. She's mad at her papa, and sad that Walt doesn't come around anymore. She misses the sweets and treats he always brought for her. Why'd Papa run him off?

Then, when she'd almost forgotten what he looked like, there he was. Walt. She sees him out the cabin window. He walks up behind Papa. The noise, so loud and the flash of...what? Papa, slumping forward into a red pool of water. Mama screams for her. The fear and panic rushes through her and forces her feet to move. They run, scrambling over rocks, and there's dirt in her fingernails. Then the cave. The dark, cold cave. No food, no water. Walt's outside, calling to Mama again and again.

"Come on out of there. I won't hurt you. Just let me have Sunshine. You know me and her are meant to be together. I won't let any harm come to her."

Mama shakes her by the shoulders, stares into her eyes and tells her to be strong. "He can't hurt us if we don't let him. We're leaving the cave."

They go out into the light, but Walt pushes Mama and she falls into a big hole in the ground. Then there are snakes and her cries of fear and pain. Drew sobs and tries to get to her, but Walt holds her back. Walt smiles when there's no more noise from the hole.

"Come on, Sunshine. Let's go home."

Drew heard Kallie calling her up from the depths of her memories. She felt the weight of them, like wet sand, on her chest. She drifted for a while in the somnolent space before coming fully aware. She knew she held all of the memories of her childhood. Everything that happened. Where she'd come from. Who her parents had been. She wouldn't lose those things now that she was back. She stayed there, in the meadow, watching butterflies, but aware of Kallie nearby.

"How are you doing there?" Kallie said.

Drew felt nauseous, the heavy emotions of her recovered memories roiling in her gut. He had made her watch her mother die. Drew shook at the remembered screams of pain as her mother slowly succumbed to the snake venom.

She opened her eyes slowly, glad to be away from her past. "The things he did…my God, he killed them."

"What?"

"My parents, he killed them. He shot my father in front of me, and my mom…it was horrible."

"Oh, Drew, I'm so sorry. That's awful. I can't imagine what you're feeling right now."

Drew took a deep breath to steady herself. "I'm not sure I want to have these memories, but they're mine now. Maybe I can get my life back."

"Did you remember anything helpful? You were pretty quiet this time."

"Yes, I remember it all. His name, and where I lived, where he took me after he killed my parents, and what he wanted with me," Drew said.

"And?"

"He wanted me to be his wife. He's an evil man. His name is Walt Sample. I know it's him. I've seen him. He's the one stalking me. He used to call me Sunshine, and I saw him talking to Wy at the movie theater. Kallie?" Drew's voice cracked as she realized what danger Cicely might be in.

"What is it?"

"He's a slave trader. A human trafficker."

Kallie paled as the words struck home. "You mean...Cicely?"

"I don't want to think that, but it's him, and that's most likely why he took her."

"We've got to call the police."

Drew nodded, wondering how they could explain the source of their information. Obviously, Kallie had done this sort of thing before. She spoke to a specific officer and had no trouble convincing them of Drew's story. She'd have been lost without her help.

Drew paced the room as Kallie worked out details with the police. She turned when she heard her end the call.

"What's next? What do we do?"

"Calm down. There's apparently a human trafficking task force at work in Austin right now. Several police agencies are working cooperatively. The agent in charge is going to send someone to interview you."

"Okay. What do I tell him?"

"Her. You just tell her everything we've brought up from your subconscious. I've explained the situation to them. I'll be right here with you. What you need to do most of all is hold on to the hope that this is the path to Cicely. That somehow, these officers will be able to rescue her and she won't be irrevocably damaged."

"I have no choice. I have to believe that."

"I believe it, too. We'll get her back."

When the officer arrived, Drew was nervous. *What if she doesn't believe me?*

"Ms. Chambliss? I'm Detective Tewes. Can you share your experience with me?"

Relief washed over Drew as she shook the officer's hand.

"Yes, of course. This is my therapist, Dr. Heidt."

"Detective," Kallie said.

They sat in her dad's office and Drew told Detective Tewes about her childhood and Walt Sample.

"He's the man whose been stalking me, and I think he abducted my girlfriend." The heaviness that had pressed in since the earlier session began to lighten. She felt the panic recede as she concentrated on working things out.

"And you remember exactly where this happened? Where he kept these women?"

"I have a sense of it, but I'd have to go there to be able to find the exact location. Detective?" Sadness nearly overwhelmed Drew, and she had to clear her throat. Kallie put an arm around her and gave her a supportive squeeze.

"Yes?"

"Do you think we could recover my parents and bury them?"

"We'll do all we can to make sure that happens. I'm sorry you even had to ask. If we can find them, we'll make sure they get a proper burial. Can you give me details to the location? Sample may still be using that area since his crimes weren't discovered. We've got an inmate record for him, but his crime was negligent homicide by motor vehicle. He was released six months ago."

"I think I can take you there, but I'm not sure I can describe how to get there. I only know the area from the inside. We didn't come into town when I was a kid. I'll have to find the place based on where they found me. Retrace my steps, you know?"

"It's possible your memories have nothing to do with our current case, but we can't overlook the chance they might. I'd like to take this grid map and try to draw in where you were. I'll set up a team to check the area as soon as possible."

Panic reared up again as Drew realized this wasn't going to happen today. She quickly circled the general area she thought it might be in, but it still felt off.

"Can't we go now? Cicely might not have much time. What if she only has today?"

"Look, I know this is hard, but we don't know for sure that her abduction is even connected. The officers working on that will get all of this right away. You have to be patient."

Drew saw the concern in Tewes's face and knew she was doing all she could to help, but that didn't stop the rush of anger at her helplessness.

"It's not right. She could be dying out there right now."

"I know, but we have to hope she's not. I'll get in touch as soon as my team has the search organized."

Bitter disappointment hammered at Drew. They weren't going to go find her now, and she could do nothing about it. She scrubbed the angry tears from her eyes and turned away as Kallie saw the detective out.

She dropped back onto the couch and pounded the pillows in frustration. *We can't sit around waiting. I can't do this.*

When Kallie came back in the room, she sat up and pleaded with her.

"I don't get it. Why isn't Cicely's abduction important to these people? Don't they understand? How can they be so vague about what they're going to do?" Drew said.

"I know you're frustrated, but this is standard procedure for them. It isn't personal. Try to keep that in mind, Drew," Kallie said.

"It's personal to me."

"Of course it is. We've given them everything we know. You described Walt to them. We have to trust that they'll follow through and get to Cicely in time."

"I have to do something. I can't sit around waiting to hear if they've found her."

"What choice do you have?"

"I have the power of my own intuition and the memory of where he kept me before. I'll hike out to that cabin and see if he's there."

"You can't do that. You'll be interfering with a police investigation. If they catch you anywhere near there, they'll lock you up."

"The hell they will. Besides, I know I can find the place. I can get there without anyone being the wiser."

"Drew, this is a bad decision. You're not thinking straight."

"Of course I'm not thinking straight. The woman I love is out there, somewhere. She's with a man who killed my parents without remorse. I have to find her, Kallie. I don't have any choice. They're not in a hurry to do anything."

"You don't know that. We have to let them do their job."

"I can't wait."

"So, what happens if you go storming in there, head full of angst? What if Sample is the person holding Cicely? What if he's in that cabin? How do you think he'll react to you storming in? You think he's going to throw open the door and welcome you home?

What if he takes you, and then we've lost you both? Think again. If you want to guarantee Cicely coming to harm, just keep on thinking like you are right now."

Drew rocked back, struck by what might happen. She couldn't be the cause of hurting Cicely, but she couldn't do nothing, either. If Walt had her, it was because of Drew. She was already at fault. She had to do something to try to secure Cicely's safety.

The memories of her childhood slammed into her present. The twisted way he regarded her. His belief that she could forgive his murder of her parents and live her life as his wife. He had a skewed perception of her. Maybe she could turn that to her advantage. She thought about the texts, the message on the refrigerator.

He still wants the life he fantasized. He believes we're meant to be together. All I have to do is figure out how to play that in a way that frees Cicely. I can do this. But not with Kallie dogging my steps. I have to make her believe I'm going to accept that we're powerless.

She tried to look defeated. "You're right, of course. There's nothing to do but wait and see what happens. It's so hard, though." She broke down then, crying real tears of frustration at the situation.

Kallie put her arms around her. Drew leaned into her embrace, thankful that she trusted her this much.

"I have to go to the office today. Are you going to be okay?" Kallie said.

"Yes, I'll be fine. Mom will keep me busy," Drew said.

"Okay. I'll head home, then. Please don't do anything rash."

"I won't."

Drew walked her to her car and waved her off. When she was sure Kallie was gone, she pulled out her phone.

"Hello?"

"Hi, Pres."

"Drew! Man, where have you been? I think you're officially taking my place on Truman's shit list. Are you changing careers, or what?"

"Nah, nothing like that. I've had some personal issues going on."

"You mean Cicely. I'm so sorry about that, man."

"Thanks. Yeah, that. I think I've figured out something I can do to keep from going insane. But I need your help."

"You got it. I'll do anything to help."

"Good. When do you get off today?"

"I'm working tonight, so I'm yours until nine."

"Sweet. Meet me at my old place in an hour, okay?"

"Sure thing. Should I bring anything with me?"

"No, but wear your darkest clothes, or camos, and your work boots."

"Okay. See you in an hour."

Drew had an hour to get everything she needed together. She changed into tan cargo pants, a pale green and brown camo shirt and her boots. She grabbed her trail pack from the garage and hopped on her bike.

Forty-five minutes later, she was sitting on her bike in front of her old house. She felt a pang of nostalgia for the place. Maybe when this was all over, she could convince Cicely to give up her apartment and they could buy a place like this one. She heard Pres approaching before she saw his car. The music was blaring, as usual. Today, though, he turned it off as he pulled to a stop.

"Hey," he said.

"Hey." Drew went around to the passenger's side and climbed in.

"What's the plan?"

"How'd you like to do some rough trail hiking?"

"Um. I don't think I'd like that much, why?"

"Because I need you to be my backup."

"Drew, what are we talking about? I mean, you know I'll do whatever you need, but what's the plan?"

"It's like this. I remembered where I grew up. There was this creepy dude who…well, he was bad news. Anyway, I'm thinking he's the person who snatched Cicely. I want to hike out to the old cabin he held me in when I was a kid. I want to see if he's there or has been there."

"Whoa. Hold on there. This guy held you in a cabin? What?"

"Yeah. I was raised off the grid, in a cabin similar to this one. My folks were back to nature people. Home-schooled and stuff. This guy took them out. He had a warped view of my attachment to him."

"And why do you think this has anything to do with Cicely?"

"I just feel it. I mean, those weird texts? That was definitely him. I think he was stalking me, and when he saw how attached I was to Cicely, he snatched her. I might be completely wrong, but I believe in my bones that he's the reason she's missing."

"So why are we doing this? Why not the cops?"

"I can't convince them, and the map I gave them was vague because I can't remember completely. They have to have more than my instincts to act. Cicely might not have the time for them to decide it's worth it to check it out. We have to do this."

"Okay, you've convinced me. So, again, what's the plan?"

"I think we hike out there, to the old place. We've both got experience with wildlife observation. This would be kind of the same thing. You know, find a blind, get hidden away and sit and watch."

"The same thing? I don't think birds are quite as adept as people at finding anomalies in the underbrush. What makes you think we can stay hidden from this guy?"

"He's not going to spot us, because we're going into this with our eyes open. We'll be extra cautious, okay?"

"Okay, I'm more than willing to try, Drew. I brought my day pack, but it doesn't have much in it."

"That's okay. I went by Hills Pro Hiker and grabbed some supplies. I figure we'll hike in today and take the lay of the land. If it looks like there's been activity, we find a good place for me to burrow in and you hike back out. Then you can check on me tomorrow."

"I'm not leaving you up there on your own. That's not happening. Give me a sec." He pulled out his phone and called in sick.

"You're a good friend, Preston."

"Thanks. You're pretty good yourself. Let's get her done."

"Right on. Head out toward Leander. The Balcones Canyonlands."

He slipped the car into drive and they pulled away from the curb.

I hope I'm not making a mistake, especially one Pres will have to help me pay for.

CHAPTER TWENTY-TWO

He decided he needed to start working the girls a little, loosen them up for their new owner. This would be a problem with the tall one awake and roaming the corral. He would need to find some way to keep her occupied and out of the way. Maybe some task he could put her to, or something. He'd figure it out. It was nice having someone around, and he found he didn't want to put her back in her stable just yet. She wasn't part of the herd he'd sold, so he'd get to have her company for a while. Until he got Sunshine back. Then he'd have to decide what to do with her. But that decision could wait.

He used the code to interrupt the current to the Mag lock and entered his domain. He could hear her moving around. He rattled the tray he was carrying to make sure she knew he was on the way in. Give her the benefit of the doubt that the previous day's antics were a thing of the past.

"Good morning, Beauty. How are you today?" he called, walking the final length of the ramp.

"Morning. I'm well," she said.

When he saw her, sitting quietly on the edge of her board, he was pleased. Maybe she had understood the lesson he'd given her. The room was in order, no unexpected messes anywhere. This was good. This was progress.

"What are you carrying?" she asked.

"Oh, some grooming tools. Not for you, though. These are for the herd. Today's grooming day for them. I'll be busy most of the day. I thought maybe you'd like to go down to the cabin. Make yourself useful. Maybe cook a meal or something. What do you say?"

"I can cook."

"Good. That's a marketable skill. Now, understand, this is a privilege, one given and easily revoked. You get up to any shenanigans down there, and I'll have you locked down in that box quicker than you can blink. Got it?"

"Yes."

"Well, all right then. I'll get your cable unhooked and we can go and check it out. You understand that I will have to manacle you. Once I have you safely inside and tethered, I'll let your hands free."

"I understand."

"Good. I'm happy to see you've decided to cooperate. That's going to make things much easier on you. Here." He tossed her a pair of nylon handcuffs.

"Put those on and sit on your bed. I'll be back in a few minutes."

He left her sitting there after watching to make certain she pulled the locking tie tight. He grabbed some cable and his drill from his out building and brought them back to the cabin.

He made quick work of mounting and stretching a new runner cable. Now he had to check for anything that wouldn't do to fall into her hands. He locked all the knives away, leaving only a small serrated paring knife for her cooking. He'd make sure that was visible on the cutting board before he got close enough for her to try anything.

He thought about the fire. She could cause all kind of trouble with that if she'd a mind to. But he had no other source of heat for cooking. He'd have to trust her a little. He made sure there was no kindling to add to the coals in the stove. They would be enough to cook. No need for flames. He put all the things he had available for making a meal out on the counter. Some chopped venison, onions, potatoes, a couple of withered carrots. A jar of cold chicken stock. That should do.

Now, what else could be a risk? There was no phone or technology in this place. That was all down in the corral. His bunk was pretty safe, just a mattress and bed sheets on a frame of stretched leather straps. The shower? No, nothing in it would be of any use as a weapon or signaling device. *It's pretty safe here. She'll be fine. And I'll sure as heck check her for everything before I move her back up to the corral.*

He returned to her, carrying his stepladder under one arm. She was still sitting quietly on the bed.

"Okay, now. You lie back on that board, and I'll come strap you down. Then I'll unhook your cable."

She did exactly as he asked. He smiled at her cooperative attitude. This was good. He could work with this kind of behavior. He tightened the straps across her upper chest and thighs, then patted her leg.

"Good girl. Keep on like this and things will only get better for you."

He was happy when she remained still and didn't mouth off to him. Things were looking up. Now he just had to unhitch her and move her down to the cabin. That should be no trouble. He used the ladder to reach the carabiner and soon had her cable untethered. He rolled some length of it around his hand as he walked back toward her.

"Okay, here's what we're going to do. I'm going to hold on to this end of your cable. You're going to walk beside me at its farthest length. I'll be holding the stun gun on you the whole way. One slip and you get a jolt. If that happens on the hillside, well, let's say the fall might not kill you, but it sure will take the snot out of you, so mind you behave."

He released the straps and tugged on the cable.

"Come on, get up."

He watched her carefully as she got up and stood.

"Now, stay there."

He walked ten feet to her left and tugged again.

"Move on up the ramp. Nice and easy."

They made their way slowly up and through the door, then down the hill to the cabin. There was only one sketchy moment when she slipped on the loose gravel and nearly dragged them both down the hill face.

When they reached the flat area around the cabin, he motioned her to the door.

"Go on in and sit in the chair."

She did as he asked without complaint.

If I didn't know better I'd think this was some other woman, altogether.

He tied her down to the chair with belts he set out for this purpose. Then walked to the opposite end of the room. He slid a step stool under the new cable he'd installed and attached her carabiner to the new line.

He looked at the length of cable in his hand. She'd have more slack than he intended, but it would do. She couldn't find anything in here to help her escape; he'd made sure of that.

"Okay, now, Beauty. I put out the stores we have to make a good meal. Be sure to keep in mind that you'll be eating whatever you prepare, first. Anything extra you toss in will be something you consume. I'm going to cut your manacles now, then I'll back out of here and leave you to it."

She made no objection as he worked his buck knife under the tight loop of nylon. He cut through it with a quick jerk, freeing her hands. Then backed away from her, his eyes never leaving her.

When he stepped out onto the porch, he pulled the door closed and flipped the hasp closed and padlocked it. She wouldn't be going anywhere now.

Whistling, he climbed the hill back to the corral. Time to groom and work the herd, then he'd come back for a nice meal with Beauty, before he went to check on Sunshine. Things were getting good indeed.

Cicely's mind raced. *Think. What can help you get out of here?* She struggled to get the belts loose and free herself from the chair. As soon as she could, she stood and walked to the kitchen area.

A cutting board with the smallest serrated knife she'd ever seen. That could come in handy. She pulled open drawer after drawer, hoping he might have left something she could use, anything.

But he'd obviously been thorough in preparing the cabin for her. She couldn't find anything that could cut the cable or be used as a weapon. Frustration filled her.

There has to be something I can use. This is the best chance I have to get out of here.

She sat in the hardback chair and looked around the room again. In one corner, his sleeping area. A narrow bed with a rudimentary mattress and an old quilt. Useless. The opposite corner held the sink and the potbelly stove. Maybe she could start a fire, attract attention. But what if no one saw it? What would she accomplish besides her own death by smoke inhalation or burning? She shivered at the thought. That would be an agonizing death.

There was the table. It was sturdy. Maybe she could drag it to the carabiner and reach it? That was a possibility. She stood and grabbed the edge. It was much heavier than it appeared. She went to the other side and shoved with all she was worth. It scraped loudly as it moved. She levered her body, her feet against the counter and pushed. The resistance lessened and she felt the table give. It moved another few inches, but now she had no surface to push against.

Move, you son of a bitch. Move.

She struggled to make headway toward the cable, but it was no use. The thing was too ridiculously heavy. She collapsed in a heap and cried in frustration. This wasn't going to work.

Think. Use your brain. What else can get me to that carabiner?

Eyeing the bed again, she was struck with an idea. She hurried to the bed and ripped the quilt and bedding off, tossing them on the floor. The mattress followed. As she suspected, the frame was a cross hatch of leather straps. Now if only the bed frame was lighter than the table. She yanked at one leg and it moved.

It moved, thank you, Lord Jesus! I'm getting my butt out of this nightmare.

She shifted forward and tugged again. It would take effort, but she'd get to the cable, she had to. Slowly, she made her way to the center of the room, pulling the bed behind her. She climbed onto the frame, near the head of the bed and reached up. She strained to reach the cable but came unbalanced and fell forward, landing hard on her knees.

She gave in to self-pity and curled up in a ball. *Damn you. You can't give up. Giving up means death, or worse. It means Drew will be gone from your life, forever, or that he'll use you against her. You can't give up.*

She straightened and tried to think of a way to reach the blasted cable. If she stood it on end, maybe she could climb it.

She slid under the frame and used the length of her body to lift it. It pivoted and rocked on its downside legs for a moment before settling. She cautiously gripped the leather netting and climbed. As she neared the top, she could feel the frame rock with her movements. She stilled until the rocking ceased. She moved farther up. Now she was even with the cable. She needed to pull the carabiner close enough to grab it.

She grasped the cable around her ankle and drew it toward her, hand over hand. The carabiner teased her as it moved, slid forward, then hung up, then slid forward again. Finally, it was in her palm. She unscrewed the lock and slipped it off the overhead cable. The movement as she tossed it down caused the bed frame to tip, slamming her to the rough wooden floor.

Pain like burning fire flashed through her left leg. She'd damaged it. To what extent, she didn't know, but it hurt so badly. She pushed up off the floor and rolled to her back. The change was like something stabbing up through her lower leg and pouring molten rock into her bones.

Shit. Shit, shit, shit. Mother of God, this hurts.

She looked down at her leg. Something was definitely not right. Her foot tilted off to one side, and when she tried to right it, there was nothing but pain. It had to be broken. No way could she walk on it, much less get back to civilization. She tried to pull herself up, but the movement caused the pain in her leg to intensify. She dropped back and gave in to tears.

Drew, I'm sorry. I can't get myself out of this. Please forgive me for being weak. I love you.

Chapter Twenty-three

Just how sure are you that you know where you're going?" Preston said. "I didn't even know these trails existed."

They'd left the car at the preserve center and taken a trail heading northeast. She'd been right that it was in this location, but the area she'd circled on the grid map was off by a good chunk. It had been two hours since they'd seen any sign of human activity. Drew wasn't surprised that Pres was concerned. If she wasn't positive this was where she'd been raised, she'd have felt the same, but this was right. The familiar smells and sounds of her childhood came back in a rush. She could hear the sound of her mother's laughter, feel the brush of the summer grass on her bare legs. This had been home.

"I'm one hundred percent sure. Trust me. We were way off grid."

"How could you even get food out here? You telling me you lived on prickly pear and armadillo?"

"Nah, we had a vegetable garden by the cabin, and an artesian well. Walt Sample was our grocery delivery guy. He'd drive out in an old Land Cruiser and bring us staples once a month. My dad had an agreement with a co-op grocer in Leander."

"But there aren't even any roads out here."

"Yeah, I know. Dad liked it that way. Probably cost him his life. Mom's, too."

"How much farther?"

"I think we're about two-thirds of the way there. I'll let you know when I see anything specific."

They trudged on, stopping occasionally for a water break. The brush was so thick in places they had to break trail. Drew regretted not wearing her Carhartt pants. This stuff was taking the cotton off her camos. Pres switched places with her at a particularly brutal patch of cedar, his longer frame making easier work of getting through.

As he broke into a thinner patch, Drew grabbed his upper arm. "What—"

She motioned for him to be silent. They were close. Very close. She could feel it.

Cicely, if you're here, hang on. I'm coming for you.

She took the lead from him and led him south about one hundred yards and stopped. There it was, almost invisible against the hillside. The rudimentary cabin more than half covered in sod and native plants. He tapped her shoulder, signaling that he saw it, too.

They found cover in a cedar break and watched for any movement. When nothing moved for half an hour, Drew signaled that she was going to eyeball the cabin. Pres nodded assent and she moved slowly from cover to cover until she was near the side wall of the place. She slowly moved toward the small window, barely breathing. She stood parallel to the window and rolled on her shoulder until she could peer in sidelong. She closed her eyes, willing Cicely to be safe in the cabin. Dread worked its sharp fingers into her stomach. *What if I'm wrong?*

Her palms felt damp with fear as she opened her eyes. The cabin interior was dark, but not so dark she couldn't see the thick coating of dust on everything inside. Cobwebs filled the window on one side, obscuring her vision. No one had been here in a very long time.

I can't be wrong. She has to be with Sample. If not, I've no idea where to look. Cicely, where are you?

She pressed back against the wall and slid down until she was sitting on her haunches. Pres whistled from the cedar break. She waved him out. No point in being stealthy now. There was no one here.

"So what's the deal? No one here?" he said.

"Nope, and there hasn't been in a long time. This is where I was when I last saw him, though."

"Let's look around, maybe we can find a clue to where he is now." Preston walked to the door and forced it open.

Drew held back, not sure she wanted to revisit this place. When he didn't come right back, she reluctantly followed him inside. Her stomach tensed as she crossed into the gloomy interior. The hairs on the back of her neck stood up. *Too many bad memories in here.* It was like it was inhabited by the ghost of her childhood.

"I'm going back out. I can't be in here."

She rushed back outside and breathed deeply. Pain hit as she remembered her time there, alone, her parents murdered by the man who had abducted her. She was glad it had been blocked from her for so long. The memories hit fast and hard now, the pain, the terror. Where? Where had he kept the underground people?

She turned and started scaling the hill behind the cabin. Up here. They were on the top of the hill. She vaguely registered the sound of Pres scrambling up after her. She moved with purpose, knowing which way she had to go.

"There's nothing up here, Drew. Let's start back to the car."

"No. I have to find them."

"Find who? There's no one here."

"There is, if you know where to look." She pushed through a thick wall of brush and into an open circle of ground. This was the place. She stood, frozen at the sight in front of her.

Pres followed behind her and stopped abruptly.

"What is this place? Why are those pipes in the ground?"

"This is where he kept them. The underground people. I had to see if it was real. If they were really here. To make sure I didn't imagine it."

"What do you mean underground people? You're freaking me out."

"He buried them. Kept them in boxes, coffins really. There, and there, and there." She pointed to the pipes still standing all these years later.

"One thick pipe for air. One thin pipe for food. He buried them. He'd take them out every few days and rape them. They screamed. They always screamed. He buried me, too." She walked to a spot where no pipes poked through the ground.

"Right here. This is where I was buried."

"Holy shit, Drew. Come on, let's get out of this place."

"See those pipes? That means they were still there. Still in the ground. He left them to starve and dehydrate. He's an evil animal."

"Come on, I mean it. Don't make me carry your sorry ass. It's a hella long way back to the car and we're leaving now." He moved as if to pick her up, but she shook off his hands.

"I can walk, cut it out. I had to see if it was real."

"Too freaking real for me. Let's go."

He hooked her arm in his and turned them away from the morbid sight. He was right. They gained nothing by staying here. Cicely wasn't here. If he had her, he'd found a new place to bury her. She felt like someone had sucker punched her in the gut. She doubled over in pain, unable to catch her breath. *How can I find you now?*

"Drew?" Pres rushed to her side and tried to help her, but it was no use. She was too wrapped up in the grief of losing Cicely, of losing her parents, her childhood. He wrapped her in his arms and did his best to comfort her.

"It's going to be okay, really. This is only a setback, you'll see. The cops will find her, I'm sure of it. Let's get you back home."

She let him guide her back toward the car, but they came out farther along the road than where they'd started and had to hike a long way to the car. With every step, a deep ache settled in her heart. *Why isn't she here? How can I find her?* She moved without awareness, numb to the slap of branches against her legs. Clouds of despair surrounded her and she walked like the air had turned to thick tar. Her eyes burned with the need to cry, but she couldn't make them fall.

At the car, he lifted her, and slid her into the passenger's seat. He reached across and buckled her seat belt.

"You sit tight, feel your feels and I'll get us back to civilization."

The sick feeling stayed with her all the way back into town. How could she have been wrong? Did this mean Sample hadn't been stalking her? Was Cicely's abduction random chance? Drew had no idea what to do with the waves of despair she was drowning in. She had no place to focus the anger and helplessness she felt.

She knew Pres was talking to her, trying to help her, but she couldn't escape the whirlpool of depression sucking her under. *How do people survive this? How do they make themselves move through life with a gaping hole in their heart?* She couldn't do it. It was impossible.

Numbness slowly replaced the pain. A cold, dead, feeling that took the pain and walled it off. She wasn't conscious of her surroundings and made no move to exit the car when they arrived at her house.

"Drew? Hey, are you with me? Drew!"

The hands that shook her barely registered in her awareness. *I can't do it. I can't.* She closed her eyes and went to the meadow Kallie had taken her to. She stayed there, refusing to acknowledge the faraway voices trying to get to her.

Then there were more hands, these less familiar, pulling her rigid body from the car. They forced her limbs flat and straps were drawn across her body. Somewhere, on a level she wasn't interested in, there was a sense of panic at being strapped down, at the feeling of being trapped. But mentally, she stayed in her lonely meadow, which was no longer bright and sunny, but shadowed and sad. Something was laid across her and she felt a prick in her thigh. Then the sweet release of sleep.

When she woke, she was in a room she didn't recognize. The bed was soft and warm, and a thick cozy blanket covered her. The room was blue gray and spotless. A dresser on the far wall was sleek and made of some very dark, almost black wood. Nothing sat on its surface. There was a window with a pleated fabric covering. She could tell it was day by the soft glow filtering through its clean outline.

Where am I?

She racked her brain, trying to remember where she'd lost awareness, but it wouldn't come. She sat up, letting the blanket fall into her lap. Plush darker gray carpeting covered the floor. She knew she'd never been in this room before. She swung her legs to the side and stood. Her toes buried in softness. As she stepped away from the bed she realized she was wearing an unfamiliar T-shirt. The burnt orange, she knew, but she didn't own this particular shirt. Goose bumps covered her legs, which were bare.

Where am I and how did I get undressed?

She moved to the door and opened it, listening for any sounds. It was quiet and still. The carpeting stopped at the threshold, sleek dark wood flooring lining the hallway. She walked down its length, searching for anything familiar, any clue to where she was.

The hall ended at the entry to a great room with an open kitchen. Very modern. Large, full length windows broke the uniform gray of the walls.

The black marble breakfast bar held the clue to where she was. A note on fine linen paper with KH monogrammed on the top read:

Drew, Preston didn't know what to do when you had your episode, so he brought you here. I gave you a sedative, so you may feel a little groggy. I had to run to an appointment. If you wake before I get home, please sit tight. Your clothes are in the laundry room. There's fresh fruit and bagels in the fridge. I won't be long. Kallie.

So, this was Kallie's place. Nice, but very different from her tastes. She found the laundry room after some exploration and felt much more herself once she dressed. The fruit was fresh and cold, ripe strawberries, pineapple, and mango. She served a bowl full and took it to the bar.

Where had she been yesterday? What had happened and why couldn't she remember?

She rinsed her bowl and left it in the sink, then curled up on the surprisingly comfy couch and watched mindless television.

She'd become immersed in the family antics of some uber rich Southern folks when the lock rattled and Kallie walked in.

"Hey," she said.

"Hey, yourself. How're you feeling this morning?"

"I'm feeling a little confused, but otherwise, I'm okay. How'd I end up here, in your guest room?"

"You don't remember?"

"No, not a thing."

"Well, Pres called me. You two apparently hiked out to the cabin you were held in when you were a kid. Something happened on the way back that made you go into a semi fugue state. Luckily, he called me, so I had him bring you here."

Drew flashed on the memories of her trip with Pres. She knew what had upset her, but for some reason, the pain didn't flare up with the memory.

"Okay, but why here? Why not take me to my folks' place?"

"I felt that the stress of your experience would be better dealt with on neutral ground. Whatever triggered that episode was powerful and connected to your past. Seeing your family might have brought you right back into the fugue."

"So, what now? I mean, what do we do now?"

"I want to talk about why you went on that wild goose chase. You should have let the police do that. It could have turned out so much worse than it did. You've only just recovered those memories. There could be things you haven't completely accepted and dealt with from that time. I wasn't at all surprised that it caused you to shut down. You're really lucky you had Pres with you. He did all the right things."

"Yeah, I need to thank him. He's my rock."

"Mine, too. Now, back to the why?"

"I thought I'd find her. That she'd be there. I was wrong. No one's been there in ages. Maybe I'm wrong about the whole thing. Maybe she's lost to me forever."

"Don't think that way. I really believe that man took her. It makes sense. We need to let the police find him, find her. She *will* come home to us. I won't accept anything less."

Drew wished she had that level of faith. The disappointment of not finding Cicely at the cabin had broken her. She was gone, and now Drew was empty and numb. She could go through the motions, pretending, but it would be a false life. Nothing would ever be right again. Not without Cicely.

"Let's be clear. There won't be any more adventures like this, right?"

"Right. Besides, I have no clue where she could be."

"I called Detective Tewes. Preston filled her in on your discovery and tried his best to give them the location of the cabin and hillside, but he got pretty turned around. She was pretty steamed that you'd gone up there on your own. You need to call her and arrange a time to give a statement. After that, I think you need to try to go back to work.

Back to the routines that were your life before this happened. I know that sounds horrible, but when Cicely does come back she's going to need you to be strong. If you're completely unraveled, how can you support her recovery?"

Drew fought down the rage that filled her at the suggestion of going back to work. How could she go back to her normal life when there was no normal anymore? What the hell? Why would Kallie say something like that?

"Drew, what happened to Cicely isn't your fault. You can't carry the weight of that. It's the fault of whoever took her. She needs you to go on. To be strong and not give in to the guilt. Going back to work isn't giving up on Cicely. It's standing up to the abductor and saying they don't have the power to undo you. That's what she'd want."

"How can you know what she'd want? What gives you the right to tell me what she'd want?"

"Isn't it what you'd want? If it were you, not her, who was missing? I know it's what I'd want people to do if it were me." Kallie's words were gentle, soothing and to the point.

That is what I'd want if it were me. I wouldn't want Cicely feeling the helpless despair I feel right now. I'd want her to be angry, defiant, but I'd want her to go on despite my absence. She's right. It's the right thing to do.

Drew felt the first shiver in the roots of her hair, then they coursed through her body, dissolving every fragment of her soul and she collapsed into a crying heap on the couch. She wept from a place so deep inside that it felt as if she were being turned inside out. Like her bone and muscle were folding in and her nerve endings were bare and exposed. If Kallie had touched her at that moment, she felt like she would have shattered into a billion irretrievable pieces.

She was a raw, burned husk of herself, and had no conception of how to pull herself back in. She cast about, seeking an anchor, something to pull against to bring herself back. She found it, finally, in the words Kallie had spoken. *She needs you to be strong. She needs you to be strong. Be strong.*

She felt herself coming together. *Be strong. I will be strong. I will be here and you will be back.* She would go on living. If the worst happened, and Cicely never returned to her, Drew would live. She felt strangely renewed, like she had a purpose now. Not knowing who she was or where she had come from had haunted her, but she had that information now, even if it was terrible. Kallie stood and held a hand out to pull her up from the couch.

"Okay, I've got to get back to my office for a three o'clock session. Why don't you call Tewes? She said something about taking you back out to that spot so you could show them where to go tomorrow, but only if you're stable."

"I will. Thanks for helping me get it together."

"That's what friends are for. Hold on to hope, and be strong."

Chapter Twenty-four

The sound of the cabin door slamming roused Cicely. She must have passed out, but had no memory of it. The pain in her leg was a constant fire of agony. She looked at the door, and saw him standing there.

"So. You couldn't do it, could you? All I asked was for you to cooperate and cook a meal, but no. Not you. You had to cast about, tear up my house and try to escape. What did that get you? Huh? Are you out there, fighting through the underbrush? No. You're lying here on the floor. What'd you do? Hurt yourself?"

She watched him walk toward her, but could do nothing to protect herself. He reached out with a cruel hand and squeezed the place on her leg that was the source of her pain.

She screamed, unable to think, to move, unable to defend herself in any way.

"You've done it well, too. You've broken your ankle, stupid pig. What good are you to me now? You know what they do to horses who break a leg."

She would have been terrified about his implication if she could focus on anything beyond her pain. Somewhere it registered that he meant to kill her. It'd be a relief at this point. She felt herself giving in to the idea of death. Sweet release from the pain, from the fear, from whatever he meant to do.

"Lucky for you, I still need you." He walked out of the cabin then, and she drifted in a haze of pain and fear before slipping back into the fog of unconsciousness.

Her next awareness was the prick of a needle in her thigh. The pain in her ankle was excruciating, and she felt hot inside, feverish.

"This is going to dull the pain, though you don't deserve it. You should feel the pain of your actions. I'm going to wrap that ankle to stabilize it. I'm no doctor, though. It'll heal as it heals, or it won't. You made this mess, so you'll deal with its consequences."

The pain began to fade and Cicely felt a relief she had no words to describe. She knew the reprieve was temporary. Hopefully, whatever he did wouldn't make the pain worse when it flared back.

He moved quickly, using thin strips of wood and tape to fasten a crude splint around her foot and lower leg. He finished it with an ace bandage, tight, but not restrictive.

"There. That's the best I can do. I've this walking stick here, I'm going to allow you to use to get back up to the corral. Once we're there, I'll take it back. No more roaming for you, girl. Now get up."

She didn't think she could do it. Her head spun as she made herself try.

"Come on. Cut out your lollygagging. I've things I need to do." He grabbed her upper arm and pulled her to her feet. The ankle shrieked with pain and she felt nauseous.

"Here," he said, thrusting the stick into her hands.

He pushed her toward the door, obviously giving no thought to her pain and lack of balance.

She couldn't help crying out. The weight on her ankle was like a knife of fire through her leg. She leaned heavily on the stick and dragged herself through the door and slowly up the hill. He'd taken the cable off her, she realized. She was completely free right now. She thought about swinging the stick down onto his head, but when she looked back at him, she saw the stun gun aimed at her middle. She continued up the hill. When she reached the top, she looked for some sign of where to go. She knew there was an entrance, somewhere, but could see no sign of it. He shuffled up behind her.

"Kneel down."

"I can't."

"You can. Now do it."

She struggled to her knees, biting back a cry at the pain. He walked up behind her and slid a bag over her head.

"If you know what's good for you, you'll leave that bag alone. Now stand up."

She tried, but couldn't find the strength to pull herself up. Not having the use of one leg made it challenging. She felt his grip on her arm as he hauled her up.

"I'm going to lead you into the tunnel. You just walk where I lead you."

She stumbled as he guided her, but didn't fall.

"Stop." He was moving off to her left. Something made a faint sound and she felt the change in temperature. He pulled at her arm again. She moved with him a few yards before he stopped her again. Then the bag was pulled free and she was in a narrow down-sloping tunnel.

"Go on. Move down the ramp."

She did as he asked and was soon in the familiar room. The room was suffused in the scent of lavender. She guessed this was from his "grooming" of the herd. How many women were here with her?

He moved her over to the far wall and her bunk.

"Lie down. You're going to be on your board for the rest of your time with me, unless I'm with you or until I need your help with Sunshine. I'll apologize now for the hunger and thirst you're going to feel. There has to be some repercussion to your disobedience. I've got a lot of things to do. I've moved up the delivery of this herd. They'll be gone next time you come up."

When she didn't move to lie on the board, he shoved her, hard. She stepped back on her wounded ankle and cried out.

"Only yourself to blame. Lie down."

She did as he asked and he tightened the straps against her chest and thighs. She watched him move to the mechanism that she knew moved her board. As she slid back into the wall niche, her box lid closed above her head. She could see light coming through the ventilation holes that riddled its dark surface.

There was barely any sound or noticeable movement, but she knew he'd lowered her down into the blackness. In a way, she was at peace. At least here, in the pit, she didn't have to wonder what he'd do next.

❖

He scowled as the box slid down into the darkness. Shame she couldn't behave. Last time he'd ever trust her, that was sure. Now he'd have to put the cabin back together before he went down to contact his buyer. He needed to get the other girls out of there. This whole thing with Beauty and Sunshine was getting complicated. Everything was unpredictable and he didn't like unpredictable.

He wanted stability. He wanted the future he'd imagined with Sunshine. He was tired of waiting. It was time to act, no matter the cost. He was going to get this herd placed and then he would make sure he had his dream. He had more than enough money in his offshore account to cover whatever means it took to make her his. No more pussyfooting around.

He slammed the niche door closed and moved quickly out of his corral and down the hill. He wasn't even going to spend time cleaning up now. He was going straight to TJ's to hook up with his buyer and to move everything forward. Time to act.

When he arrived at the storage unit, he was met by an unpleasant surprise. TJ was filming one of his streaming vids. *Damn fool.* That kind of stuff was going to come back and bite him on the ass. Walt was even more resolved to finish things and get out of here. He would get Sunshine and they would head south. Mexico offered him the life he wanted and she'd adjust.

When the others finally shut down their filming, he made his way to the computer terminal and logged in to his account. He found the email of his buyer and sent an inquiry about stepping up delivery.

His normal practice was to rent a truck to ferry the herd down from the hills and make the transfer of goods in a separate, secure location. This change was going to screw that up. He had to work through channels to keep his identity off all paperwork. Knowing he was never going to bring another herd to the cabin and corral, he decided it was worth the risk to have the buyer drive out to his spread. There was an old farm road that led back up behind his site, and the hike in wouldn't be too hard, even for a novice.

Come on. Answer the damn message. I'm ready to do this thing.

He finally got his reply. They couldn't make the transfer today, as he'd hoped, but could do it first thing in the morning. He felt an unfamiliar tightening in his gut.

Am I doing the right thing?

The hell with it. He'd had nothing but good experiences with this group of buyers. Even though this particular guy was new to the group, there was no way he'd have gotten invited in if he was in any way fishy. Walt's operation would be safe. He made the arrangements and set up an email with directions to be sent automatically at four the next morning. He'd have the girls up and lucid by the time they arrived to collect them.

He moved to a foreign property sales site and searched for a place to start up his next phase. There were so many options. West coast, near Mazatlán? The Yucatan? Somewhere near the coast, so he'd have access to vulnerable tourists. He searched ranches and found a mango plantation for sale that looked interesting. He messaged the realtor, using the false identity he'd prepared.

When he finished in the morning, he'd come back and make his purchase. All that would be left would be to secure Sunshine and use his connections for safe passage to their new home. In a few months he'd have his new home set up for a herd, and Sunshine would be his forever.

He drove out to the house he'd last seen her in, but he didn't stop today. He would do nothing else to tip his hand. Tomorrow he would make her his. He'd do whatever it took.

Back at the cabin, he put his sleeping area back together. He wanted a good night's sleep tonight. Too many things were happening in the morning to risk being fuzzy due to lack of sleep. He washed and slid into his bunk, ready for tomorrow to be done.

When his alarm woke him, it was three thirty in the morning. He needed to deal with Beauty and then get the herd up and lucid. He'd shackle them as a group to avoid anything unexpected coming up.

He opened her niche and called her box up. He watched as the box opened and she slid forward. It was a shame, really, her injury. He could have added her to the herd, or even kept her as a friend for Sunshine. Now he'd have to get rid of her. He'd done it before, left behind those who didn't fit into his plans. She was moaning and shivering as she moved out. *Must have some internal infection or something around that break.*

No doubt, she was feverish. He considered her situation. She was already struggling, might as well let nature take its course. He wasn't cruel; he didn't need to hurry her on her way. Besides, she deserved a little suffering after the way she'd behaved. He pushed the button to send her back down. She could rot down there for all he cared. She'd brought that on herself. He'd hoped having her there would help control Sunshine until she calmed down enough to understand that they belonged together. Unfortunately, that wasn't an option now. He wasn't going to cart around a sick filly. Sunshine would have to adjust on her own.

He brought the others up, one by one. They were all relatively fresh, having been groomed thoroughly the day before. He dressed the first girl before bringing the next to consciousness. They were, as a group, docile and easy to control. The drugs he kept them on ensured that.

When the first girl was ready, he led her to a bench in the tunnel and fastened a manacle around her ankle. That would keep her on the bench and out of the way. He then did the same with each girl in turn until all seven of them were sitting quietly in a line.

"All right, ladies. The time has come for us to part ways. It's been a real pleasure getting to know all of you. You are each special in your own way. I have a gentleman coming to collect you. I can't say if he'll keep you all together, or not, but I can guarantee you'll all be treated with the dignity you deserve. I'm going to ask you all to cooperate and not give me any trouble on this stretch of our journey together. We are going to move down to my cabin. Each of you is responsible for all of you. Walk slowly, and be careful."

He unlocked the chain on the bench and hefted its length.

"Come on. Let's get moving." He pulled them along slowly, giving them time to adjust to the rough terrain. They moved down the slope, until they reached the cabin.

He led them inside and had them sit against the far wall. There was a ring in the wall to lock the chain to. He checked the time. Four fifty. He'd made better time than he expected. Wouldn't be long before his collector arrived. There would be no sign of the corral if the buyer was curious. He didn't share his secrets with anyone.

He made a pot of coffee while he waited. Wouldn't be long now.

Chapter Twenty-five

Drew finished her shift. Overnights were tougher than she remembered. The green space on Ladybird Lake had been entirely too peaceful last night. She'd had a hard time staying awake.

Now it was almost five and she was more than ready to clock out and head home for some rest. Truman had been gentle with her, but hadn't given her a pass on night duty. She'd been prepared, she thought, but now realized it was going to take a while to get back in the groove. She hadn't minded the idea of an overnight. Nights were her hardest time. She couldn't get the thought of Cicely and what she was going through out of her head. Her nightmares hadn't returned since she regained her memories, but now she had this new trauma to contend with in sleep.

She groggily climbed onto her bike and headed for home. Before she knew it, she was sitting in front of the old house. *Nope.* This wasn't her home anymore. She needed to find a new place, soon.

She drove on to her parents' place as the sun came up, happy at the thought of a soft bed and later, a warm cup of coffee. As she walked through the house, she dropped her helmet, her gloves, her jacket and boots, so that by the time she entered her room, she was in her khakis and an undershirt. Her mom would kill her for that later, but for now, she didn't care. Tewes was coming by to pick her up in the afternoon, and she desperately wanted sleep before she had to face her childhood prison again.

She kicked off her pants and flopped onto her bed, the pillow calling out to her as she formed it around her face.

Cicely. I miss you so much.

She drifted into a fitful sleep, peppered with visions of Cicely being tortured by a sinister dark shadow. She had no image to fill in that blank. Now that her theory of Walt Sample had fallen through she had nothing. Cicely had no way of showing her how to help. Not even in her dreams.

She was running, chasing Cicely. Someone had her arm and was forcing Cicely to keep running. "Stop! Stop!" She screamed until her throat was raw, but the figure pulling Cicely only moved further and further ahead. And something was buzzing, chasing behind her as she ran, buzzing.

What is that? What's buzzing?

She pushed herself up and grabbed her phone from the table beside her. It was an incoming call. Kallie.

"Hello?"

"Drew. Get up and get some coffee. I'm coming to pick you up."

"Huh? Why? What's up?"

"I just got a call from the information officer connected to the task force. They made an arrest an hour ago."

"What? Say that again?"

"An arrest. In the kidnapping and human trafficking case. He didn't know if it had any connection to Cicely, but he thinks we need to come down."

Could this be it? Would they find something out about Cicely? The thought of facing the man who'd done all he'd done to her life made her nauseous. But for Cicely…

She shrugged back into her work pants, grabbed a T-shirt, and pulled it on over her undershirt. Her mom was in the kitchen, where she found her work boots. She hooked a chair out from under the counter and slipped into the boots.

"What's up, honey? You're not going back to work already, are you?"

"No, Mom. I'm going to the police station with Kallie. There might be a break in Cicely's case."

"Oh, God, I hope everything's going to be okay. What do you know?"

"Nothing. Not yet. They called Kallie and said there might be a break and we should come to the station."

"Do you want me to come with you?"

"Don't you have a class this morning?"

"Well, yes, but I can call in."

"No, that's okay. We don't even know anything."

"You're sure?"

"Yes."

"Okay. Have some coffee. You've barely had any sleep. And call me once you know anything."

"I'll grab a cup on my way out. Thanks, Mom."

True to her word, Kallie pulled up almost exactly ten minutes later. Drew grabbed the two travel mugs she'd filled and headed to the car.

"Here. Mom said drink some coffee." She handed a mug to Kallie.

"Thanks. Buckle up. I want to get there as quick as possible."

They made good time, despite the traffic. When they'd found a parking spot and gone into the reception area, they were directed to the second floor, where they were met by detective Tewes.

"Ms. Chambliss, Dr. Heidt, follow me, please."

She led them to a conference room, where she invited them to make themselves comfortable. She left them alone.

"Do you think this could have something to do with Cicely? Do you think they've found her?" Drew said.

"I'm as clueless as you are. All we can do is hope," Kallie said.

The door swung open and Tewes and three other people filed into the room. Two wore the uniforms of Austin PD, and the third was a state trooper.

"Ladies, good morning. Thank you for coming in. As you know, we made an arrest this morning. We recovered several women in the operation—"

"Cicely?" Drew interrupted. She couldn't help it; she needed to know.

"No, none of the women match her description, but there is an interesting fact. The man we arrested? It's your guy. Walton Sample. You mentioned that you thought he might be connected to Ms. Jones's disappearance."

Drew felt like the wind had been knocked out of her. Her whole body reacted to the news as if she'd been struck. She sucked at the air, trying to get a breath. Walt Sample. *It was him. He had to have taken her. He had to.*

"Are you okay, ma'am?"

She managed to pull it together. "Yes, yes. I'm okay," Drew said. "I knew him when I was a kid. I told detective Tewes. He killed my parents. He kept me prisoner in a cabin in the hill country. But he wasn't there. I went back, but he wasn't there. He has to have her. If you haven't found her, that means she must still be buried."

"Buried?"

"Yes. Don't you people talk to each other? He buried them. All of them. I had to feed them. They died there. Some of them died out there."

"Ms. Chambliss, I can see how upset you are, but none of these women was buried. They were all in a cabin, clean, and unharmed, and a good distance away from the area your friend Preston told us about, even if it was off by a mile or two. They certainly suffered some abuse, but they definitely weren't buried. They were kept drugged and in the dark somewhere. That's all they remember. Of course, they were groggy from the prolonged sedation. Something might come back to them after a few hours."

"They were. They had to be. That's what he does, trust me. There's a cabin, but there's also the underground part. I know."

"He may have, in the past, but it doesn't appear that he did this time. There was nothing else there. Nothing but the cabin. We searched the surrounding area thoroughly."

"That's how he likes it. He keeps them separate from the cabin, underground. Ask him."

"We have asked him. He refuses to speak with anyone but his lawyer."

"He'll speak to me. He thinks he loves me." The words were out of her mouth before she had time to think about them, but she knew she was right.

"I don't know about that."

"We have to try. He has to know where Cicely is. Please. Please let me try."

"Give us a minute."

They stepped out of the room, leaving Kallie and Drew alone again.

"Do you think that's a smart thing to do?" Kallie said.

"I have to. It's our last chance to find her. At the old cabin? The one Pres and I went back to? He'd left them there. Buried. Left them to die. If he had Cicely, and she's not with the women they recovered, then he's buried her somewhere. Talking to him is our only shot at finding her."

Kallie nodded.

Drew was glad she didn't have to fight Kallie on this. She knew she only had her best interest at heart, but Cicely was way more important than anything talking to that monster could bring up.

The door opened again, but it wasn't the officers. It was Preston. Drew felt a wave of relief at him showing up. He was such a good friend.

He walked to the table and held his arms out to Kallie. She went easily into his arms and he folded her into an embrace.

He reached a free hand out to Drew and held on to her as well.

"How's everybody holding up?"

"Tired. Just waiting to talk to that bastard to find out what he did with Cicely."

"Sounds good. I'm here for the duration. I'll do whatever you need, both of you."

"Thanks, Pres."

They waited. Drew became more and more anxious as time dragged on.

Why haven't they come back? Don't they know she only has so much air? She could die because they're being so slow. Hang on, Cicely, hang on. I'm coming for you, I promise.

When the door finally opened again, Drew jumped up from her chair.

"What took so long? She's dying while we sit here. Come on."

"Calm down, Ms. Chambliss. We have to go through proper channels. We've been able to get Sample to agree to talk to you, on one condition."

"Yeah? What's the condition?"

"He wants to talk to you alone. No officer present. That's against our policy."

"To hell with your policy. Cicely doesn't have time for this shit, she's dying. Don't you get that?"

"We don't know that he even has anything to do with Ms. Jones."

"You can seriously think it's coincidental? That he was my childhood abductor, that he's been stalking me, and that my girlfriend is missing? Seriously? I know it was him. Let me talk to him, please?"

"We've discussed it and here's what we've come up with. We will let him talk to you at the visitor's center. That means you'll be talking through a phone with glass between you. That's the only way we can proceed."

"Fine, fine! Let's do it."

Tewes showed her to the visitor's center. She had to go through the search procedure, like anyone visiting an inmate. It wasn't the search that bothered her; it was the time it was taking away from Cicely. Finally, she was seated in front of a large glass wall with Plexiglas dividers between her and the next chair. The room was empty except for her. She waited. He was walked in from the cell area and seated opposite her on the other side of the scratched glass wall.

He looked much the same as he had that day at the theater. Lanky and spare of build. Greasy hair, less of it now, and more lines in his face. A tattoo on his neck didn't figure in her memories either. He wasn't old, probably around forty, but he carried himself like a younger man. She knew he had been around twenty-five when he'd had her before.

He picked up the phone receiver and pointed to hers. She picked it up, dreading the sound of his voice.

"Sunshine. You came to see me, huh? You finally accept that we are meant to be? Is that why you came?"

"Walt. You look like the shit you are. I'm here to find out where she is."

"Who? Where who is?"

"You know who. You took her. What did you do with her? Where is she buried?"

"I don't know what you're talking about. I never buried anybody."

"Cut the crap. You and I both know you like women buried. Weak and helpless, so you can manipulate them in to doing what you want."

"You're crazy, kid. I never buried anyone. All I did was agree to wait at that cabin for someone to pick those women up. I had nothing else to do with it."

"Save it for your trial. You know what? You forgot to clean up your mess. You know the old cabin? In the Balcones? They're still out there. No one's been in that cabin since we left it. That means regardless of how you sway things with these women, you're going down for murder. Your prints are all over that cabin, and I'll testify against you."

"Sunnygirl, you're my wife. You can't testify against me."

"Not true on either score. I'm not your wife, never was. You can't marry an eleven-year-old, asshole. Besides, the law states wives can't be compelled to testify. It says nothing about volunteering."

"Why would you do that to me? I never harmed a hair on your head."

"No? Burying me doesn't count, huh? How about murdering my parents?"

"Didn't happen."

"Where is she?"

"I still don't know who you mean."

"Then rot in here, where you belong." She went to slam the phone down, but he was talking, screaming something. She put the receiver back to her ear.

"You're my wife. Nothing can undo that, not your laws, not this wall, not that damn bitch, either. She's never coming back to you. She's gone. Dead. Buried." His face was close to the glass as he stared at her, wild eyed, his yellowed teeth bared like an animal's.

"Where? You buried her where? Tell me, Walt."

"Your Beauty, she was nothing but trouble. I never should have taken her, but I thought she'd help me get to you. That crazy bitch tore up my cabin and broke her damn leg. She's better off where she is."

Her stomach churned with acid as she realized Cicely needed help more than ever. She had to get him to tell her something. *Play the game.*

"Where is she? I'll never forgive you if you don't tell me what you did with her."

"Now you're talking, you do what's right by me and tell these cops to let me go and when I'm out we can go find her body."

"Damn you. That's not going to happen, you bastard. You're going down for this and everything you did to me and my family." *So much for playing the game.* She couldn't stomach much more of him and his demented words.

"You'll never find her, you know. It's not like before. I didn't have to lift a shovel to bury these fillies. You'll never find your way into the corral."

"You're wrong. I'll find her."

She slammed the phone down. He was nothing but a soulless piece of garbage. He knew where Cicely was, but he'd never help Drew find her, not now that he'd been caught. And he hadn't given her enough to find her.

Where are you? What can I do?

She rocked back and forth in the chair, barely registering them taking him back to the cells, not paying any attention to the threats and pleas he was screaming over his shoulder as they dragged him away. *Think. Think. Where is she?* She sat up suddenly, realizing she knew. If he followed the same pattern he had in the past, she'd be able to find her.

She practically ran back out of the visitor's center. Kallie, Pres, and the officers were all outside.

"Where? Where did you find the women? You have to take me there."

"That's an active crime scene, no civilians allowed," Tewes said.

"Make an exception. You heard him. He knows who I was talking about. He had her up there. If you take me, I can find her."

"We've searched the entire area."

"But you don't know what to look for. I do. I'm your best help right now. If I find where he held them, you're bound to find something to make your case stronger. If we find Cicely, and she's alive, she can help, too."

It took another half an hour. Half an hour that Cicely might not have, but they finally agreed to take her to the scene. Kallie and Pres had to stay with the vehicles, but she could go up to the cabin.

It was in a completely different area of the hill country, west of town. But when she climbed out of the cruiser, she felt an instant recognition. This was the same terrain she'd grown up in. He'd have been as comfortable here as she was. Now would he have kept to the same routine as before? She saw the cabin, and knew immediately that he had. It could be the same building she'd been held in, but for the location. She walked to the south wall of the cabin and began to mount the incline.

"Ms. Chambliss? Where are you going? There's some really thick brush at the top of that hill. Wait. Hold on."

She could hear the officers scrambling after her. They didn't know him. She pushed her way through the thick brush, not stopping even though it seemed to be getting thicker the farther she went. Finally, she broke through.

There it was, just as she knew it would be. A clearing. But no pipes. Where were the pipes? She scanned the area, looking with her trained eye for any discrepancies in the brush. She missed it the first time, but on her second scan, she saw it. It wasn't much of a groove, not even really a difference if you weren't looking properly.

She walked out across the empty space to the overly thick brush. Not a natural pattern of growth, but a sculpted pattern. One meant to conceal. She moved the brush aside and found a tunnel of sorts. She made her way into it until she came to a door. It was disguised as a limestone outcropping, but again, it didn't fit the surroundings.

"Here. There's something here!" she called. She needn't have shouted, they were right behind her.

"Let me get in there, Ms. Chambliss."

She moved back to accommodate Tewes.

"Looks like a magnetic lock. There has to be a power source. If we cut the power, it'll open."

"But what if the power is all that's keeping her alive? You can't cut the power."

"Just briefly. A single thirty-second interruption will give us access. That shouldn't cause any harm, okay?"

Drew nodded, still unsure, but helpless to find another way into the rock.

It took another fifteen minutes for them to find the power source. He'd hidden a solar panel and battery array higher up, at the top of the hillside. He'd definitely gained some significant knowledge in the time he'd been out of her life.

The interruption of power happened quickly, once they found the source and an officer pulled the door open before the power was restored. A slanting ramp led down into a wider space.

Drew was afraid they'd make her stay out, but they only told her not to touch anything and stick with the officer who opened the door. She followed the officer into the circular room below. He'd created a whole subterranean complex. There was a cistern of some sort in the far corner behind a partial partition. The walls were lined with smooth panels every few feet. There were twelve in all.

But no pipes. Not one. Drew felt dread weigh her down. Maybe she wasn't here. But where else could she be? She had to be here somewhere.

"What are those panels?" she said, watching as an officer explored them. He was wearing gloves and was careful where he put his feet. This whole place was now a part of the crime scene. She understood the care they had to take.

Her guardian officer stood beside her, making it his job to keep her out of the way. Suddenly, one of the panels shifted and slid upward into some kind of niche. Tewes, who'd opened it, leaned into the column of darkness, looking up and down. She found something on the side that held her interest and then there was a humming sound. A large box came into view, the top lifting to the side as it reached the opening. A bare board with straps slid out of the passage into the room.

This is how he's doing it now. He's become more technically advanced, but he's still burying them. She had to be in one of those niches. She had to be.

"Check them all! Please! Cicely has to be in one of them. She might not have much time. Please!"

The officer moved to the next panel and several others spread out to check them faster. Soon all but one had been opened.

That's the one. That's where she has to be. Please, please, let her be in that one.

Drew dropped to her knees, unable to stand any longer. She'd never been much on religion, but she felt a prayer coming on strong. *If you're up there, if you exist at all, please, please let her be there. Let her be okay.*

The final panel slid up, and the humming started again. There was the box, like all the others. It seemed to move with exquisite sluggishness, the lid tipping almost in slow motion. There was someone there. A body, terribly, terrifyingly, still.

"Cicely!" she cried from the center of the room.

The officers rushed to the prone figure on the bed, talking excitedly, but over their noise, she heard it. Unmistakably, she heard it. Faint, but very definitely, Cicely had said her name.

She's alive! She's safe! Relief washed through her, making every muscle turn to water. As desperately as she wanted to go to her, her body felt like water and she couldn't find the strength to stand. Plus, she was surrounded by law enforcement.

They made her leave the space, then, and walk back out into the open clearing. Drew didn't argue with them. She was alive. That's all that mattered. Soon there were more officers outside the space. They'd somehow disconnected the board and carried Cicely out, still strapped in place.

Tewes walked over to her, holding out her hand. "Ms. Chambliss, she's asking for you. You can come with me, now."

Drew felt weak with anticipation. She was going to see her.

"Is she okay? Is she going to be all right?"

"We think so. She'd dehydrated and has a fever. Leg injury. We've called for a helicopter from Seton Medical. Let's get over there and let her see you, huh?"

And then she was standing beside her, looking at the face she loved. She gently stroked her cheek and bent to kiss her forehead.

"You're safe now, love. You're going to be okay. I'm here and I'm never leaving your side again."

"Drew?" Cicely's voice was weak and cracked.

It hurt Drew to think of her thirst. "Can't we get her some water? She's burning up."

"It's best to let the doctors start an intravenous line. That will have her hydrated much faster, and they can give her antibiotics. Water might make her throw up. It won't be long now."

Drew heard the sound of rotors drawing near. "They're coming, baby. You're going to be fine. I promise. No, don't try to talk yet. We've got time. Plenty of time. We've got forever. I love you, Cicely. I love you so much. I'm so sorry he took you because of me." Tears flooded her eyes now that she knew Cicely would be okay.

The helicopter touched down and a medical crew ran to the board. They had an I.V. started and were working on her leg.

"She's stable. Let's get her loaded and away."

"This is her partner, Ms. Chambliss. She's going on board," Tewes said.

The doctor nodded and led the way. Drew followed, ducking instinctively as they reached the whirling blades.

The trip to the hospital took almost no time at all. Drew held Cicely's hand the entire way. When they landed, a second crew met them with a gurney. They transferred Cicely to the bed with practiced ease.

"Follow us," the new doctor called to Drew.

She followed them down to the fourth floor, where she was ushered into a waiting room and handed a clipboard. The board held paperwork for her to attempt to fill in. She did the best she could. She knew most of the basic information, but had no idea about some of it. She couldn't answer questions about past hospitalizations and illnesses. They'd never really discussed that kind of thing.

She sat, staring at the blank lines that grew larger as she looked at them. *Why don't I know these things?*

"Drew," Kallie said. She rushed into the room with Preston hot on her heels. "Oh, Drew, thank God. Thank God you insisted on going up there. You found her. You saved her."

"I didn't—"

"Don't even. You made them hear you. You made them look beyond the obvious. You saved her."

"I don't—"

"Stop denying it. You made it happen."

"Kallie. Stop. I don't know what to fill in on these forms. Could you help me?"

Kallie laughed with relief. "Of course I can. I've got all her information in my phone. No problem."

Drew was happy to hand the forms to her. This was all becoming overwhelming. All she wanted was to hold Cicely. To take her home to the apartment and lie down beside her. Just hold her.

CHAPTER TWENTY-SIX

Two hours later, Cicely was given a room and they were able to see her. Drew, Kallie, Preston, and Drew's parents went in together.

Drew was happy everyone wanted to be there, but she couldn't help feeling a little disappointed not to have some time alone with her. *Oh well, we'll get some time to ourselves, soon.*

Everyone needed to see for themselves that Cicely was going to be okay. They waited outside the door, arranging themselves in a loose group. Drew entered the room and walked to Cicely's side. She was in the bed, her leg in a boot. She looked worn to the bone, but had no other signs of injury. What had happened was in the past. She'd help Cicely heal. *Together. We'll heal together.* She reached out and held Cicely's hand. Her bruised looking eyes flittered and opened.

"Hi, baby," Drew said.

"Drew?"

She sounded so much better than she did at the cave. Drew felt a thrill of happiness run through her. *She's really okay.* "Yes, love, it's me."

"I'm safe? He's not here, is he?"

"No, he's not here. He's in jail where he belongs. You're in Seton Medical Center. Your ankle is broken, but you're safe and no one can hurt you." Drew slipped her hand away to open the blinds a bit.

"Drew! Don't let go, please, don't leave me."

"I'm here. I won't be leaving you. There are some other folks who want to see you, though."

"Other—who? Who else is here?"

"Kallie, Preston, and my folks."

"Really?"

"Yes, really. You feeling up to seeing them?"

"Yes."

Drew opened the door and motioned for the others to enter. Kallie walked to the far side of the bed and leaned in to kiss Cicely's cheek. Preston stood to one side of the bed, and her mom stood at the foot.

"Hey, everyone," Cicely said.

"Hi, beautiful," Kallie said.

"Welcome home," her mother said.

"We missed you, kiddo," Preston said.

"I missed you all, too. So much."

Big tears rolled down Cicely's face, breaking Drew's heart. What had she gone through under that hill? She wanted to kill that scumbag.

"We wanted to see you. We'll leave you two alone, now. We aren't going far though. I'm kicking Drew out in an hour so you and I can have some time, too," Kallie said.

Drew leaned down as the door closed behind their family.

"I love you, Cicely."

"I love you, too. Please don't ever leave me."

"I won't. I'm yours forever."

"You promise?"

"I promise."

"I love you, Drew." Cicely's lids grew heavy and she was soon sleeping again.

Drew watched her, a smile on her face and a warm feeling in her chest. She had everything she needed to move forward with her life, and she'd live every day grateful to have the love and answers she'd always longed for.

❖

Drew watched as they lowered the coffins into the gaping black holes. There was no anxiety this time. Seeing the caskets lowered filled her with peace. Her mother and father were finally known to her, and now, they were being buried. This was the last piece she needed to have closure regarding her childhood.

She felt the warmth of Cicely's hand holding hers. They stood side by side at the graves, with the members of their family around them. Wy and Javon dropped roses down onto the caskets, followed by the others, until only she and Cicely were left.

Cicely's hand slipped out of hers and she stepped forward, dropping her peach roses among the others, then she slid back into place. Drew stepped up, her heart pounded and she felt the tears on her face. This was her final good-bye to them. Since she had regained her memories, she knew them. She could remember the joy they took in their simple life, how much they loved her. Now they could rest. She dropped the sunflowers she carried onto the top of each coffin, and turned to take hold of Cicely's hand once more.

Walt Sample was in jail, awaiting trial. The official charges against him included rape, human trafficking, kidnapping, attempted murder, and murder. She and Cicely would be among those testifying against him. The police had recovered several trafficked women thanks to records they had found at the storage unit. They'd also exhumed and identified the women from the original corral Drew had led them to, and thanks to Drew's memory of the area, they'd also followed her to her childhood home, where they'd been able to recover her parents' remains, which Sample had buried in a shallow grave behind the old house. There was so much evidence against him, there was no question he'd spend his remaining time on death row.

Drew and Cicely walked to the car, to join Kallie, Preston, and Drew's family.

"Thank you, everyone, for being here with me," Drew said.

They all took turns hugging her and giving her their best. This was her family, and she couldn't be happier. The nightmares were gone, her fears were gone, and she and Cicely were building their life together. They were buying a small house west of Austin with a little bit of land, not too far from Lake Travis. It was time for both of them to move forward.

Kallie and Preston were living in Kallie's place, a short twenty minutes from the new house. Drew knew they'd always be there for them. Her parents were solidly behind her relationship with Cicely and loved her as much as they loved Drew.

"Hey, let's go get some food. I'm starving," Wy said.

Drew laughed. "You're always starving. Where should we go, kiddo?"

"Let's go to the Clay Pit."

"Indian food? You're branching out."

"Well, Charlie's working there now and, you know."

Back to Charlie, guess he's grown up in the past few months. Drew smiled and nodded. "Yeah, let's go." She took Cicely's hand and they all headed to their cars.

Later, Drew and Cicely sat on a floating dock in a secluded cove on Lake Travis. Cicely's leg had healed well enough for her to make the climb down the staircase to the dock. The limestone cliffs surrounding them formed a grotto that made Cicely feel like she was in another world. One that didn't include the occasional nightmare from her experience. One where all that existed was Drew and what they were building together.

She slid her hand over Drew's and scooted as close as she could get without sitting on her lap.

"Drew?"

"Yeah?"

"When I was in that black hole, thinking of you kept me sane. It made me realize how much you mean to me."

"I'm so sorry about him taking you."

"It's not your fault, you know that. And as horrifying as it was, it made me face my faults. I'm sorry about how I was, before."

"What do you mean?"

"I mean expecting you to tell me everything immediately. Asking you to give me so much, when I could barely give you my trust. That wasn't fair." Cicely interlaced her finger's with Drew's, liking the way they fit together, and the way Drew's touch made her feel so safe. "I love you and I trust you. If you have to keep some things to yourself, I know you have a good reason and I'll accept it." Cicely felt the weight of old hurts and past insecurities lift. She needed to heal from her ordeal, but there was no question she could. She had friends and family who loved her, and she knew she could trust in them, and in herself.

"I won't keep things from you, love."

"I know, but if you do, it's okay. I trust this. You and me. I want this forever."

"I want this, too. I love you. I promise to be open, and loving, and all yours."

Cicely sighed and rested her head on Drew's shoulder as the last of the sun dropped and orange and pink filled the sky. They'd been through unimaginable horrors, but together, life was going to be better than either of them had ever had it. She closed her eyes and let the promise of the future fill her.

About the Author

Laydin Michaels is a native Houstonian with deep Louisiana roots. She finds joy and happiness in the loving arms of her wife, MJ. Her life is also enriched by her son, CJ, and her fur kids. Her love of the written word started very early. Her first novel, *Forsaken*, was a finalist for a GCLS Goldie in Romantic Suspense. She has also written *Bitter Root*. *Buried Heart* is her third novel.

Books Available from Bold Strokes Books

A Quiet Death by Cari Hunter. When the body of a young Pakistani girl is found out on the moors, the investigation leaves Detective Sanne Jensen facing an ordeal she may not survive. (978-1-62639-815-3)

Buried Heart by Laydin Michaels. When Drew Chambliss meets Cicely Jones, her buried past finds its way to the surface—will they survive its discovery or will their chance at love turn to dust? (978-1-62639-801-6)

Escape: Exodus Book Three by Gun Brooke. Aboard the Exodus ship *Pathfinder*, President Thea Tylio still holds Caya Lindemay, a clairvoyant changer, in protective custody, which has devastating consequences endangering their relationship and the entire Exodus mission. (978-1-62639-635-7)

Genuine Gold by Ann Aptaker. New York, 1952. Outlaw Cantor Gold is thrown back into her honky-tonk Coney Island past, where crime and passion simmer in a neon glare. (978-1-62639-730-9)

Into Thin Air by Jeannie Levig. When her girlfriend disappears, Hannah Lewis discovers her world isn't as orderly as she thought it was. (978-1-62639-722-4)

Night Voice by CF Frizzell. When talk show host Sable finally acknowledges her risqué radio relationship with a mysterious caller, she welcomes a *real* relationship with local tradeswoman Riley Burke. (978-1-62639-813-9)

Raging at the Stars by Lesley Davis. When the unbelievable theories start revealing themselves as truths, can you trust in the ones who have conspired against you from the start? (978-1-62639-720-0)

She Wolf by Sheri Lewis Wohl. When the hunter becomes the hunted, more than love might be lost. (978-1-62639-741-5)

Smothered and Covered by Missouri Vaun. The last person Nash Wiley expects to bump into over a two a.m. breakfast at Waffle House is her college crush, decked out in a curve-hugging law enforcement uniform. (978-1-62639-704-0)

The Butterfly Whisperer by Lisa Moreau. Reunited after ten years, can Jordan and Sophie heal the past and rediscover love or will differing desires keep them apart? (978-1-62639-791-0)

The Devil's Due by Ali Vali. Cain and Emma Casey are awaiting the birth of their third child, but as always in Cain's world, there are new and old enemies to face in post Katrina-ravaged New Orleans. (978-1-62639-591-6)

Widows of the Sun-Moon by Barbara Ann Wright. With immortality now out of their grasp, the gods of Calamity fight amongst themselves, egged on by the mad goddess they thought they'd left behind. (978-1-62639-777-4)

18 Months by Samantha Boyette. Alissa Reeves has only had two girlfriends and they've both gone missing. Now it's up to her to find out why. (978-1-62639-804-7)

Arrested Hearts by Holly Stratimore. A reckless cop with a secret death wish and a health nut who is afraid to die might be a perfect combination for love. (978-1-62639-809-2)

Capturing Jessica by Jane Hardee. Hyperrealist sculptor Michael tries desperately to conceal the love she holds for best friend, Jess, unaware Jess's feelings for her are changing. (978-1-62639-836-8)

Counting to Zero by AJ Quinn. NSA agent Emma Thorpe and computer hacker Paxton James must learn to trust each other as they work to stop a threat clock that's rapidly counting down to zero. (978-1-62639-783-5)

Courageous Love by KC Richardson. Two women fight a devastating disease, and their own demons, while trying to fall in love. (978-1-62639-797-2)

One More Reason to Leave Orlando by Missouri Vaun. Nash Wiley thought a threesome sounded exotic and exciting, but as it turns out the reality of sleeping with two women at the same time is just really complicated. (978-1-62639-703-3E)

Pathogen by Jessica L. Webb. Can Dr. Kate Morrison navigate a deadly virus and the threat of bioterrorism, as well as her new relationship with Sergeant Andy Wyles and her own troubled past? (978-1-62639-833-7)

Rainbow Gap by Lee Lynch. Jaudon Vickers and Berry Garland, polar opposites, dream and love in this tale of lesbian lives set in Central Florida against the tapestry of societal change and the Vietnam War. (978-1-62639-799-6)

Steel and Promise by Alexa Black. Lady Nivrai's cruel desires and modified body make most of the galaxy fear her, but courtesan Cailyn Derys soon discovers the real monsters are the ones without the claws. (978-1-62639-805-4)

Swelter by D. Jackson Leigh. Teal Giovanni's mistake shines an unwanted spotlight on a small Texas ranch where August Reese is secluded until she can testify against a powerful drug kingpin. (978-1-62639-795-8)

Without Justice by Carsen Taite. Cade Kelly and Emily Sinclair must battle each other in the pursuit of justice, but can they fight their undeniable attraction outside the walls of the courtroom? (978-1-62639-560-2)

21 Questions by Mason Dixon. To find love, start by asking the right questions. (978-1-62639-724-8)

A Palette for Love by Charlotte Greene. When newly minted Ph.D. Chloé Devereaux returns to New Orleans, she doesn't expect her new job, and her powerful employer—Amelia Winters—to be so appealing. (978-1-62639-758-3)

By the Dark of Her Eyes by Cameron MacElvee. When Brenna Taylor inherits a decrepit property haunted by tormented ghosts, Alejandra Santana must not only restore Brenna's house and property but also save her soul. (978-1-62639-834-4)

Cash Braddock by Ashley Bartlett. Cash Braddock just wants to hang with her cat, fall in love, and deal drugs. What's the problem with that? (978-1-62639-706-4)

Death by Cocktail Straw by Missouri Vaun. She just wanted to meet girls, but an outing at the local lesbian bar goes comically off the rails, landing Nash Wiley and her best pal in the ER. (978-1-62639-702-6)

Gravity by Juliann Rich. How can Ellie Engebretsen, Olympic ski jumping hopeful with her eye on the gold, soar through the air when all she feels like doing is falling hard for Kate Moreau, her greatest competitor and the girl of her dreams? (978-1-62639-483-4)

Lone Ranger by VK Powell. Reporter Emma Ferguson stirs up a thirty-year-old mystery that threatens Park Ranger Carter West's family and jeopardizes any hope for a relationship between the two women. (978-1-62639-767-5)

Love on Call by Radclyffe. Ex-Army medic Glenn Archer and recent LA transplant Mariana Mateo fight their mutual desire in the face of past losses as they work together in the Rivers Community Hospital ER. (978-1-62639-843-6)

Never Enough by Robyn Nyx. Can two women put aside their pasts to find love before it's too late? (978-1-62639-629-6)

Two Souls by Kathleen Knowles. Can love blossom in the wake of tragedy? (978-1-62639-641-8)